CONTINUE BREATHING

Continue Breathing

A novel
by

JOSH GREENFIELD

Adelaide Books
New York / Lisbon
2020

CONTINUE BREATHING
A novel
By Josh Greenfield

Copyright © by Josh Greenfield
Cover design © 2020 Adelaide Books

Published by Adelaide Books, New York / Lisbon
adelaidebooks.org
Editor-in-Chief
Stevan V. Nikolic

For any information, please address Adelaide Books
at info@adelaidebooks.org
or write to:
Adelaide Books
244 Fifth Ave. Suite D27
New York, NY, 10001

ISBN: 978-1-954351-29-5

Printed in the United States of America

For Dr. Harry Reiss and Stanley R. Greenfield

Contents

"Two roads diverged in a yellow wood,

And sorry I could not travel both,

I wandered off into the underbrush and got lost."

Robert Frost (adapted)

Prologue

It has been a longstanding habit with me to spend some part of the late morning or early afternoon hours sitting in a café with a notebook before me and, in all likelihood, a cup of coffee. If all has gone well, I've done some writing earlier in the day. Sitting in a public place allows my thoughts to settle. It provides an opportunity to think about how the story might develop. It also gets me out of the house, which has to be a good thing. The following account came together in two such establishments in the West Forties, just to the north of Times Square and just to the west of the theater district.

I say there were two. One, however, came first and was more important: the Europan Café. That is the way they spell it, with 'an' at the end. I have reason to believe that the café is part of a chain of cafés, with others situated around the city. I think there may be one on Seventy-Seventh Street and Broadway, but I'm not completely sure. The one that became so important to me is on Eighth Avenue, between Forty-Second and Forty-Third Street. The first time I went in I thought I was just going to have a cup of coffee.

The entrance on the east side of Broadway opens into a congested space. Every square foot of the Europan Café is accounted for. Inside the double doors, white with glass windows top and bottom, and immediately to the right, is the part of the establishment devoted to pastry and coffee. This, I suppose, is the European part. A glass case displays a rich array of cakes, sliced into individual pieces and encased in individual paper wrappers: carrot cake, cheesecake, both plain and strawberry, chocolate layer cake, and German chocolate cake, to name but a few. The glass extends some eight or ten feet to the left of the cash register, and some eight feet off the floor. It is too high for the employees to see over.

They interact with the patrons at the opening on the right-hand end where the coffee is served and the finances are transacted. Facing the street to the servers' left is an additional supply of pastries, and cookies, large round chocolate chip cookies, and circular Linzer tarts with raspberry jelly oozing out the sides. But the feature attraction of this section of the Europan Café is the coffee. I ordered a medium, the conventional American, caffeinated, with extra milk. On that first day, I had a Linzer tart as well.

I was served by a young woman who was short in height, but not cowed by either the location of the café in the midst of Midtown or the flow of world travelers through its tourist attractions. She prepared my snack and served it with a smile. I found a seat at the back of the shop, in the row of small tables against the wall beyond the beverage display. There was also a counter serving tossed salads and fruit smoothies, but, on that first visit, I paid it no mind.

It was a Tuesday in the early afternoon, and the rows of two-person tables were only partially filled. Nobody stayed very long. They had, I suppose, better things to do. Out the windows to my right was an unobstructed view of Eighth Avenue. On the sidewalk, right out in front, an older man was trying to sell glazed nuts. There wasn't anybody buying them, and the salesman seemed to have lost all hope of making a sale. He sat on a milk crate on the uptown side of his cart, with its stained and tattered orange awning, studying the cracks in the sidewalk. There were individual packets of glazed cashews and peanuts in white wrappers arranged on the front of the cart, but no one was stopping to buy them.

Behind this failed business operation, the cars and buses of Eighth Avenue made their way uptown. The flow was not consistent, halted intermittently by the traffic light, or by the undue congestion of tourist buses moving slowly and stopping to pick up passengers. Through the gaps in the stopped traffic, I had a view of a bit of New York City history, an X-rated peep show on the west side of Eighth Avenue. These used to be the defining feature of the area, before Mayor Rudy Giuliani took the bull by the horns and cleaned up the neighborhood. The only remaining vestige of the old Times Square was right across the street. Beside it was an independent movie house showing a scary movie for the benefit of the area's new denizens. Further to the left, across Forty-Second Street, was the Port Authority Bus Terminal, with a large electronic billboard on its side, trying to entice the foreign visitors to take a side trip to Philadelphia.

I had left home that morning carrying more than my black-and-white-speckled notebook and my dog-eared copy of the AA Big Book. I always had these in my black shoulder bag. I had included an oversized tan notebook as well. I'd brought it with me despite the fact that the contents were not backed up on any kind of hard drive. With my computer in the shop one morning, I had started a new project longhand. When the computer came back, I kept at it. I had even purchased a distinctive notebook for the effort. There seemed to be something comforting in setting my thoughts down in blue ink on white paper. I never lost my shoulder bag. Umbrellas, yes. Shoulder bags, no.

And, strange as it may seem, there in the back row of tables in the Europan Café, my story unfolded before me. I saw the chapters. I felt where I was going and where I would wind up. I got a pretty good idea of what I was writing about: placing myself in the hands of my Higher Power. As the years had progressed, He had helped me along and in no way had this been more true than in the progression of my writing. I saw where my book would end. And when I closed the large tan notebook that first day, I expressed my gratitude as best I could.

I kept going back there – going back being a severe obsessive compulsive's greatest strength. We'll go back to check if the gas stove is turned off. We'll go back to a girlfriend we should have left long before. And we'll go back to a coffee shop on Eighth Avenue. Even as I began writing in earnest, I continued to stop in, to shape the book and elaborate on my outline. The employees came to expect me. I was a standout in an establishment with a steady turnover.

Why exactly I felt so at home finding a structure for the book in that particular café, I really couldn't say. I was a solitary man making the acquaintance of strangers, just as was the protagonist in my account. I was an obsessive alone in the big city, another apt description of my book. I skirted a romantic involvement with the Greek woman who was in charge. I found a way to connect my Kindle to the WIFI of the hotel next door. But I remained fundamentally alone, a condition of many writers no doubt, and for better or for worse, the rest of the human race.

The writing was my occupation and my joy. It gave purpose to my day. It kept me sane.

CUTTING THROUGH THE KNOT

Chapter One

I'd Only Have Turned on You — 1984

The only way to look back at all this is with something resembling a smile. The breakdown happened when I was twenty-one years old. It was June of what should have been the end of my senior year. I'd finished three and spent one screwing around. I had a part-time job in a vegetarian restaurant. I was a waiter, though on some days I helped in the kitchen. It was communal in that way. I was staffing the dining room one Sunday morning, but there wasn't a whole lot to do. The spinach had been washed, and the fruit juice bottles carefully arranged, all by people more functional than myself. The wooden interior was inviting, with the morning sun flooding in through the large picture window. In the kitchen, the corn was quietly sautéing in garlic sauce, and the brown rice was nicely puffed. All we needed were some customers.

A man and a woman entered to the sound of the tinkling bell above the door, not that we would have overlooked them in the rush. They took a seat at a table for two against the wall. The woman wore a long maroon skirt, and the man had his hair pulled loosely back in a ponytail. Ready to serve, I approached the table and offered the couple menus. I looked at them. The woman smiled, the man nodded. They consulted the bill of fare in silence.

I stepped back behind the wait station and began to contemplate the water glasses. Five filled, two empty glasses on the end.

I could fill them, or not...

If I fill them I'll have to refill the pitcher, which means walking into the kitchen.

If I don't fill them I'm going to run out of water glasses. Unless I fill them later...

It might get busy and I won't have time. I could fill the glasses but let the water level in the pitcher drop. How much would it drop? If I got a smaller pitcher, it wouldn't drop as much. At least it wouldn't look like it had dropped as much.

No one is going to look at the pitcher.

I could take the empty glasses off the end of the shelf. Then at least I wouldn't have to think about them. I could also put them under the counter.

There, now all the water glasses are filled. But three don't have any ice. The empty glasses under the counter don't have any ice either. They don't even have any water.

What will people think when they see empty glasses under the counter? Nobody puts empty glasses under the counter.

Better put them back on the shelf...

There.

The couple had been ready for ten minutes. I walked over to take their order.

"I'll have the soup and salad. With cornbread, right?" the woman asked.

I looked at her but did not fully comprehend the question. I nodded. I made some effort to write down her request. The writing was not coherent. These people had water. But the man had no ice, or very little. They needed ice.

"The choices?" she asked again, smiling a little more forcefully.

I tried to focus. "There's blue cheese. There's also Russian and… a French." She ordered the French. I got something down on paper about the man's order and retreated to the wait station. The ice glasses were still there. I counted them again: five filled, two empty. Of the five filled, three didn't have any ice.

It's getting warm outside. It's going to get hot.

No ice. The ice is in the kitchen. I could fill the pitcher and get the ice at the same time. What would Corey think? Doesn't everyone fill the glasses with water and ice before the meal, during set up? There are two glasses filled with ice. That's enough for one more table of two. What if it's a table for four? Two would get water with ice and two would get water without ice. Maybe they wouldn't notice… Better get the ice now.

This process proceeds indefinitely, or until interrupted. Some prisons have no walls.

The order slip with the pencil scratch marks on it was crumpled and placed in the front left pocket of my denim apron. It remained there. The couple was quietly looking at one another across the table for two. The kitchen staff were leaning against the stove perusing the Sunday paper. Nothing was happening. Forty-five minutes went by in this condition of suspended animation. The couple refrained from registering any form of complaint; they were very polite.

There are limits to what even vegetarian restaurants in college towns will put up with. I lost the job. All functioning effectively stopped. I wandered around, lost in my own world, a world of exquisite pain. By the middle of June, I resembled a washed-out rag left too long in the sun. I slept, I guess. I ate when I thought about it. I stumbled through parking lots, unable to get to the far side without stopping to pick up the crushed soda cans and windblown newspapers.

Before the city cleared out for the summer, there had been some contact with other students, but with my housemates gone, I let myself go. I spent nights in a top-floor room strewn with clothes and three-day-old plates of dried spaghetti. I hadn't paid any rent, but I'd lived in the house a long time and it was summer time. It was the same house where I'd wandered the halls singing Carly Simon's "I Haven't Got Time for the Pain." I was trying to convince myself, but I was not successful.

I'm not saying I was ignored. People had tried to intervene.

"Why don't you go see someone?"

That question really pissed me off. I'd heard it from friends, from family members. I just snapped back. I had no great logical response. I just wanted nothing to do with it.

College towns do really clear out after graduation. At least this college town did. Just about everyone was gone. One friend was still around. We were standing around in the basement room that had been home for three: Pete, my roommate since freshman year, who had pulled out right after graduation, and now Gary, who was preparing to move back to his parents' house across town. He was quietly placing some shirts in a duffle bag. The room was largely underground, but it did have a line of windows, high along one wall that opened out on street level. One of the beds was on a platform, even with these windows. Pete had slept on a mattress beneath. Since my return, I'd been camped out in a sleeping bag somewhere in the middle of the room. They'd taken me in upon my return from a second internship in Washington, D.C., along with my nine cardboard boxes of important papers.

Gary looked up from his packing, "I didn't say anything," he said quietly. He wanted reinforcement for the tact he had shown.

I didn't miss a beat. "I'd only have turned on you," I came back.

Gary finished his packing and later that afternoon, he moved out.

What was I supposed to acknowledge? That there was something wrong with my head? That I could no longer walk without stopping to pick up trash? That everything, I mean everything, had come to a stop? I had no idea what was going on. I had no way of thinking about what was going on. Above all, I had no idea that there was anything that could be done to fix the problem.

Someone tells you, "You look tired."

You say, "Yeah, I was out late last night." Maybe you go to sleep early the next night. Someone tells you, "It seems like something is wrong with your head." You snap. I'm afraid that's just the way it works.

Help did eventually come. It started with a phone call to my brother-in-law in New York. I think it was the ten-minute pause in our conversation that gave me away. Something must have tipped him off because when I came home that night, my father and sister were sitting on the front porch. I walked up Oak Avenue and saw them swaying on the metal swing beside the front door. Something went off inside, a recognition that maybe there was really something going on here. I sat down on the swing and rested my head on my sister's lap.

"You're the only brother I've got," Anne said. She'd been dragged six hours across New York state to salvage a fucked-up brother, but she spoke with conviction.

We took a walk, my father, my sister and I, up Oak Avenue, through the western New York night, and sat down on a grassy hillside.

"He'd have to be smart," I said.

"There are smart doctors," Anne said. She wanted me in that car. She also knew how to talk straight. I wasn't accustomed to addressing the subject of psychiatry in any manner.

The grass was damp, and it was pretty late. They were anxious to get going, to drive me back to New York City. And I got in the car with them.

It doesn't sound like much, but it was a big deal closing that car door. I sat in the back seat, my sister sat up front with her earphones in and my father drove. He drove the car, but in a sense, he was driving more than that. He was driving me toward some form of help. By getting in that car, I had conceded that help was in order and I had turned things over to him. Had I chosen to walk away into the night things would have been different, but a lifetime of devotion had earned him that respect.

We arrived in New York at daybreak. My sister got out of the car on West Ninety-Ninth Street to shower and go to work. With her out of the car, something clicked, and I unloaded.

"You can't do this! This is the one thing you can't do!" I screamed at my father as we pulled out of Central Park at East Eighty-Fourth Street. I was referring to the whole idea of interfering in another human being's life on such a fundamental level. I'd gotten in the car with my sister there, but with her gone, I couldn't figure out why.

"I know," my father replied. He kept his eyes on the road. He kept driving. There are times when even the most fundamental laws of individual respect must be abridged.

Later that morning, he walked me over to Rubin's office. And the whole thing got started.

Chapter Two

And He Was Smiling – 1984

The first morning in Dr. Rubin's waiting room, my father and I sat side by side on the cream-colored sofa. Off to the left was a polished, circular wooden table that supported three Smithsonian's, an art catalogue, and a year-old copy of *The New Yorker*. In the center of the table, toward the back, was the figure of a Japanese Bodhisattva, her loosely fitting garment covering only one breast. With her right arm, she reached out to the patients who had enough awareness to register her presence. Beside the statue was a miniature ceramic figure of an ancient Japanese man consulting a scroll and smiling at his own joke.

My father wore a jacket and tie, a white shirt. I was in the same clothes I'd been wearing for at least two days. We waited for Dr. Rubin to entertain us, my father with the concentration of a man engaged in his life's work, myself with the attention of a three-day-old dandelion seed pod about to be blown away by an evening breeze. I remained stationary and in the upright position only through the force of my father's will.

In short order Dr. Rubin appeared and he was smiling. Call it remarkable or downright inappropriate, but he had a grin on his face. He welcomed my father and me into his office, the consulting room where he held his sessions.

"So, why did you bring him here?" Dr. Rubin looked at my father.

My father began to recount a series of incidents that had occurred in the last year. There were any number he could have chosen: the weekend our day's canoe outing turned into a prolonged bout of crying and introspection by the side of a lake, the endless phone calls about which course to enroll in, my seeming inability to hold my political views in any kind of reasonable perspective. He chose to emphasize the fact that I had called to change a dinner date some twenty or thirty times.

Dr. Rubin felt he had heard enough. He escorted my father back to the waiting room and asked me what I thought about his remarks.

"Well...I mean...come on..." I said. I wasn't big on whole thoughts at the time. I tried to answer his questions. I was too intimidated to be impolite. The doctor's words were very few that first morning. At the end of the session, Dr. Rubin gave me his business card. I noted the home address in New Rochelle and made some attempt at a humorous aside about living in the splendor of Westchester County.

"That's what will make you well," Dr. Rubin said. "Humor cuts through the knot."

We walked back to the waiting room where my father was seated quietly on the sofa. There were tears in his eyes. Rubin noted the tears. "It's a good sign," he said.

Both of these simple statements reflected thirty years of practice in the psychiatry business. Rubin had made the walk before.

Dr. Rubin scheduled another appointment for two o'clock that afternoon. As my father and I walked down the gently sloping incline that led away from the Park Avenue building, my father said, "You're lucky he could see you again on the same day." I slowed a step, in silent awe of my father's knowledge of psychiatry.

That afternoon, Dr. Rubin and I sat alone in his office.

"Jordan, you've had an emotional breakdown," he explained. He smiled again. "We're going to make you well." There was not the least wisp of doubt in his statement.

I had made it to the office. I was sitting in the chair. I heard his words, but I had no perspective on what I was experiencing.

Dr. Rubin rose slowly from his office chair and walked the two steps to the wooden cabinet on the adjacent wall. He was a gray-haired man who kept himself trim, but he wasn't as light on his feet as he'd once been. Rubin opened the top drawer and removed a small plastic bottle. It contained lithium carbonate. He handed me the bottle.

"I want you to take one of these three times a day. Take them with some milk or food," he said. That was it.

Dr. Rubin's simple, straightforward statement did not invite a response. I held the plastic bottle in my right hand and looked at this strange human being before me. I didn't trust him. I was still wearing the same stretched out t-shirt and blue jeans with a rip in the right thigh. My abundant supply of brown curly hair was still not combed. I was twenty-one and up a creek.

Two days later, I still had not taken the pills. Who goes around putting unknown, possibly addictive substances in their body? It was a Sunday afternoon and I was walking in the East 60s. I took the business card out of my pocket and called

Rubin's New Rochelle phone number. I began to articulate questions, questions about the nature of the drug, its qualities, its side effects.

"Take your medicine!" Rubin interrupted me.

I got off the phone and walked across Lexington Avenue into a small neighborhood restaurant called Serendipity, known for its ample supply of Tiffany chandeliers. I sat down at a table for two and ordered the Welsh rarebit. I think it was the Welsh rarebit – whatever it was, it had a lot of cheese. I set the lithium capsule on the placemat on the far side of the white plate, in front of the water glass. I looked at it. There was certainly an element of risk here. What did I really know about this character? Once you start in on these pills, there might be no turning back. I tried to focus.

Rubin's tone of voice on the phone carried the day. I picked up the lithium pill and washed it down with a gulp of cold ice water. I looked at the cheese on the plate. I didn't eat anything.

The remarkable thing is that I think the capsule made me feel better. Something eased in my mind. A little of the pressure was taken off. The balloon had been stretched to the breaking point. It might not have exploded, but it was still pretty uncomfortable. The lithium capsule eased the pain, just a bit. Sometime later I learned that lithium carbonate is a clay found in the waters of some European resorts. For centuries, manic-depressives went to these resorts to "take the waters." They didn't know why, but they knew it helped. Then some brilliant doctor took the clay and put it in a capsule. I lucked out because they don't have those springs in New York City.

I remember this story about the kid who couldn't stop washing himself, but what isn't always so clear is that the same mechanism that makes him do that can affect every aspect of the human thought process, everything until the whole brain just about shuts down and comes to a screeching halt, like the 7:15 from Ronkonkoma crashing into an eighteen-wheeler stalled out at an intersection: Wheels flying, steel rails bent, seats sticking out windows, flames, women screaming, men in suits looking like children lost at a state fair. It's kind of like that – only all this is taking place inside your head, and it's with you every waking moment, from the time you wake up in the morning, until the drugs knock you out at night, until it starts all over again the next day. Any drug is welcome, but there is really nothing you can do but decide not to kill yourself and show up at your doctor's office on time.

The other thing that helped me out was realizing that lithium is found in some foods. Well, it's in nature, so it could be in foods. How would I feel if a doctor told me to eat a lot of asparagus? I don't mind asparagus, but the point is, I wouldn't have a problem with it. It's a food. How bad could it be?

Anyway, it worked. That's a bit strong when you consider the pain I was feeling at the time, but I did walk into our next session a little more open to what Dr. Rubin had to say.

Chapter Three

Ocean Liner Cables – 1984

Sessions in those first few weeks went something like this: Dr. Rubin would invite me into his office. "So, how have you been?" he would begin. He would be matter-of-fact, not overly concerned. It was then my job to try to explain what I had been doing since the last session.

The room would distract me, however: The tapestry of swirling, muted oranges and blues on the wall behind Dr. Rubin's chair; the floor to ceiling bookcase filled with medical volumes; the swiveling black leather chair I sat in. When I couldn't amuse myself with looking around the room, I played air guitar. Or I played air guitar and looked around the room at the same time. I tried to avoid answering any direct questions.

In any case, there wasn't a whole lot to report. "I went to the museum," I would sometimes say. That usually worked, unless I added that I had been at the museum on a Monday – the Metropolitan Museum of Art was closed on Monday.

This was one of the advantages of crashing in an eleventh-floor apartment of a building at 1010 Fifth Avenue, literally across the street from one of the world's great museums.

"I was in the park." That was another winner. The bottom line here is that there just wasn't a whole lot going on.

"Whenever I have a free hour, I go over to the museum. I always learn something new."

Dr. Rubin encouraged me to take advantage of my proximity to this fine cultural institution. Unfortunately, my principal activity was sitting in this courtyard and sorting through old postcards. I would sit on a marble bench between two large nymph statues and a slowly trickling fountain, rearranging these important documents.

When Dr. Rubin wasn't asking about my activities, he generally let me have the floor.

"So how long is this going to take?" I asked him.

Dr. Rubin had no response; time frames were off the table. "We're going to have hundreds of hours together," he replied.

There he went again. That was clearly ridiculous. Wasn't I an activist for the Nuclear Weapons Freeze Campaign? At the time, this noble endeavor was my one and only concern, but I was a man with a life. I was on leave from an Ivy League university. I was long accustomed to doing great and interesting things, performing in a children's theater company, working in an Alaskan salmon cannery. Didn't I have things to do? I tried to do the math.

Three sessions a week for roughly fifty weeks was a hundred and fifty hours a year. Was this guy kidding? Years? He thought I would be coming in here for years? That's rich, I thought to myself.

It was the case, however, that from the very start, Rubin had a way of saying things that threw you off your guard. Rubin was leaning forward in his chair, the way he did when he really wanted to make a point, when he said this: "A professional tennis player demands complete silence so he can hit a bouncing yellow ball with a large round racket. A professional baseball player stands in the middle of thirty thousand screaming fans and tries to hit a small white ball coming at him at upwards of ninety miles an hour with a wooden bat. The point is that we're creatures of habit. The way we've always done things is the way we expect them to be done. Changing habits is never easy."

I would just listen. Rubin's insights never hit me right away.

There was one central concept Rubin would spend the next decade trying to get me to understand the importance of anger. Anger and its cousins had the common effect of leaving me zoned out, detached, like I was floating alone and apart. This was a chemical reaction, and once I fell into that state, I was sure to fall in deeper. Only on occasion did this "anger" exhibit itself visibly, but it left me unable to carry on the simple interactions of everyday life.

And then, just like that, the session would be over. Forty-five minutes as carefully registered on both clocks, one clearly visible from my swiveling, black leather chair. It would be time for me to go.

I would start for the door. The session might be brutal, but the world outside that building was all the darkness ever known to man. Through good fortune, I had a safe, dry place to retreat to at the end of the day.

My mother was to leave shortly to spend an academic year at Harvard's Kennedy School. My father and I were on our own. Anger, to the severely obsessive-compulsive, is more than a transitory reaction to a particular stimulus. It is a state of mind. In this condition, everything has the power to exacerbate the anger, whether that be the sideways glance of a passerby, a car hesitating at an intersection, or the friendly greeting of a well-wisher. When you are *that* angry, anything can make it worse.

The anger went hand-in-hand with the obsessive rumination. When I walked out of Rubin's office, I would immediately feel compelled to pick up the loose trash I passed on the sidewalk. As New York City neighborhoods go, the Upper East Side was relatively clean and orderly, but this is still a losing proposition. I walked past a piece of a crumpled gum wrapper and resisted the urge to go back and pick it up, only to find that I was confronted by a license plate with two *R*s. Or had there been three *R*s? I walked five paces, overwhelmed by waves of anxiety. Had it been two *R*s or three *R*s? My life, the life of my loved ones, the future of the planet rested on knowing the correct answer to that question. I took three steps more and inevitably turned back to retrieve a definitive answer.

By giving way to the compulsion to return, I had strengthened its power to hold me the next time, but there is just so much a body can endure.

I would go into Central Park during those first few weeks. I used to join in pick-up softball games.

I was commended for my positive attitude by the family friend, another psychiatrist who had chimed in about the lithium and the asparagus. I wasn't depressive by nature. I was making the effort, but the drugs slowed me down; if things weren't entirely in reverse, the vehicle had downshifted.

My hand-eye coordination was a little off. I had a little trouble going to left. I always had trouble going to left. Actually, I usually grounded out to the second baseman. But the drugs made things worse. Once, a slow line drive that I typically would have caught bounced off the center of my forehead and went for an infield single.

This experience dampened my enthusiasm a bit, and I refrained from future participation. I didn't know if the drugs affected my mouth and tongue, but I knew that it often was difficult to articulate my thoughts. I would have the idea clear in my mind, but it just wouldn't quite make it out of my mouth.

Most of my time apart from Dr. Rubin was spent in thought, whether I was walking up Madison Avenue, or in a wooded area of Central Park, or stalled out in the entranceway of the bank. I could get started on just about anything and run with it. I'd start in on some obscure point and develop it from every possible angle. This would go on and on, until I was composing a three-volume treatise on the arrangement of eating utensils. It was exhausting.

The obsessive rumination and anger, which were my ever-present states of mind, were really both a part of the same condition. If you can hold on to thoughts about the alternative arrangements of the knife and the spoon on the placemat, you can also hold on to the resentments of the day. This obsessive rumination inevitably leads to acting compulsively. Cutting down on the time spent on obsessive rumination cuts down on the time spent with anger.

That first year, there was one long nightmare from which I did not know how to awaken; it engendered a profound confusion I utterly lacked the capacity to understand. I felt a terrible pain I could not control.

It was a double dip. Two scoops. Vanilla and Butter Pecan. Manic-depression is no joke. Before lithium it was just about fatal. Some glorious tales of fortunes made and lost, and creative journeys undertaken, only to be followed by terrible depression and, seemingly more often than not, suicide. With lithium, the highs and lows can be controlled and a normal life can be achieved. That was the first scoop.

The second scoop is always the winner. The one you know you really shouldn't have, but you do anyway. That was the O.C.D. That was the one that took all the work, because once it gets a hold on your head, it really doesn't want to let go. Call it a monkey on your back, if you like, or being tied to the ground with ocean liner cables. That's good, too.

I had a partner. On the very first day we had met, Dr. Rubin had declared, "I would so much enjoy working with you!" Rubin wasn't going anywhere. It was up to me to take advantage of the resource.

Chapter Four

I Stayed in the Park and Played Softball – 1984

I missed my third session. I just didn't show up. I stayed in the park and played softball. Dr. Rubin rescheduled, and I saw fit to show up the next time. My biggest reservation about Dr. Rubin in those first few weeks was that he wasn't right for me. I don't remember knowing how I came to this conclusion because I'd never been treated by a psychiatrist before, but I was absolutely certain. Dr. Rubin heard me out on this point.

"Well, maybe you're right," he finally conceded, looking at me thoughtfully.

"Hold on here," I thought, "What's the big idea? You're giving up so easy? I was tearing into you, and now you just up and give way?" Something was wrong.

"I'll never blame you for anything," Rubin came back, and he never has. I wasn't proud of what I was doing. In fact, I was a little concerned.

I tore into him every way I knew how. I questioned his competence, the drugs, the profession of psychiatry.

"I've been worked over by professionals," he reassured me with a smile, after one prolonged berating. And when the forty-five minutes were up, I got up and left.

Dr. Rubin had more drugs to give me. In the first few weeks, I started in on the clonidine. The lithium was for the mood swings, and the clonidine was the first of many drugs designed to lessen the power of the obsessive thinking. Taken at bedtime, it also ensured a good night's sleep. Dr. Rubin tried not to upset me. He knew I was having a hard time with all the pills. But he didn't sugar coat the process either. He was matter-of-fact and straightforward. He might have liked to have taken another blood test to monitor the lithium levels, but he refrained from having me do so. He knew that would have pushed me too far.

We sat in his office at the appointed hour, me attired in a worn blue sweatshirt with a ventilation hole under one armpit, Dr. Rubin in a smart, white, striped shirt and a simple tie. Rubin was ready for bear, keenly aware of the clock. He was entirely focused on the task at hand: Think Roger Federer, down five-four in the fourth set at Wimbledon, waiting to return the serve, but appearing a relaxed conversationalist at the same time. Rubin had his own scoreboard, measuring categories I could not have understood had they been patiently explained to me, which they certainly weren't. He knew what he wanted to accomplish and in what order.

"I have a track record, you know," he said, with a touch of modest pride, "of getting paranoids to trust me."

I looked at him. Maybe I blinked. I stared at the titles on the vertical bookshelf, without registering any of the names. I played my imaginary air guitar. Specific songs were not relevant; the distraction was.

I looked at him again. Speech did not come easily at this point, just yelling. And I wasn't interested in yelling right then. He seized the advantage.

"The longer you hold onto that anger, towards me or anyone else, the longer you'll hold on to the anger against yourself. It doesn't turn on and off so easily. You can let it go." He had my attention, so he continued.

"There was a circus performer in Great Britain in the nineteenth century who taught himself to swallow coins, and then to bring them back up into his mouth. He conditioned his muscles to do this. What do you think of that story?" he asked.

I made no response. I was astounded, but I failed to see any connection between his story and what was happening in the room. Rubin waited.

"Must have taken a lot of practice," I finally got out.

"Exactly!" Dr. Ruben responded. "Through practice, we can learn to do things that might seem impossible at first. It's a matter of habits. You'll hear me say that a thousand times. We are creatures of habit. Change is never easy, but we're going to change your habits, from losing habits to winning habits."

It was time to go.

I started for the door. Dr. Rubin was smiling, not so much to cheer me on through the next day and a half, but because he was happy that he'd gotten some things said. I had heard him. How much I had understood was another question.

Dr. Rubin's principal task in those early days was getting me to understand the importance of letting go of anger. When you held a grudge against the guy at the newsstand who looked at you funny and held on to it all day, something had to change.

Another session went something like this:

"I talked to a girl from school. She asked if we were going to talk about my childhood."

"If it comes up," Dr. Ruben answered, not unduly impressed. He kept his eyes on me, but he was inscrutable. Through some form of observation and intuition, he had to determine which drugs to give me and in what amounts. He must have been making these appraisals, but for all intents and purposes, he was just having a conversation.

"I'm actually more interested in what's happening today. If we do okay with today, whatever comes along some other day will probably work out too. It's the same the same thing with those distant days in the past. Perception is everything."

There he goes again, I thought, saying these incredibly logical things that have the ring of everlasting truth as though he'd just thought them up this morning.

"If you hold onto that anger today, it will be with you next time around. If you can let go of it, you'll be free of it the next time. It's all about habits, and the anger is at the top of the list. You, above all, have to be very forgiving." He was looking directly at me. His tone was calm, but there was no doubt he was conveying information that my future and my life depended on.

This has, indeed, been a lifetime endeavor: choosing to forgive when every fiber in your body wants to hold onto blame. Letting the cool waters of forgiveness begin to flow.

I had no answer, no reply. First of all, everything he said was coming in through a buffer of water three feet thick. That's the anger. That's the chemical reaction to the anger. Dr. Rubin was working on it with the drugs, but none of them could take the place of my own effort to let go.

Anger isn't only about yelling and punching walls, although I did that on occasion. Anger is about being so zoned that all perception is in slow motion. But there was more than this. This doctor still didn't get it. I didn't even belong here. Yes,

I was taking his fucking pills. Yes, I made the effort to show up on time, but I was an anti-nuclear activist. The world was still in peril, and I had work to do, important work. This was all a big distraction.

Dr. Rubin had words to contribute here as well: "There are many good people working on that problem."

And he was right. He got me to see it. There were Secretaries of State. There were ambassadors and negotiators of all kinds. It might have been possible that at least some of them had their heads in the right place.

But Dr. Rubin would have even more illuminating things to say. In one session, Dr. Rubin pointed out to me the connection between anger and fear. He put it this way: "Say you're walking down the street, how do you know what the people you pass by are thinking?"

"You don't," I said.

"Right. The logical human solution to this problem is to assume that they are thinking the same thing you are thinking. That's the way it works. If you walk down the street in a rage, you will assume that everyone you pass is also in a rage, and you will be afraid. On the other hand, if you walk down the street thinking kind and loving thoughts, you will assume that all the people around you are also thinking kind and loving thoughts. The world will be a pleasant place to live in. Perception is everything."

Once again, he was leaning forward in the scientifically designed office chair that supported his back.

That one got through right away. It was that clear and logical, but Dr. Rubin wasn't done.

"You can't change anyone else. The only person you can change is yourself. You'll hear me say it a thousand times, but if you can change the inside of your own head, you can change the world you perceive. You can change the world you live in."

This was all pretty good, even for Dr. Rubin. I'd grown accustomed to hearing mind-bending stuff in this room. That's what I showed up for.

Chapter Five

You Won't Kill Yourself – 1984, 1985

For the time being, returning to Cornell was not an option, and finding some kind of gainful way for me to spend my time was essential. I began attending class twice a week, spending my off-hours in the Columbia undergraduate library. A trip to campus might involve three circular routes between my parents' Upper East Side apartment and the campus itself, but I usually got there.

Butler Library may not have had the charm of Cornell's Uris Library, but it was a safe and clean environment in which to pass the day. I looked around way too much, people looked at me, and I didn't make many friends, but I withdrew the books from the reserve stacks, and tried to read them.

I took two classes that first semester. One was in art history, an appropriate class to take in New York City, with its access to world-class museums. I was right at home in the museums. I could sit in front of a Renaissance painting for hours. Part of my attention was attracted to the elements of the painting, its primary colors, and symmetry, but I came to the exercise with an advantage. I could just sit there and think. That is the nature of obsessive rumination, and it has very little to do with art appreciation.

The other class was entitled "Peace in the American Tradition." This professor had worked out a syllabus that focused on the Quakers and the Mennonites, and the other fringe elements that had protested against wars. It led right on up to Dave Dellinger and the 1960s, one of the direct forerunners of the anti-nuclear movement of which I still felt myself a part.

I had to secure special permission to enroll, as I was not a regular student in the college, a prerequisite for this class.

"Rules are made to me be broken," the professor told me, a lively, rotund man who enjoyed his work. I told Dr. Ruben about this in session, and he approved. He looked at me with a light in his eye and said, "I see you, someday, saying the same thing to one of your students."

There he went again. I could barely make it across town, and he was projecting ahead to a day when I not only had a college degree but a Ph.D. and employment as a professor. I looked at him uncomprehendingly. He had a way of keeping you motivated.

The next semester, I took a course that had something to do with Russian politics, contemporary Russian politics, and it employed a text, written by the professor, that included the same paragraph over and over. This professor may have shared my problem. I sat next to a pretty girl who had been a year behind me at Andover. She seemed to enjoy my slightly spaced out behavior and somewhat incoherent conversation. One evening we even went out to a local bar, *Augie's* on 106th street. She took my arm, walking down Broadway. We sat at the bar and discussed mutual prep school acquaintances.

"Barry's been in bad shape," she said, bringing me up to date on a remarkably talented and creative classmate. "He was in the hospital with DTs."

I was shaken up and immediately wanted to rally our friends to help out. Dr. Rubin set me straight. "You'd only make him paranoid," he said at our next session.

But that was how I looked at things. If I didn't tell a friend to start seeing a doctor, I probably didn't like them very much. In the course of a few months, I'd become a believer, a convert.

Before an appointment with Dr. Rubin, I had to select a shirt to wear. In some ways, I had become more functional, but I was still regularly caught up in tangles by the simplest decisions. Having two blue shirts in the closet can be a good thing. But to the obsessive, it can be an obscure form of hell. How do you choose between them?

One is better pressed. But the other is a little warmer. It could be sunny today. Then again, the radio is predicting a heat wave for later in the week. That was one radio station. The other radio station is predicting rain. The second radio station is never reliable. Everyone knows that. I'll just take the shirt that's further to the right. That will solve everything. But I think I rearranged the shirts last night. Yesterday the other shirt would have been on the right. I'll close the door, open it fast, and whichever shirt I see first, I'll wear. There, I did it. No, I saw them at the same time. I'll try it again. This time I'll open the door on the count of three. One, two, three. There. No. That was no good. The door opened too slowly. I'll open the door on the count of five, and whichever shirt sways out, I'll wear that one. No more thinking. Just do it. One, two, three, four...

This process proceeds for forty-five minutes. Then you throw the damn shirts on the floor and wear a T-shirt. You move on to the next decision.

Three mornings a week, I showed up at Dr. Rubin's office. I was on time. On this particular morning, it had been rough.

"That's not what you said!" I confronted him.

"I say a lot of things." Dr. Rubin's demeanor was placid.

"How could it work?! How could it work?! I'm not functioning, not at all!" I was close to an explosion.

I took the next step. "I've been at Columbia for a year and I don't know anyone!" I'd lost it, in my hyperbole.

Dr. Rubin sat quietly, watching me intently. A long moment passed.

"I don't know how you get there, but I know it isn't that way."

There was one dark afternoon that stands out. It may not have been any darker than all the others. I was still looking forward to rainy days when I could avoid looking at anything except the underside of a black umbrella in front of my eyes, but for some reason I could not have identified or explained, I had reached an impasse. I was standing at a pay phone on Madison Avenue and Eighty-Forth Street and I called Dr. Rubin in his New Rochelle office. He was with a patient.

"Excuse me. This is Dr. Rubin," he said, his standard greeting to let the caller know that there was a patient in the room.

"This is Jordan," I said.

"Yes, Jordan." He was ready to listen.

"I think we should take a break," I blurted out.

"What brings this on?" Dr. Rubin was taking time with me.

"I just think we should take a break," I repeated. I had absolutely no insight into why I was making this proposal. I was stalled out on Madison Avenue in the '80s. All was awash. Fortunately, Dr. Rubin did.

"Well, there are breaks. I take vacations. You may be away for a week or so this summer."

"I mean, now…" I was aware that I was taking someone else's time, and I didn't like it.

"Jordan, would you like me to come into the city?" Dr. Rubin asked a question only a lifetime of practice could have taught him to ask.

"No, no. I just think… I don't want to hold you up. I just think…"

Dr. Rubin stayed on that pay phone with me for forty-five minutes. What his patient did, I'm not certain, but a psychiatrist is a shared commodity. His patients never meet one another, but they learn to share when necessary. Before I hung up, Rubin was satisfied that I would be at the next session.

And there was a next session and another one after that. Dr. Rubin had seen me through the storm. We met in the morning on Mondays, Wednesdays, and Fridays, without fail. I showed up on time, even if it meant running the last few blocks to get there. Dr. Rubin got to you that way. He didn't allow smoking in the office. I didn't smoke, but some of his patients did. Dr. Rubin told them they could go outside if they needed a cigarette, but it was on their time. They gave up the need to smoke. Every moment in that room was valuable to Dr. Rubin, and I guess I came to see it that way as well.

I had a metaphor for the pain. You're walking up the slope of a huge pit. At the heart of the pit is a massive fire which burns you as you walk, and the ground on the slope of the pit is covered with metal spikes. You keep walking because there is no alternative. I kept walking.

I did consider taking my life, at least conceptually. I thought that through. The way I saw it, you're alive on this earth for some seventy or eighty years, then you're dead for a gazillion years, actually, gazillions and gazillions. There is no question about that part. The only part in play was the time here on Earth, which is of strictly limited duration. There was an outside chance I might be able to make something out of it. It seemed worth the attempt.

Dr. Rubin had an opinion on this as well. "You won't kill yourself," he said. Don't know how he knew that, but he did. He assured me that he'd had patients who had committed suicide before and that mine wouldn't jeopardize his reputation. But still, he pointed out, "If you think about it, you'll try it."

So, I tried to stay away from the issue. There is a lesser-known view of Hell, the poor schmuck standing at the foot of the hill unable to decide which boulder to start pushing.

Another image that stayed with me at the time also involved motion. I'm walking through the heart of a dark, swamp-infested forest, deep in the heart of a hidden valley somewhere. It is night. I can't see more than ten feet ahead of me. I struggle on through thorny brambles and vaporous, stinky mud holes. I have no idea where I'm going. At the same time, Dr. Rubin is standing in the clear air and sunshine, high on a mountain ridge that overlooks the valley. From up there he can see a hundred and fifty miles in every direction. Three times a week, he comes down from the mountain ridge to speak with me and give me my bearings, to point out which way I'd best be going. Along with the mountain ridge image is another that had a particular resonance at the time. I'm walking along, and I fall in a mud hole. The time it takes for me to claw my way out is best measured in eons, eons of painful and almost hopeless effort which finally result in a position at the base of a tree. From there, another period of eons pass, during which I climb onto an elevated branch.

From there, things aren't half bad. They are almost acceptable. There is a little breeze, and above all, I am finally out of the mud hole. I sit back and begin to relax a bit. Then it happens. I see a piece of fruit hanging out at the end of one of the smaller branches. In my gut, I know the smaller branch won't support my weight, but the fruit is ripe and oh so tempting. Am I content with my new-found position in the tree? Afraid not. I inch my way out on the branch and, against all better judgment and experience, reach for the fruit. The branch gives way and I fall. Once again, I am in the mud hole, and the interminable ascent begins again. This is the nature of the obsessive. We cannot live with uncertainty and incompleteness, and it leads to our fall, over and over again.

I was trying to get better. I thought it was possible, and I was giving it my best shot. That was until I systematically destroyed everything I had going. The psychiatrist's vacation has been written about before. There was a popular novel in the '80s called *August*. I think I can say, in all modesty, that I took the patient's reaction to a shrink's vacation to an entirely new level. Dr. Rubin took a month-long vacation to Japan.

Dr. Rubin had been planning that trip for years. Japan was big for Dr. Rubin There was the Bodhisattva in the waiting room and I knew he'd been there before. The whole Zen thing lies right at the heart of his philosophy, along with the workable ideas from every other philosophical tradition. He wasn't making this trip lightly. He knew there were liabilities and risks involved, but he had decided to take those risks.

A break is especially in order for a psychiatrist. Lives lie in the balance in his office every day: relationships, marriages, career choices. In just seconds, Rubin makes choices about what to say that can have repercussions years into the future. And if someone calls in ready to walk out on a ledge, what about that? It may not happen every day, but I know it happens. So, if a hard-working, dedicated doctor decides to take some time off, who can say anything about it? You can wish him bon voyage and settle in for the duration. But with that first vacation, I didn't know how to react. I just freaked.

I knew he was in Japan, wherever the hell that was. Of course, I knew where Japan was. Didn't I have three-fourths of an Ivy League education? It's just that, to a guy who has difficulty negotiating his way down the block, let alone across town, the idea of a country five thousand miles away has a certain degree of unreality. I knew he would be gone for a month, a length of time that was also essentially meaningless. At the time, he was renting part of his office to another psychiatrist. I was supposed to go in and talk to him, and I did, a few times. I would launch into one of my forty-five-minute explanations of why I was writing a letter to a girl I had met in Washington, and he would be interested. He entirely missed the minor point that this kind of explanation wasn't interesting: it was the problem. My anchor was gone. I floated up and away from the earth, like a hot air balloon cut free from its tether. Day by day, the towns, the cars, the people, all signs of civilized life began to recede from view. The air grew colder and I was alone.

Chapter Six

My Own Place – 1985

I was living in the den of my parents' apartment. They'd taken me in, which, given the state I was in, was no small thing. They gave me a place to sleep, put food in the refrigerator, and paid my tuition bill, not to mention Dr. Rubin's hourly fee and bill from the Lascoff pharmacy on Lexington Avenue. It's not every set of parents who puts up with a son who screams, yells, and punches holes in the wall. As a house guest, I left much to be desired.

The den had a bed built into the wall. It folded down. When it was folded up, it was closed in by these two doors. They'd had it installed when they moved in, in case my sisters or I ever needed a place to stay. One wall of the room was covered with books. I'd read the first half of a lot of them. I never finished books. Don't know why. I'd achieved a fairly high level of education without finishing books. I'd fake it. I had a pretty good idea where the author was going. I'd just set the book down somehow, and never get around to picking it up. Some people avoid stepping on cracks in the sidewalk. I read the first half of books. Maybe it was something like that.

The room also had the television. I used to watch the Weather Channel with the sound turned off. It was soothing. But that was only on bad days.

But with Dr. Rubin off jet-setting in the Far East, I decided to move out. There must have been some justification for this decision at the time. I'd take a room closer to Columbia. That may have been how I thought it through.

"Got to get closer to the library. Got to study more," I convinced myself.

I found a real estate agent who specialized in low-rent apartments, and I told him I wanted something cheap. As to where the money for the rent would come from, I sort of overlooked that minor issue. I was moving out. The rest was detail. Was I thinking, "I'll stick it to Rubin?" No. I don't think I was. But that is exactly what I was doing. If he can leave town, I can leave my parents' apartment. If he can fly off to Japan, he won't have me as some kind of big success story. No chance of that.

The real estate agent must have taken me seriously when I asked for some place low-end. Maybe it was the way I was dressed. I tried to explain that I needed a room in the vicinity of campus and that I didn't have a lot to spend. What I communicated may have been something entirely different. For whatever reason, he led me to a building that could best be described as challenged. How can a New York City apartment building be challenged? If it never faced a day with a sense of hope. If it displayed from the front windows a profound disregard for every living being that passed by. If on every possible occasion, it stood for the agony of birth and the garbled few moments of life. This was the building the real estate agent led me to.

In the parlance of New York City real estate, it was a single resident occupancy, or S.R.O. They were a phenomenon of New York City in the '80s. During that period of enormous growth, in the construction of apartment buildings for the super-rich, city housing activists succeeded in passing into law a mandate that a certain number of buildings be set aside for the old and the infirm. They were symbolic of the divide in that city, the divide between the high life of the successful and the minimal existence of those barely getting by. In the summer of 1985, the S.R.O. was a part of New York. It did not provide social services so much as it provided a place for the old and the sad to pass their days alone. A solitary walk to the supermarket, the occasional visitor: these were the highlights of the day for the aged who had managed to avoid more draconian forms of institutionalization. I accepted the arrangement.

The room the agent showed me was at the back of a small suite. Maybe ten by ten, its one window looked into an interior air shaft. There was no chance for the sun to make its way into this dark interior. The suite had other single rooms. How many there were was not clear on that first visit. It also had a kitchen and a bathroom. The agent remarked, "Just 'til you find something better."

I gave him some form of deposit, and he handed me a key. I was on my own, my own place in the big city. I wouldn't say I had visions of wild parties and a carefree bachelor's life, but I had succeeded in removing myself from my former place of residence.

I shared the suite in the S.R.O. suite with just one other person: an elderly black woman. I only saw her a couple of times, but I had some sense that she was around. For one thing, she had covered all the fixtures in the kitchen with silver foil. She may have been in worse shape than I was. I know that. I'm very much aware that mental illness is prevalent in our society. I always had a roof over my head. I always had food to eat. I was educated with an opportunity to advance myself. There was plenty of pain, but I was receiving the best care possible. Just walk through New York City sometime and see the men sleeping in empty doorways. Then you can have some idea what rough is. How many of those people could be straightened out with nine hundred milligrams of lithium on a regular basis? How many of them just aren't getting it? Even at my lowest point, I was being protected by a safety net. I might have done my best to go crashing to the ground, but there were always doctors and family members looking out for me. I was always amongst the fortunate few.

Chapter Seven

I Was Alone – 1985

With Rubin out of the country, dangerous thoughts were taking shape in my mind. Those thoughts can be summarized by one word: fear. Paranoia is a common phenomenon. Crosby, Stills, Nash and Young sing about it in the song about almost cutting their hair. It goes around. But there are different degrees of paranoia. In later years, I would think about beating it back with a stick. That's actually pretty good. At this stage, I knew nothing about beating it back with a stick. I knew nothing about paranoia. I knew that I was lying on the floor of a small dark room with my clothes and few possessions scattered about me. I was unable to focus my thoughts, and they were taking me into a landscape of fear I had no way to control. The central thought was that Rubin was actually an evil man who was using the drugs to keep me under his control. From this small beginning grew a fear of enormous proportions. How I was able to break free from its power is at the heart of this story.

At some point during those first days, I went out and bought a small color television. I lugged it back to the room and lay on a mattress on the floor watching TV. The room was completely unfurnished – just a small square space. There was a mattress lying at a diagonal on the floor and a meager supply of clothes and papers scattered about. There was certainly no cable hook up, but I got some reception. I watched a soccer game between two South American powerhouses. 1985 was not a World Cup year, but for some reason, one of the networks was carrying the game. I had the sound turned off – not low, off. No one would have complained, but I didn't want to attract attention. At some point, I got up and tied the door closed with a yellow bandanna. Master locks don't always work, but you can always count on the yellow bandanna. With the door securely fastened like that it was hard to go out of the room, and I did need to piss. I pissed in a small wooden chest, purchased on a family trip to Switzerland that had somehow made the progression to my current abode.

I was afraid. Fear, like anger, however, doesn't always have a specific point of focus. Fear can become a general state of mind that, once inhabited, comes to seem as natural as any other. I was isolated. No one knew where I was – my parents, my siblings, no one – and with each passing hour my own conviction that Dr. Rubin was an evil doctor using the drugs to manipulate me were growing stronger. Days went by in that condition, days and nights. How many, I couldn't say, but there was little distinction between them. During the days before I went cold turkey, the drugs were taken sporadically, which is bad enough in itself. A divergence from the regular time table of even a few hours, of even one of these powerful drugs, can throw you so far that any hope of return becomes problematic. I was playing around with six. There was the lithium and the clonidine, and four others designed to control the obsessive thinking. What I should have seen as signs of trouble, my warped mind took as signs of greater clarity. As I drifted further and further out to sea, I thought I was understanding everything clearly for the first time.

Rubin has been using these drugs to keep me under his control. Now I see. Now I see what's really going on. I had to wait for the effects to wear off a little to really understand. It went something like that. I lay there on the floor of my upscale digs and watched the shapes and colors on the twelve-inch TV screen. There was very little sound, save for the muffled street noises filtering their way up from West Ninety-Fifth Street. The room was darkened. I was alone.

Chapter Eight

Down the Drain – 1985

I crossed the line from being afraid of the drugs, to deciding I wouldn't take any more. I have a visual image of the toilet basin filled with an assortment of colored pills, capsules and tablets in reds, oranges and greens. There is a loud sound of pressure being released as the pills swirl around and disappear down the drain. A stillness returns as the pool of water comes to rest. The pills are gone.

It's a dramatic memory. But I'm not sure it really happened that way. I did stop taking the pills, the capsules – everything. That, I'm sure of. And as my grip on all that was real became more and more tenuous, I became more and more sure that I was finally seeing things clearly. If I had been slipping slowly toward a steep precipice, I was now over the edge, in free fall. I felt liberated when actually I was rushing down toward the chiseled rocks at the base of the cliff.

At this point, there was no turning back. Even if the pills were still nestled somewhere among the clothes and papers on the floor of my room, I could not have returned to where I had been. For one thing, my body was already out of sync. My mind and body were scrambled. Even if I had wanted to get back on the program, it would have been virtually impossible. But there was a bigger problem. I was convinced that I had done the right thing. I saw myself as a courageous freedom fighter, striking back at the forces of evil, Dr. Rubin, the villain. He was a very bad man who had infiltrated his way into my family and taken over my life. I was prepared to take whatever steps were necessary to secure my freedom.

I was driven by an overarching and pervasive fear. But once I had moved into this space, it felt entirely natural. This was my world. It was the world I knew and accepted. I moved through it without questioning its validity. Steps had to be taken.

I realized that the first thing to be done was to get word to my father, to let him in on the discovery I had made. But this had to be done with the utmost care. He had to be contacted with meticulous attention to detail, for he, too, was under the control of the evil psychiatrists. I determined that I had to meet up with him on some neutral ground where he would be free to listen to the truth– Truth with a capital *T.* I needed to find a place where I would be able to speak without interruption, to explain the whole situation. If only I could get him to see what was happening, there might be some chance of breaking free. It was a long shot. But I had to try.

I settled on the chess sets near the carousel in Central Park. I decided I had to meet up with him somewhere in the park where we would be able to talk in peace and quiet, where I would be able to make the whole thing clear. I wasn't particularly familiar with the spot, but my father likes playing chess, so I thought this would be a good place. There would be no telephones, no distractions, and I would have the chance to make him understand.

I wasn't sure I would be successful. My father had such a firm belief in Rubin, but I had to try. There was no other way. A telephone call to set up the meeting was out of the question. They would be on to me. They would try and get me back into Rubin's office, back on to the drugs, and that was not going to happen. I had to find some other way to get word to my father. I settled on a plan. It was a long shot. But steps had to be taken. Lives were lying in the balance.

I found a piece of paper and composed a note. It was short and to the point. The details could come later. The important thing was that I get him to the chess sets in Central Park. If I could meet up with him there, everything else would be okay. Did I recopy the note thirty or forty times? That would have been the usual pattern. Things were different now. I set it down in one try. There was no time for equivocation. I stated the time and place and asked him to meet me.

Bringing the note to the apartment was entirely too risky. The apartment was in Rubin's realm. It was part of the world he controlled. To go anywhere near there was to risk being drawn back in, to risk being put back on the drugs, maybe this time for good. I couldn't chance it. I trusted my father. He might be under Rubin's control, but at least he was open-minded. I felt he could still listen to reason. I just had to get to him in the right way. He had an office in mid-town. I would bring the note there. Until my father got this note, my parents had no idea where I was. I don't think the note did much to allay their concern.

Chapter Nine

The Doors of the Ambulance Closed – 1985

Psychiatric medication is a wonder, a wonder that has helped millions of people. But these drugs must be accorded the highest degree of respect. There is, I believe, no way of conveying this fact to the patient taking them for the first time. Aspirin can be taken for a while and then stopped. Vitamins certainly, even antibiotics can be halted abruptly without consequences. With these psychiatric drugs, that just is not the case. I don't know how many people act out and stop taking their medicine. I don't know how many people wind up in the hospital as a consequence. It is not likely that many break off as radically as I did, but I don't know even that. I do think it is probable that most psychiatric patients screw around at least once. I would like to think that most get a little phased, and learn their lesson without serious consequences. In my case, the lesson did not come easy. There was a support net in the city of New York, but I was letting go of the trapeze at the highest point in the arc. I was falling.

By this point it had been days since I'd gone off the drugs, and with each passing hour my system was going further into collapse. My limbs were moving, but the circuits upstairs were jammed. Electrons were firing in the wrong direction, and chemicals were flooding areas they had no business being. The whole thing was a big mess. It was not a sustainable situation.

I must have walked south through the park. I don't recall. I do know that by some system of advanced path-finding I made my way to the grassy area adjacent to the Wollman Skating Rink. The rink has a different name now. It was rebuilt with Trump money, I believe, but this part of the park also held rich associations. It had once been the site of the Shaffer Summer Music Festival, which later became the Dr. Pepper Summer Music Festival. The concerts took place inside the rink, but the music could be heard by people sitting on rocks outside. I'd heard my share of concerts both inside and outside the rink.

The concerts had always been about fitting in with the big kids. The afternoons I had spent playing softball or throwing a football with my friend, not far off, were not. On a Thursday morning in early autumn, the crowds had long ago dispersed. The ice had not been laid down for the winter. The rink was empty. Individuals walking dogs and the occasional tourist strolled about. The sky was slightly overcast. It was cool, but not cold.

Slowly, steadily, I walked down a sloping black pathway that led from an upper level toward the plateau adjacent to the rink. It's easy to feel lost in Central Park. That's part of its charm. You never know exactly where you are. But I must have still felt I was on the way to the chess sets. As the path curved its way downward, my mind must have become increasingly stiff. All was not well. I reached the foot of the black path with the grass and dirt on either side. I looked down at a medium-sized round stone on the ground to my right. I continued to look down at the medium-sized brown stone to my right. I had no inclination to do anything else. I stood at the foot of that black path with the brown dirt and scruffy grass at my feet and fixated on that stone. I don't think I was inclined to pick it up. I don't think I was inclined to walk past it. I just stood there and looked at it. The obsessive gets stuck on one idea. The obsessive who has gone off his medicine without a doctor's consultation gets stuck looking at one rock.

I don't know how long I stood in that position, staring at that damn rock, but at some point, I fell to the ground. I fell to the ground and stopped moving. My eyes were open. I could hear the sounds around me. I just stopped moving. I was frozen. It is tempting to look back on this behavior as some form of temper tantrum of a spoiled child. I concede that may have been a part of it. But there were chemical problems. I had a lot of growing up to do. There is no question about that. But on this occasion my behavior was facilitated by the chemical imbalances inside my head. The circuits were shorted out. The mixture of components that make it possible for the human being to function normally was profoundly screwed up. I would like to say that this was my most embarrassing moment, lying still on the ground beside the Wollman Skating Rink, but unfortunately, it was just the beginning.

New Yorkers will come to the aid of someone in trouble. At least that was my experience. From all sides, people came running. I heard their voices. When they were in my line of vision, I saw them, but I didn't move. One young man called out: "He's well dressed!"

Maybe I should add that New Yorkers will come to the aid of someone in trouble if he is well dressed. At any rate, a small gathering of people stood around, and some moments later, an ambulance pulled up beside me. You would think that at this moment I would stand up and say, "Hey, thanks, but I'm O.K. I just fell down. I must have hit my head. I'm O.K. really. I can just walk it off. No, I'm really O.K."

You would think I would say something like that. No such luck. Knucklehead that I was, I just lay there. I lay there stiff and still without moving a muscle. My eyes darted around to the left and the right, and I was aware that I was being placed on a stretcher and lifted into the back of the ambulance, but I didn't move, at all. The doors of the ambulance closed.

It was symbolic, I think, the doors of that ambulance closing. They were closing so that the ambulance could drive to the hospital, but they were also closing on my chance to walk around as a free person. The word 'freedom' comes up frequently in discussions of Patrick Henry and the founding fathers. You also hear it in the context of debates about the Cold War and the Berlin Wall, but using it in the context of daily life in New York City sounds pretentious. It just seems inappropriate to use such a grand word to describe going to the deli to pick up some bagels and a half a pound of Munster cheese, or taking the 7 Train to Flushing to watch the Mets. These things are so ordinary, so commonplace, that the word 'freedom' seems overblown. But that is what it's really about.

I'm just saying that once these basic liberties have been taken away, their value can never be taken completely for granted again. Once the door of that ambulance closed, I was in the custody of strangers. I was in the custody of men and woman who were operating according to an agenda of their own, an agenda regulated in part by a fear of massive lawsuits. Not even Rubin had the power to dictate the actions of these people. Through my own actions, I had placed myself in the control of the mental health system of New York City, a better mental health system than is found in most parts of the world, I imagine, but a system with its own rules and regulations.

So the ambulance pulled out onto the park drive with me strapped in the back. We drove south and out of the park at Fifty-Ninth Street. I know we turned right and traveled west to Ninth Avenue. I know we turned left on Ninth and went south to Fifty-Sixth Street. I know all this because I know we wound up at Roosevelt Hospital, which lies between Ninth and Tenth on Fifty-Sixth Street. All things taken together, I would recommend taking a taxi for a trip of this kind. You get to sit up, and when you arrive at your destination, you can pay your fare and get out. These people had something entirely different in mind.

My next memory is of being tied into some kind of raised platform on one side of the Roosevelt Hospital Psychiatric Emergency Room. They must have carried me in, because I'm quite sure I didn't walk. It was clearly an emergency room for psychiatric patients; there were no broken bones or bleeding ulcers being treated here. This was strictly for those individuals who had lost it big time. Not like an all-out fight with a significant other in the kitchen. Not like a sobbing breakdown after losing a job. This room was reserved for those who had stepped over the line, to a point where deep breathing and a long walk weren't going to do much good, people who had lost it so severely that they were really quite powerless to get it together on their own. I fit right in.

So there I was, strapped down, and as frightened as I had ever been. I had begun moving and talking. Don't ask me why. My platform was on one side of a large central corridor. Doctors, nurses, and attendants were moving about. On the opposite side of the corridor was a series of four or five small rooms which opened out on to the central area. In one, a man was screaming and yelling at full volume. I had no idea what he was so upset about, but the effect of his contribution was to raise the energy level of the room. I wasn't aware of any other individual patients, but there was a general air of activity.

A senior doctor took a position beside my bed, or platform, or whatever it was. I don't call him a senior doctor because of his bedside manner, but he was an older man, and he was definitely taking an interest in me. The main thing he wanted was telephone numbers. I may have started moving and talking, but on certain essential matters I was not giving way. The drugs were a disaster. They were evil, to the extent that I had a conception of the word. They were a tool used by bad men to control vulnerable people, to keep them under control and take away their freedom and their money. On these fundamental issues, I remained steadfast. I knew what I knew. There was no room for discussion. None. This man, or doctor, or whatever he was, wore a white coat. He was in league with Rubin and the rest of them, and if given half a chance he would put me back under, put me under in a way that I would lose sight of the clarity I had gained. Put me under so that maybe I would never come up again.

I knew all this. I also was aware that I was powerless. I was tied down. My resistance was by necessity passive. I was not confrontational. I certainly was not violent. I interacted and conversed, and at some point, I must have given him my sister's telephone number. It was a weekday, and I must have given this doctor my sister's work telephone number. I remember telling my sister Anne I was tied in, "like on a sailboat." When a sailboat is moving rapidly toward the wind, it keels over on its side. The crew, in an effort to keep the boat from going too far over, can lean out over the topside. It's called "hiking out" and sometimes the crew will tie their feet into the cockpit of the boat to make sure they don't fall out. So that is what I told my sister.

"Like in a sailboat."

She appreciated the allusion. I would like to point to this as an example of keeping some humor in the most stressful of times. Maybe it was.

Sometime later, my father was standing at the entranceway to the emergency room. There are many joys to parenting – seeing your child take his first step, watching him grow, watching his school graduation. Coming to see your child in the psychiatric emergency room of a major city hospital may not rank high on this list. But if you're in for the long haul, you show up anyway. My father had gotten the note slipped under the door of his midtown office and had shown up as instructed at the Central Park chess sets. He still had the tuna fish sandwich he had bought for the occasion, also as instructed, with him when he walked in the emergency room door.

Chapter Ten

What a Salesman – 1985

The doctors were trying to calm me down. That must have been their first order of business, as I had become extremely agitated. They wanted me to take two pills. One was Haldol, and the other was supposed to do something to complement the Haldol. I refused to take the pills. There was no anger in my refusal. There was, I felt, despite my extreme agitation, a great calmness. I wouldn't do it. I would explain to anyone who would listen why I wouldn't take the pills. But I simply would not take them.

I kept talking. I don't recall what I said, but I kept trying to make my position as clear as possible. At some point, the nurse came to me with a needle to give the drugs by injection. I didn't fight her, and she injected the drugs, which were certainly in order.

"What a salesman," she commented with a smile.

They do exist, these mental health workers who conduct themselves with humor and humanity under stress. My father's presence was supportive.

"That's what the second drug is for," he said facetiously, sharing an unspoken agreement that there were, in fact, potentially dangerous consequences to these drugs. He didn't believe it, but in spirit, he was a comrade in arms. There wasn't a whole lot he could do, sitting there beside me. But he was there. And when he stepped away, he was making plans to have me taken to Payne Whitney, the best in-patient psychiatric hospital in New York City.

Others had not been so detached. Plans had been made. A place had been secured for me at the Payne Whitney Psychiatric Hospital, a division of the Cornell New York Hospital. The medical authorities at Roosevelt Hospital had no intention of turning me out onto the street, and my parents had been left with the unpleasant task of finding a hospital that would take me in. They chose Payne Whitney. I couldn't speak to their thought process, but over the years I have gathered that the hospital they chose is reputed to be among the finest in New York City. It does not garner headlines for treating celebrities on the mend, but as psychiatric hospitals go, it has a first-rate reputation. It is difficult, even now, to utter those words, "as psychiatric hospitals go." That, however, was the position in which my family was placed. One of their own needed the care of the medical community. They rose to the occasion and made plans to send their son to the best the city had to offer.

Once again, my means of transportation was taken care of. The Fifty-Ninth Street cross-town was not an option. A private car service was similarly ruled out. They were sending me to the East Side the way I had arrived – in the back of an ambulance. My sister Anne, who had also shown up, rode with me. "Make doctor friends," She said, with her penchant for speaking directly, as we traveled east.

The ambulance wouldn't need its siren, and it wouldn't have to run any red lights, but it would ensure that I arrived at Payne Whitney unharmed and in one piece. The Roosevelt Hospital Emergency Room had performed its duty. It had scraped me off the pavement of a path in Central Park, injected me with the drugs required to calm my hyper-excited state of mind, and delivered me to the hands of a responsible in-patient institution. They were in no way liable. Whether or not I actually belonged in a hospital of the kind to which I was being sent was not a question that concerned them. I had at no time attempted to harm myself, or to take my own life. I had stopped taking my prescribed medication. That was all it really amounted to. That was why I'd fallen apart. Ideally, I'd be put back on them.

Chapter Eleven

You're a Fighter – 1985

The admissions interview is the first order of business when you arrive at a mental hospital. I guess they just have to make sure you're crazy enough to get in. And I can proudly state that I passed with flying colors. A willing audience asking me what I was so angry about, and man, did I let her have it. I was speaking to some kind of psychologist or nurse while the real doctor sat in a chair along the wall. The woman smiled while I spoke and encouraged me to get more involved. It was my longest, angriest rant. The doctor didn't say a word. He sat there. I think he was smiling as well. The woman who was doing the talking asked some questions. They were the same questions I was asked a number of times by various nurses and attendants. They asked me if I wanted to hurt myself, and they asked me if I heard voices. Frankly, these questions mystified me. I actually had no idea what she was referring to. At no time, anywhere on the dark road had there been any voice in my head other than my own thoughts. That was in no way a part of the picture. As for the other question, the answer was a resounding no. I may have thought conceptually about ending my life, but I had never taken any steps in that direction, and I had certainly never wanted to hurt myself.

Still, the medical team in the admissions department must have been satisfied with what they heard because this middle-aged woman with white hair was prepared to usher me into the elevator and up into the confines of the Payne Whitney Psychiatric Hospital, which, near as I could tell, occupied a number of floors on the upper reaches of the Cornell New York Hospital, there on the corner of Sixty-Eighth Street and First Avenue.

"Just like Betty Ford," I joked as we walked across the hall toward the elevator. She didn't appreciate the humor and was quick to point out that I shouldn't expect the surroundings to be too luxurious. The elevator took us up to the seventh floor.

Someone led me to my room. I shared the room with one other patient. My roommate was an older man, at least in his sixties, who seemed quite at peace with his surroundings. Some days later, his wife and daughter came to visit, and they all seemed content that he was where he should be, doing something useful for his health. No *One Flew Over the Cuckoo's Nest* overtones here. Unfortunately, I did not share his placid outlook. I was scared, I was stoic, and I was not talking. I would have been scared anywhere with the state my brain was in. But here, I was really scared. I knew I was confined. It was not a topic of conversation, but I knew the front door was locked. Not locked like you come home and throw the latch to keep people out. It was locked from the inside – like you needed a key, and you wanted to keep the people inside from going out. No one talked about it, but there was an unspoken understanding that no one could leave.

There were other indications that this was not the Holiday Inn, despite the placid demeanor of my older roommate. For one thing, there was a small, square window in the doorway that led from the room to the hallway, and a number of times during the night, one of the nurses would walk by and point a flashlight through the window. She pointed it at both beds, to make sure we were still there. I don't think this would go over real well at the Hilton or the Marriott Marquis: room service, complimentary continental breakfast and 2:00 a.m. bed checks. There are many joys of living in freedom, joys you just don't appreciate unless you've spent some time in a place like that. One of them is being able to lock the door to your apartment and to be free of flashlights pointing at you in the middle of the night.

It was the loss of freedom. It was the fact that I had not had a lithium capsule in something like four or five days. I'd gone cold turkey off six drugs. It was a deep-rooted fear of what might lie ahead in this place. I tried to put a positive spin on it all, to compare it to a house I had shared with college classmates, but all things taken together, I was a little concerned. My future plans before the breakdown had become increasingly abstract. I always wanted good grades, but after concluding my work for the Freeze Campaign, I had seen my-self traveling the world for five or six years, working as I went. None of this had I foreseen.

Before each meal, one of the nurses distributed medicine to each patient in a little white paper cup. My cup had one pill – a Valium pill. Call it hutzpah. Call it ignorance. But no attempt had been made to ascertain what I had been taking or to restore the chemical balance. I know they had spoken with Rubin, but it seems that the medical authorities at the inpatient section of the Payne Whitney Psychiatric Hospital prized their independence more than the advice of another member of the fraternity. One Valium. That was it.

During those first days, the doctors themselves were relatively unobtrusive. I sat down with the doctor assigned to my case once. There was, however, a ritual which really made an impression. On an assigned day, at an assigned time, the entire medical staff walked around the floor in a group and came to visit each patient at his bed. I wasn't raging against anyone. I was trying to get along, as well as I could. I must have told this floating brain trust what they wanted to hear because they left smiling.

Yes, they were smiling. I'm not saying they were cheerful (maybe it had something to do with their own group dynamic), but they went about their business with smiles on their faces. The psychiatric profession is notorious for keeping their thoughts to themselves. That may be one of the questions on the application for the psychiatry specialty. "Can you say the exact opposite of what you mean with a straight face?" I'm not knocking it. It is a useful skill. I'm just saying I had no way of knowing what those doctors really thought.

There was, however, a certain amount of community there on the seventh floor. Activity centered on the lounge area in the middle of the floor. There were a couple of large couches, a table, and a bookshelf with an assortment of board games and paperback books. Patients who weren't hiding out in their room congregated here before meals, after meals, at all hours, and I can truthfully say some became acquaintances. One guy was either on his way to or from Sing-Sing, a well-known New York State penitentiary. He walked around with a large pile of lottery cards. They kept him busy. He wore a blue jean jacket with the sleeves cut off and had three day's growth of a dark black beard. This guy was into big things, much bigger than the seventh-floor lounge. He was going places, or he had been places. He was only here for a short stay, entirely by accident.

There was a short woman who was much more Upper East Side. Her name was Doris, and her ambition was to get over to Bloomingdale's to buy some cosmetics. She dressed well and had a refined but not a stuffy attitude. She participated in the book group, which read and discussed novels, and she welcomed me to join them. Doris also helped maintain a chart of the floor's residents, who was in which room. Like the rest of us, she was floating, overmedicated or undermedicated, grappling with her own array of demons. There were occasional field trips led by one of the staff, so it was not unrealistic to assume that she made periodic trips to Bloomingdales. Either she could afford the cosmetics, or she was putting on a pretty good show.

Another member of our group was in his thirties and preoccupied with getting back to his studio apartment, which, he was proud to recall, had a V.C.R. He consistently wore blue button-down shirts, not tucked in at the waist. Wilber, that was his name, complimented me on the job I had done rearranging the bookshelf: Responsibilities had been allocated, and mine had been to do some straightening up.

"Looks like a normal person did it," he remarked.

I did have that distinction. I came across in this company as pretty well put together. I had my acoustic guitar, and from time to time I brought it out and played in the lounge. I played songs I knew by heart, Neil Young and James Taylor.

"Who would think you'd hear something like that in here?" Trey, another patient, asked.

I had an audience: a middle age man who'd been around before.

"She came to visit me every day," he proclaimed, proud of his girlfriend.

"Sounds like hell," I responded. Maybe I was just jealous, or maybe the idea of being exposed in such circumstances rubbed me the wrong way. I did in fact have visitors: from both my parents who brought my clothes and guitar; from my brother-in-law, an attorney, whom I consulted on legal means of getting out, and from a first cousin who left me a box of orange Tic-Taks.

Taken together, these associations were not insubstantial. Every one of us belonged in Payne Whitney. The reality may have been that Rubin could have straightened me out and gotten me back on the right mix, but for the time being I was in no shape to be standing on the Ninety-Sixth Street platform waiting for the 1 Train. The others had more substantial problems, but I wasn't looking for their shortcomings. I was one amongst many and had very little interest in judging anyone crazier than myself.

There were professionals on the floor – the psychiatric nurses. They dressed in street clothes, but they had training in how to interact with the mentally ill, the slightly deranged, and the overmedicated. They were the clear-eyed people in the land of ghosts. They saw the world with a clarity the rest of us could only attempt to recall from an earlier existence. As far as I can tell, their responsibility was to sit around and engage any patient who was so inclined in making conversation. I think I can say that, in general terms, their heart was in their work. They smiled. I was trying to give everyone the benefit of the doubt.

Two of the nurses had supervisory responsibilities, one during the day and one during the night. They oversaw the work of the junior nurses on the floor and hung out in a small office opposite the lounge area. These two women were in charge of day-to-day affairs. One of them was an older woman, an African-American, in her sixties. On Sunday mornings, she took two or three of the patients to church services. She made the effort to connect with me. "You've got a young mind, you're a fighter, and you've got your whole life ahead of you," she said.

I was holding on, and not by a whole lot. Her remark was born of a life's work, and it sustained me. I really don't know how long I was in there. We were indoors all the time and the days had a way of drifting by. It could have been a couple of weeks.

There were organized activities for our merry band of the mentally ill. At certain times of the day, on certain days we were assigned to meet together in small groups to talk about stuff. These were quiet, sincere exchanges. We sat in a small room, in a circle, and talked to each other. One participant in my therapy group was an older Irish man, heavy set, with graying hair, who seemed to have a particular skill at listening. Mr. McEnery always made eye contact and always seemed tuned in, like he'd been in that very same place himself. He took the time to listen. Maybe that was it. He wasn't going anywhere. He'd be there for as long as it took.

One evening in the dining room, Roby, a young patient who always dressed in shorts, started talking about a shampoo commercial. "It's all a big fake. No shampoo makes that amount of suds. It's not the shampoo. They make it look like the shampoo, but it's all a lot of chemicals." Roby was just getting started. When he got on a roll, there was no telling where it would end. Mr. McEnery sat beside him and laughed. He was really enjoying himself, and when it was time for him to leave the floor, he told Roby he would miss him. He told me he would miss me too.

Roby was not the easiest guy to like. Like me, he was a severe obsessive-compulsive, but in his case the illness had verged over into psychosis. I only knew this because of some of the comments he volunteered at a floor meeting. Periodically, the staff on the seventh floor held floor meetings which all the patients were supposed to attend. The senior doctors spoke about how things were going on the floor, and the patients had the opportunity to share whatever was on their mind. You wouldn't have caught me dead opening my mouth at one of those meetings, but many patients did. Roby had come to the conclusion that the pay phone on the floor was being tapped by aliens. This was his rational appraisal of the facts as he saw them, and he let his views be known. "Something needs to be done here," Roby said gravely.

His comments were duly noted, and other business was attended to. One of the doctors couldn't understand why no one had taken the initiative to set up a folded ping pong table at one end of the hall.

"Because, we're all scared shitless…" I thought to myself.

It could have just been me, but I kind of felt that no one would have been at ease preparing to play anything. Another doctor wondered if there couldn't be more support on the floor of one patient for another. This comment was received like a lead weight in the middle of a flat pond. We were all doing what we could.

We had been going around the room during group therapy one day, and Mr. McEnery mentioned that he had to "get back to meeting." He didn't explain himself. He didn't say what meeting, or what kind of meeting. He just said he "had to get back to meeting." And like the words from the supervising nurse, those words never left me. Sometime later, standing around in the hallway he also said he "had to do thirty meetings in thirty days." He wasn't preaching. He made no effort to be more explicit. He was just speaking out loud a simple fact that was of great importance to him. He said other things. He jokingly admitted that he was wanted in two states. Nothing seemed to faze him. Nobody questioned him. Nobody asked why he was wanted in two states, what he'd done. I just knew, or in hindsight came to recognize, that I had met a remarkable man.

I use the word "remarkable" advisedly. There was a quality about the older gentleman that was unique. It was partially in the way he carried himself – there was nothing about him that was looking for a fight. Quite to the contrary, his hopeful confidence rubbed off on every troubled person he talked to. It was partially in his sense of humor. He could be serious at times, speaking about how his sons needed to do more to help their mother, but the humor was never far off. Imagine yourself standing on a hillside at dusk and seeing a unique shape of cloud float by in a distinctive shade of violet and green. It's there one moment and gone the next. How could you truly capture in words what you'd seen? It was like that with Mr. McEnery. He certainly wasn't looking for any pat on the back or trying to single himself out in any way. But when he left the room, you noticed his absence. The lights had dimmed, the air grown just a little stale.

So I had settled in. I ate my meals, hung around the lounge and went to activities. I didn't communicate much – I just didn't have the words – but I wasn't disagreeable either. I had very little sense of the future, or of the past. I passed the time from day to day. I might have continued on in this manner for some indefinite period of time. But a particular event jarred my routine, shook me up, and propelled me into action. I was walking down the far right-hand hallway, the one that led to a series of patient rooms, one of which was my own. I was returning from breakfast. Just as I was making the left, in my usual casual but distracted fashion, one of the floor psychiatrists came out of his office, which was also in that corner. His name was Dr. Stein, and he was all of thirty-five. He wore a long white coat and he had glasses.

"Mr. Fineman," he caught my attention. "May I speak with you for a moment?"

I paused in my walk and came to rest in front of him. I didn't say anything.

"Mr. Fineman," the doctor began, "we have a group of student psychiatrists that meets here at the hospital every week, Wednesday afternoons. We discuss issues relevant to their education as young doctors. From time to time we invite a patient here at the hospital to appear and answer some questions. Nothing intimidating. Just a conversation, really." He paused and smiled. "I was wondering if you would consider coming to speak with us next week. Nothing formal, really. I do think you might learn something about yourself." He smiled and paused again.

I didn't say anything. I stood there facing him. I was holding a deck of cards that I carried around in case I needed to strike up a conversation, but this one took me by surprise. I looked at him a moment longer and continued down the hallway to the left. I returned to my room and lay down on my bed. Something had to be done. The thought of being on display before those students was not acceptable.

Chapter Twelve

Herman's Sporting Goods – 1985

Shortly thereafter, I walked out the front door. I walked out the front door alone, with the kind of destination only a crazy person could contemplate achieving. I wasn't crazy with a big *C*. I wasn't psychotic. I had never been psychotic. I was a poor shmuck who had stopped taking all his medicine, and I was about to take things into my own hands.

I have a distinct recollection of the moment I made the break. There was a large armchair in the corner of the hallway. To the right were some of the patients' rooms, and to the left was the lounge, the dining room and the nurses' office. Just in front of the armchair, a little to the left, was the main door that led out onto a small receiving area and the elevator. The door was locked. No one was supposed to go out that door without permission or supervision, but there was no great vigilance about the matter. It was more or less assumed that the patients would conform to the rules.

I knew I was leaving. I was absolutely resolved. There was no specific fear of the appearance before the student psychiatrists. I wasn't dwelling on the conversation with Dr. Stein, but undoubtedly this had stirred something down deep. There was an understanding that something had to be done. I have explained that I had difficulty speaking. That was still true, but the difficulty also extended to other aspects of my thought process. I didn't know where I was going. I just knew I was going.

Someone came in the door from the outside. It might have been a delivery. It might have been an administrator. As the door was closing, I slipped out of the armchair and through the opening of the closing door. No one saw me leave. In the general commotion of the floor, my action went unnoticed. I descended in the elevator and walked calmly past the main reception desk.

New York City is a big place, a large anonymous city of some eight million people. In distinct neighborhoods, it is not uncommon to run into an acquaintance who shares your routines. But the likelihood of running into someone you know, randomly, in some unfrequented part of the city is pretty slim. It happens, but not every day. Today was one of those days. Walking south on First Avenue, I ran into a girl I knew from school. She was ready for a chat, to catch up a bit, and share some news on mutual friends. I couldn't quite get up the enthusiasm necessary for the exchange.

"Can't do it," I thought.

I kept walking. She called after me a couple of times, wondering, I suppose, what the matter was. I just kept walking up a large hill in the low 60s, and out of the range of her voice. There just wasn't a whole lot I could say.

There is one remarkable fact worth noting here. I had my bank ATM card. Through my stay at the S.R.O., through my experiences in the park and Roosevelt Hospital and the various ambulance rides and even through the stay at Payne Whitney, I had held onto the blue and black Citibank ATM card. Call it a lifeline to freedom or an attachment to plastic, I still had it. It was tucked away in an inside pocket along with some cash, for I began my excursion with some financial resources. I hailed a taxi. I needed to get to an ATM. This was early autumn 1985, before mini-machines had appeared in every deli and convenience store. I recalled that there was a Citibank on Sixty-Fifth Street and Amsterdam Avenue. It was clear on the other side of town, but I could picture it. There was no ambiguity. I asked the cab driver to take me there.

My father had been anxious for me to continue my education. He knew that the activity was therapeutic. He'd gotten me through three years before things went awry, and he remained hopeful he could bring me the rest of the way. When I started worrying about the cost of the tuition, he had wanted to allay my concerns. In an act of perhaps excessive generosity, he had placed a huge sum of money in my checking account. He had simply wanted to show me that the money was there for my education.

I walked into the sunlit branch office of the esteemed American financial institution, approached the automated teller machine, and proceeded to withdraw all the money. I hesitate to remark that I was now in possession of nearly ten thousand dollars. Looking back, it seems unlikely that one machine would have dispensed so much cash at once. All I can say is that the money was in there, and before I was through, I had spent it all. I don't recall ever needing to access another ATM machine. I was not awed by the amount. I was not unduly impressed or concerned about the risks of traveling around with such a large sum in cash. I had the money. That was all.

My immediate concern was with the temperature. I had walked out of Payne Whitney in nothing more than a cotton shirt. Once again, I chose a destination that I could clearly conceptualize. In those days, the principal sports retailer in the city was Herman's Sporting Goods, and one was located on Forty-Second Street, off Eighth Avenue. I knew exactly where it was. I had been there before. I was also reasonably certain that they would have some kind of windbreaker. I arrived there at night. How I passed that afternoon, I really couldn't say. I can say that I didn't call anyone for a movie and a bite to eat. I didn't touch base with a family member or college classmate.

There are many ways to be alone. Making an unauthorized exit from a mental hospital is one of them. There is just no one you can call in that condition. You just can't do it. Try any way you like to visualize the phone call, it isn't going to work out.

I bought a blue pullover windbreaker with a fleece lining. It had a zipper that pulled its large collar snug up around your neck, and it served me well. Maybe it was the fleece. The night passed. I have no idea where I spent it. I don't know if I ate. I'm quite sure I didn't sleep, but in the early morning I was standing in line at the Greyhound bus line ticket area in the Port Authority Bus Terminal.

It was autumn. The Yankees had concluded their season in the Bronx. Kids were back in school. The Broadway season was in full swing, but Shubert Alley was still awaiting the evening audiences to come that night. I had settled on a destination. I would return to Ithaca. I had an attachment to the community. I had been a student there, but I had also lived there for a year or so as a non-student. I knew people there, a few other college dropouts, people who, like me, had decided to stop taking classes and put down tentative roots in the city. So that was where I would start a new life. As I stepped up to the counter, the ticket agent asked my destination. Then, for some reason he turned and walked behind the partition that separated the service area from the private region where the employees conducted their own business. Probably he needed some more change, or maybe a new supply of ticket forms. During the minute or two that he was out of sight, however, a new idea took hold in my head. The agent had been told to look out for me, he was now calling the authorities. Which authorities, I could not have explained, but he had contacted someone.

An obsessive doubt begins very small, a mere speck of sand that lands somewhere in your mind and that, with constant attention and careful nurturing, grows, takes on a life of its own in shapes and colors that defy description, grotesque colors of neon green and distorted shades of purple, shapes unknown in the world of men. The piece of sand had landed. I was completely alone without any outside force to counter the impression it had made.

And the obsessive doubt was powerful indeed. I got on the bus and took a seat by the window. I still thought I was going to Ithaca. With my conscious mind, I was still preoccupied with my plans, the madness I thought I was leaving behind. The bus pulled out of the darkened parking area of the bus station, and briefly into the sunlight as it descended the ramp toward the Lincoln Tunnel and then suddenly entered the darkened underwater tube, illuminated only by a yellow fluorescent light that led to New Jersey.

Chapter Thirteen

People's Express – 1985

Bristol, Pennsylvania. I may grow in my capacity to live one day at a time, but I will still recall sitting in the waiting room of the Bristol, Pennsylvania bus station. The bus had a layover, and I sat alone on one of the plastic chairs connected to eight other plastic chairs on one side of the bus station waiting area. I shared the room with ten or twelve other morning travelers. In front of me was the wooden facing of the ticket area, with its two windows for servicing customers. One of the windows was in use. To the right of the window was a rack holding schedules and blank luggage tags. And as I sat there waiting for my bus to reload, I gradually came to the conclusion that if I got back on that bus, the authorities would be waiting for me at my destination. I had been living with bone-crunching fear for quite a while, but this realization shook me to the core. Yes, walking alone without permission out the front door of a psychiatric hospital touches a rarely accessed region of the human soul. But I got up and walked out of the bus station.

I walked down the gravel road that led away from the Bristol, PA bus station, pursued by an unnamed fear. I saw a clump of bushes down the embankment to the right of the roadway. I descended the embankment and crawled under the bushes and tried to decide what to do next. You know you've arrived when you are hiding under a clump of bushes beside a bus station in western Pennsylvania. I tried to think it through. I ran through all the people I might try and get in touch with and came to the flat-out realization that I was in this one alone. I studied the situation from every angle and decided that my best option was to return to the hospital.

I say, 'studied the situation from every angle.' It makes it sound like I was in some kind of boardroom, considering options for the next fiscal year. My thought process was more like watching a fireworks' display on an unusually cold Fourth of July. Ideas were flying off in every direction. When I saw a good one, I tried to hold onto it. I had deep-rooted fears about interacting with the medical authorities in Payne Whitney, or anywhere else. I was afraid of how they would react to someone who had gone A.W.O.L. But I decided to find a way to make it work.

With my newfound resolution, I walked up to the ticket window and bought a return ticket to New York City. This was supposed to be a funny story. I set out to find some laughs in a tough time, and here I am trying to recount the internal thought process of a young man "on the run" and trying to make the whole thing sound plausible. Deep-rooted, all-pervasive fear is not easy to recall, write about, or laugh at. It's like standing at the water's edge and being drenched by huge ocean waves that come rushing in, one after the other. There is no sunshine on this beach, but there is always an active mind, plotting, thinking, striving for some way to alleviate the intolerable pain. I concluded that there was only one way to go, and that was back to the hospital. I got back on the bus.

Unfortunately, my resolve did not last. Somewhere between Bristol, Pennsylvania and the Port Authority Bus Terminal, I decided that the whole plan was unworkable. I developed a new plan. I would go to Washington State and pick apples. A friend of a housemate had done it. It sounded like the way to go. Leave everything else behind and start over. It was a clean plan. It was workable. I'd be able to live free from the interference of troubling doctors and bothersome hospitals. Once again, I had a plan. I stumbled forward through some combination of dumb luck, intuition and memory and arrived at Newark Airport.

I had money, thanks to my father's scholarship fund, but I was anxious not to squander it. I was going to fly People's Express. People's Express was a short-lived experiment in low-cost air travel. Stewards and stewardesses would introduce themselves as school teachers and electricians holding down a second job. Every effort was made to keep costs low. People's Express never crashed a plane. Passengers arrived at their destinations, but it was a little like flying on a plastic toy you found in a cereal box. It might be fun, but you wouldn't want to make it a regular routine.

In what was, I assume, an effort to cut costs, tickets for a People's Express flights were sold in an airline hanger. At least that was the way it worked for me. I was standing in a bustling crowd of expectant passengers crowded around a woman who appeared to have the responsibility of dispensing tickets. There was no ticket counter, no baggage check-in, just a huge cavernous room with the single woman in a stewardess' cap, trying to cope with too many responsibilities. I made it to the front of the throng and requested a ticket to Seattle for that evening.

"No more flights to Seattle today," she responded, making an effort to sustain some vestige of professional behavior.

"What about San Francisco?" I inquired.

What could this poor woman have been thinking besides, "I need to look for a new line of work."

But now I had a ticket, a real airline ticket on a real, if struggling, airline. I was going places now. The friendly skies, the wide-open spaces, it all lay before me. I had led a privileged life, and as a child, had flown regularly on vacations to Europe and to ski weeks in Colorado. There was one single fact I chose to ignore entirely. I was a sick puppy. I might have been a smart cookie, but I was still a sick puppy.

I was in absolutely no condition to work in an apple orchard, toss burgers in a ski lodge, or cross town unescorted. My brain was fried and sorely in need of professional psychiatric care. Payne Whitney had made no effort to remedy the chemical imbalance that had been created when I flushed the drugs – the lithium, the clonidine and the three or four others that went swirling down the drain. I was walking around a zoned-out shell of a human being. And this zoned-out shell was about to take off for the coast. At no time during my travels since leaving the hospital had I considered that the problem was with the drugs or the fact that I had stopped taking them. I blamed the controlling psychiatrists and the evil institutions which subjugated the good people I had come to know in Payne Whitney.

They gave me a seat by the window. And in an irony befitting a B movie, I was seated in the first row, just behind the emergency exit. I sat for three hours staring at the large lever that opened the emergency escape hatch. I was not that kind of crazy. I had no desire to send three hundred people to their death in a cornfield in Iowa. Still, you would think that there might have been more suitable places for me to sit. In a second, somewhat more understated irony, the man seated to my left was a businessman anxious about some upcoming project awaiting him in California. He was anxious to talk, to let off some steam about the things that had him worried. I made some effort to listen, although I'm quite sure I didn't reciprocate with any news of my own. It was nighttime. The sky outside the window was dark. I was speeding, at hundreds of miles an hour, away from any form of assistance.

I should add here that there are some memories of this journey that I just can't account for. I was on a direct flight to Oakland, California. Of that, I am relatively certain. But the fact remains that I have a memory of sitting on a row of cushioned airport seats in an empty airport lounge somewhere. It wasn't the Newark International Airport, and it wasn't the Oakland Airport. The fact is, I don't know what airport it was. I am half reclined on this cushioned seat, half asleep. There is no one else about. A security guard walks into the room but has little interest in me or what I'm doing there.

This happened. It has some of the qualities of a dream, but it was not a dream. The thing is, I can't place the airport. Days had gone by without food. My brain chemistry was scrambled to high hell. I was moving forward continuously, but where I was, or where I was going, was not always completely clear.

I am certain that I was seated in a window seat of a large commercial airline when the plane landed in Oakland, California. It was the heart of the night. I had no luggage, but I stood up with the other passengers and prepared to disembark. During the five-hour plane trip, when I wasn't interacting with my businessman seatmate, I had decided on a destination. I had decided that I would go to Fort Bragg, California.

Destinations are always a good idea, but on this occasion having one was particularly important. I had the idea that when I walked through the airport gate, I might be approached by a follower of Sun Myung Moon or one of a number of other organizations that practice similar recruiting strategies. They'd seen their heyday in the late '70s, but the model still worked. A low-budget flight from New York to California arriving in the middle of the night? Somehow in my gut, I just knew I needed someplace to go, something to propel me through the receiving area and out the door of the airport. Without one, I was liable to find myself holding hands with a group of other new recruits in a darkened field and wiring my parents for whatever funds I could access to contribute to the general welfare of our leader.

I wasn't mistaken. As I stepped off the exit ramp and into the airport terminal, a middle-aged man in a plaid shirt beckoned to me, with just the shade of a smile. I walked right by. I had places to go, things to do. I was going to Fort Bragg, California. Mr. Moon, or whichever cult leader this gentleman worked for, would have to look elsewhere to fill his quota. Sun Myung Moon is no longer in vogue. In the late '70s and early '80s, he loomed large. Grade schoolers were fed stories of older students who had been indoctrinated by his cult, and only "rescued" through hours of intervention in locked hotel rooms. Pairs of agents, a man and a woman, wandered the streets of New York inviting impressionable young people to potluck dinners devoted to the subject of world hunger. The threat was real. By 1985, it may have been on the wane, but I was still aware of the possibility of this kind of interaction. In some ways, I remained acute.

I was out the door of the Oakland Airport into the line of travelers waiting at the taxi stand. My choice of Fort Bragg was in some sense arbitrary, but it was in Northern California and a step closer to the Northwest, where I could make a living picking apples. Mostly, it was someplace to go, straight ahead, without getting confused.

The taxis were waiting in an orderly queue in front of the terminal. An attendant in a red and black hat asked the recent arrivals where in the city they wanted to go to and loaded them into an appropriate car. I shared the back seat with a young woman with long, straight, blond hair. She smiled at me. It's not done in New York, but this wasn't New York. I registered her reaction and silently moved my lips to convey some kind of greeting. The taxi driver was ready to go. He was a young man of Asian descent in his late twenties.

"Where can I take you?" he asked the pretty lady.

She rattled off an address, evidently somewhere in the suburbs that meant nothing to me.

"And yourself?" the driver addressed me.

"Could you just take me to….the bus station?"

The words came out of somewhere. I heard them. Clearly, I had spoken them, but they were still from a long way off. The driver pulled away from the curb and started for the city.

"You traveling?" he asked the young lady.

"Boston. A business trip," she tried to sound a little bored, but this was still new to her.

He turned onto the freeway, and we drove in silence. I looked out the window. Get to the bus station. Get on a bus. Head north. That was all I had. The driver made his way through a series of turns in downtown Oakland. He pulled up beside what appeared to be a large shed, a cement enclosure topped by a domed roof.

"The station doesn't actually open until six. This is the best place to wait." The driver said.

There are some people who have simply decided that all fellow human beings should be accorded a reasonable amount of respect and courtesy. This cab driver gave me more than my share despite my bedraggled appearance. There was no luggage to take out of the trunk. I had none. I paid him and climbed out of the car. The car drove off.

I walked aimlessly about in this darkened shed, an outdoor area that seemed to resemble an ice skating rink without the ice. I know I was not completely alone. There were a couple of other shades of a real person, seemingly like myself, awaiting the opening of the Oakland bus station. I couldn't say why they chose to arrive hours in advance of their departure time, and I certainly wasn't asking any questions. I wandered, or stumbled around in the darkness. There was very little light. But somewhere off to one side there was a small group of people sitting down.

One member of the small party was a beautiful woman who I stopped to look at. I did more than stop and look. I fixated. She wasn't offended. She may have even laughed or smiled. But she didn't seem to mind this gawking stranger. Maybe some psychologist or philosopher has addressed the matter, Carl Jung, or Joseph Campbell or someone like that, the power of beauty to touch and captivate. Maybe it has something to do with the Beauty and the Beast story. For whatever reason, I was unable, or not inclined to, move from that spot in front of her. She was as soothing as a small stream of cool water on a fevered brow. Here, again, I couldn't say why they chose to sit on the side of this darkened shed waiting for a bus, hours before their departure.

At six o'clock in the morning, the back door of the bus station opened. The sky was still dark, but in the bus station itself there was already a great deal of activity. It was a large, well-lit room, lit with a bright yellow light. The main entrance stood opposite the back door that led into the shed and opened on to one of the major thoroughfares of the city. The waiting room itself was bustling. Maybe I spaced out for a while, but by the time I entered the station, it was filled with morning travelers. On the left were the ticket windows: four apertures in a facade, with some form of grating dividing the windows from one another. Behind the row of ticket windows was the Grey-hound's running dog logo. Where that damn dog was running, I couldn't say. Maybe, like me, he really had no idea where he was going. Maybe he was just running for the hell of it.

I still had a destination. I was still going to Fort Bragg, but I was no longer quite so intense about it. The danger of the Moonies had passed. The recruiting division of the Moonies does not look for new enlistees at the break of day in the city bus station. There's no money in it. If you're traveling by bus, you probably aren't their man. At least that is the way I saw it. I was also no longer so preoccupied with the "mental health police," who I had evidently given the slip with my quick turn-around in Bristol, Pennsylvania. Either that or they had just given up. For whatever reason, they were no longer my pri-mary concern.

It was long about them, The Good Lord intervened. I witnessed a scene that sent me headed back to New York City. In the front row of the waiting area was a young mother with long, straight brown hair pulled back in a loose ponytail, sat with her son, a blond-haired boy of about five or six. Together, they were waiting for their bus departure gate to be announced. Across the waiting room, in an alcove to the right of the ticket windows was a set of vending machines, standard bus station fare, a coke machine, a candy machine, and a couple of the machines with a turning central column that present yogurt and three-day-old sandwiches to pull-back windows. The kid wandered over to them. He actually started off at a run, and his mother, concerned for his safety, got up and brought him back to his seat. A moment or two passed, and the little tyke did it again. Up he jumped and started across the room at a run. Once again, the young mother grabbed him by the arm and escorted him back to his seat. But the kid was persistent. Who knows? Maybe he was a future obsessive. On the third occasion, the mother lost all patience. She jumped out of her seat, lunged after her rebellious offspring, and grabbed the kid around the waist, hoisted him over her right shoulder, and strode back to the row of seats. She firmly planted him in his seat and resumed her seat on his left. The kid didn't move. He sat there beside his mother and, like her, awaited his bus ride.

Something about this interplay between mother and son struck a chord. Something resonated in the back of my mind. What it said to me was that I still had work to do, simply that there were still unresolved aspects of my character that required professional attention. And as I sat there, it occurred to me that Rubin might very well be the best person to help me out here. Forgotten were all issues of medication, or vacations, or evil psychiatrists. I was left with the simple realization that Rubin was a competent professional who could probably help me work through some things that needed work.

Chapter Fourteen

Readmission – 1985

It is remarkable to note that, along with my bank card, I had managed to hold onto Rubin's business card, the same card that had given us a laugh on my first day or one of its fellows. I took out the white card with its small black letters and placed it on the silver metal shelf that jutted out beneath the black pay phone. For a moment, I looked down at the card, and as I looked at it, a troubling thought arose.

"What if he is professionally prevented from treating a patient who has made an unauthorized exit from a mental hospital?" It was possible that that was the way the psychiatry business worked. It took me only a moment to reformulate my plans.

I had to get back to Rubin, and if the only way to get back was by re-admitting myself to Payne Whitney, that is what I would do. The decision was swift and firm. I would return. I might be three thousand miles away, standing at dawn in a city bus station. But I knew where I was going. The die was cast. I picked up the white business card, with its black letters and returned it to the same safekeeping that had preserved it to this point. I started on my return journey.

The next thing I know for certain is that I was standing at a ticket window in the Oakland Airport. I paid cash and walked away with my ticket. Since the flight wasn't scheduled to leave for a couple of hours, I went into a coffee shop to have myself a real breakfast. I took a seat by a large picture window that took up almost the whole front wall. Food had been a low priority.

The waitress placed before me a plate of scrambled eggs with buttered whole wheat toast and a glass of orange juice. The morning sun shone in through the window as I ate my meal. Did I feel any better with my new-found resolution? Was there any sense of relief in deciding to return to New York? The issue here was not destinations, or even eggs and orange juice. The issue was lithium carbonate, and unfortunately, that was not on the menu. I had decided to return. If I could do so moving in a relatively straight line, I would proceed. There just wasn't a whole lot else I could think about at the time.

With some more time to kill, I wandered around the airport terminal. I stopped into the gift shop and bought a paperback book. It was a prop to keep out of unwanted conversations, but I leafed through the pages. The book was by Joseph Heller. It was called *Good as Gold*, and a few sentences stayed with me. The main character is a middle-aged man with a difficult twelve-year-old daughter. In the midst of one of their disputes, the daughter threatens, "I'll have a nervous breakdown! I'll bleed you dry!" or words to that effect. The central character shudders and responds, "Once a week! Group therapy!"

I got a kick out of that. The father also exclaims, "Don't they teach you anything at that school I send you to?"

This time it's the daughter's turn. "They try, but I'm too smart for them." I got a kick out of that, too.

The public-address system announced that my flight was boarding. I sat in another large airplane, this time preparing to take off for New York City.

I spent the flight sitting beside a teenage girl traveling home on from some kind of family vacation. She was with her parents and a younger brother. The contrast was striking between this domestic scene and my own position, traveling east to readmit myself to a psychiatric hospital.

I was not quite so tactful with the taxi driver who escorted me away from the airport. The plane landed at LaGuardia Airport in the early evening. I exited the terminal, still ensconced in my blue fleece-lined windbreaker, and found a cab for the trip into the City. I gave the cab driver the address of the hospital, on 68th and 1st Avenue. Here, however, my polish must have worn thin. Riding taxis in New York City is a skill unto itself. If the cab driver speaks very little English, communication may be at a minimum. But on many rides, there is at least a certain amount of give and take. Not only, *Where are you going?* But, *Which route do you want to take?* And any number of small private asides may be shared. Some experienced taxi passengers are skilled at keeping these exchanges to a minimum.

1985 was a year when New York City taxi cabs were equipped with electronically activated glass partitions that could be raised by the driver. This taxi driver sensed that he had a strange bird back there and the partition slowly ascended from the back of the driver's seat. From that point on the driver and I were only connected by a small plastic window with a movable tray that could be opened from either side of the dividing wall. The tray could be used to transfer the fare from the passenger to the driver, and the change from the driver to the passenger. We passed a billboard advertising Wrigley's Double-mint Gum. Two police officers on horseback, evidently closely related, smiled down on me from fifty feet above a dimly lit highway entrance, twins offering double the fun Doublemint gum. There were no particular thoughts in my mind. To call it a dream would be to overemphasize its clarity.

The driver did get me where I needed to go. I may even have tipped him. I got out of the taxi and, by my own free will, began the long walk up the circular driveway back toward the hospital I had so unceremoniously departed from some days before. I had the idea that getting back in might be a more involved process than getting out. I may have asked someone for directions. Something like, "How do you get in this place?"

I determined that getting readmitted involved going through a public admissions area. The grounds were nicely landscaped, and I walked through the autumn night amidst the grass and shrubbery, toward the massive building that housed the Payne Whitney Hospital.

As it turned out, the receiving area was in a large room below ground level. It was reached by descending a short flight of stairs and entering through a double green door. Inside was an open space that resembled the waiting area of a major city train station. It was filled with people sitting around. No one much wanted to be there and everyone had been waiting far too long. Who knew there were so many people willing to come out on a perfectly nice fall evening just for the chance to get into a mental hospital?

The procedure seemed to be that you gave in your name at the front window and took a seat. Then you were just sup-posed to sit there until your name was called. Kind of like the "Group W Bench" in *Alice's Restaurant*, but no one came up to me, or asked me any questions. I just took my seat and waited my turn. You would think that, at a moment like this, I would have some degree of misgiving or unresolved emotions. Here I was, preparing to readmit myself to the mental hospital I had made such a Herculean effort to leave behind. But I had no misgivings, no doubts. The decision was made, in a moment, in front of a pay phone in the Oakland Bus Station, and it remained unchallenged. I had moved forward, in my equivalent of a straight line, and I was not about to start doubting myself now. There had been times in the recent past when it had been difficult to proceed from one street corner to the next without waves of indecision and physical reversals, but on this occasion, I held steady.

They called my name. I was summoned to the front of the gathering to be consulted about my mental health and competency to remain a free man. But not only was I called upon, I was brought straight to the front of the line. My name had set in motion an accelerated process. I was given star treatment. A call had been made to the seventh floor, and word had come down that I was to be accepted. They wanted me back. It seemed my absence had been noticed.

I can explain this in a couple of ways. First of all, it appears that Payne Whitney is embarrassed when patients walk out the door and leave for a couple of days. They have some responsibility for maintaining the health and safety of their patients, and when one of them disappears, it doesn't look good. But there may have been something more at play here. My psychiatrist might well have been aware that my exit came shortly after he proposed a show-and-tell before an auditorium of student psychiatrists. The timing of my leave of absence would suggest that his request upset me. That may have been part of the reason they were happy about having me back.

The next step was the readmission interview. Like my initial interview at Payne Whitney, this friendly chat took place with two people. On this occasion, however, they were both doctors in white coats, one a man and one a woman, and they had very different approaches to their jobs. For the man, it was another day at the office, an office he'd been going to for too long a time. You did what you had to do, took care of what you had to take care of until it was time to leave.

The woman didn't see it that way. She showed up for her job with an awareness that it was in her power to brighten someone else's day, and she accomplished her objective.

The male doctor assumed I had spent my time away from the hospital wandering around the streets and asked a question intended to establish that fact. I quietly pushed aside the paper that was covering my return plane ticket from the Bay Area, disclosing the reality that he was off the mark on that one. Maybe I just showed it to the woman, but I made the point that I had indeed been busy.

The two admitting psychiatrists escorted me to the next doctor, who was to conduct a physical exam before I could actually return to my own place of temporary residence. They walked me down this long hall. You would think two psychiatrists would have more to do than walk a returning patient down a long hallway. But that is how things were done. The nice woman and I had a moment of connection as we were approaching the end of the hallway. It turns out we'd attended the same prep school: Phillips Andover Academy in Massachusetts. This connection did not please her more morose colleague, who looked at the people who came under his care as being from another world entirely, to be examined and possibly prescribed for, but still, never to be connected with.

It is clear that I still harbor some resentment toward this fine doctor. I think the resentment is larger than that. It is a resentment toward all mental health workers who somehow deny the humanity of the people they are interacting with. I'm not proud of this resentment, but it is borne of long experience with telephone crisis hotline workers. I first called the hotline based in Ithaca when I still lived in that city, and I continued to call down through the years.

Doubtless, the decision to commit valuable time to taking care of the mentally ill is noble and rooted in good intentions. Nevertheless, there is a distinction that can be drawn here. There are some mental health workers who recognize that we are all carrying a load of some indeterminate weight, some heavier than others. These are the ones who are able to see that we are all human beings. There are others who choose to overlook this fundamental reality. Maybe they are seeing the other guy through a lens of some textbook they've read. They stick to the script. For whatever reason, it is the ones who understand that every one of us is crazy, to a greater or lesser extent, who will always get a tip of the cap from me.

At the end of the hallway we parted ways, and I was entrusted to another doctor for the physical examination. At this time, I was talking – talking a lot. I was into explaining where I had been and what I had been through. Maybe I wanted to connect with this doctor and follow my sister's practical advice to make doctor friends. Maybe I was just frightened, or terrified, or just strung out from the chemical imbalance in my head, the lack of sleep, the lack of food, and the indeterminate number of days wandering around the country. For whatever reason, I was talking. The thing is, when he concluded his exam he gave me a lithium capsule. Three hundred milligrams. It seems instructions had come from upstairs that this drug was to be administered.

There is a question here. Why did they keep me under their care for however long it was, weeks at least, and consistently refuse to give me a regular dosage of lithium? Why did they refuse to give me any lithium at all? This is a mystery. I know there had been phone conversations between Rubin and my Payne Whitney psychiatrist. They knew I was manic-depressive. They knew I had been taking lithium for more than a year, yet they chose not to provide me with any. Something had changed. It took a three-thousand-mile plane flight, in each direction, and a journey best suited for the Twilight Zone, but they now saw fit to give me the substance that was then, and remains, and will remain until my dying day, as essential to me as food and water. What changed? I really couldn't say. But there it was, in a little white cup, one three-hundred-milligram capsule, in green and white.

There is something that needs to be said, and this is as good a time as any. It's about the anger. It was my anger that landed me in the hospital in the first place. I got in a wicked rage at my doctor and it took away my freedom, literally. But anger does the same thing every day in a million smaller, less conspicuous ways. Here I am, bearing a resentment toward mental health workers. Does it imprison me, literally? Evidently, not. But it takes away the laughs. It takes away the sunshine. I'm still free to walk out the door to look up at the sky, but I don't see the light. Not in the same way. Sure. I'm right. I'm filled with righteous insight, but I'm also just a little bit less free. There is no other way to look at it.

Chapter Fifteen

You're Just Here for the Rest – 1985

The hospital must have had the difficult task of informing my parents that they had kind of lost track of their son. When I did return, I spoke with both of them from the pay phone in the hall. My only specific memory is of being flattened by a speeding eighteen-wheel truck traveling at high velocity. What they went through during this trying time, I am in no position to judge.

While I was traveling about, my bed had been given to a new patient, so I was moved in across the hall to another large double room: two beds, and two large windows, this time looking out to the east. It was on one of those beds that I hung out for the next week or so. I lay there, I sat there, I raved a little, I was brought my meals by the nurses, and my badly shell-shocked system tried to establish some kind of equilibrium.

There was one window just to the right of my bed, and if I sat up I could look out at the East River flowing beneath. The water was moving forward, flowing down toward New York Harbor, past the Statue of Liberty and out into the Atlantic.

From there, who knows where it went? East to Europe? North to Newfoundland? Or south to Rio de Janeiro? The water was flowing day and night with no time off for recuperation. At least I was lying down or sitting up in one place.

It was the normal procedure for the patients on the seventh floor to gather three times a day, in the dining room for a meal. We weren't waited on, but we picked up our meals and sat in an orderly fashion at a nicely presented table to eat. The nurses on the floor were aware that after my unescorted excursion, I just wasn't up to this form of participation. One of the nurses brought me each of my meals on a tray. And I just lay there, day after day. I guess I got up to use the bathroom, but I don't recall any attempts at psychotherapy. In the back of my mind was the idea that I just needed some time for the lithium to start working. Manic depression is a hereditary illness, and there was a legend passed on in my family that after nine days, things would kick in. So in the back of my mind was that magic number. If I could make it to nine days of regular lithium, things would be better. I kept some track of the passing days. They were giving me regular dosages of lithium. Maybe not enough, but they were giving me some.

I said I was "raving," and I know for at least a while, I was. I was calling out the name of this guy I knew in high school, or prep school, or whatever you want to call that place I passed my teenage years, and I was telling him that I had had a "hell of a time." But mostly I just lay there, or sat up and looked out at the East River, and, day by day, the time passed. And, day by day, I recovered. Day by day, some sense of normalcy returned. No one from outside visited me during these days, which was probably just as well.

Payne Whitney was about locked doors and huge hospital bills. It was also about, at least to a certain degree, psychiatric treatment. But it was also about a community of patients. Big word, "community." Big and overused. But Payne Whitney was about spending time with other people who were also struggling with mental illness. Sometimes, in the dark days of that first year, I compared my experience to that of a foot soldier in Vietnam, for the sheer darkness of the whole thing, and then I would think that the Vietnam foot soldier had the camaraderie of the other soldiers, which was something I didn't have. In Payne Whitney, I learned what it was like to share my experience with others.

At no time was that more true than after my return from my trip to California. I entered a support system, a support system of other crazy people. During those first few days, I was quite alone: lying on that bed, eating my meals and raving to my high school classmate who wasn't there at all. But as time passed and I calmed down a little, my new roommate reached out.

"I was worried about you," he said. It was Roby. The same guy Mr. McEnery had befriended in the dining room. "Do you need anything? Can I get you anything?" Roby was in earnest. He had privileges to go off the floor, and he was trying to be helpful.

"Could you get me an orange soda?" I asked.

"Yes," Roby replied.

And he did it. He went and got me an orange soda. The floors of the hospital were marked with colored lines to keep us crazy folk from getting confused. He returned sometime later and handed me a twelve-ounce can of Sunkist orange soda, and I drank it.

Some days later I began to feel a little more put together. The floor was firm under my feet, and I ventured out into the common area. I took a seat, tentatively, at the card table.

Wilber was there, and so was Doris. They didn't make any big commotion about seeing me again. Slow motion was the order of the day for all of us, but they were also letting me feel my way. I picked up a deck of cards and began to absentmindedly cut the deck and look at the card I had turned face up. Wilber came over and sat beside me. He was still wearing a blue button-down shirt. It was still not tucked in. He looked straight ahead.

"It gets easier," he said.

I don't know how much my absence was noted, or whether it was noted at all. People came and went, and most of the patients were pretty involved in their own stories, but I was received into a community that had some sense of what I was experiencing. I also don't know anywhere else I could have found such a group of people. Each of us was walking a walk apart. We had been called out for not caring at a floor meeting, but we were confined on the same floor, and we shared an understanding, an understanding not fostered by school, or work, or common friends or relations. We took different prescriptions and had different lives, different futures. But for at least those few days, we were acquaintances who looked out for one another when we could. We may not remember what took place, and we certainly remember it in different ways, but we knew and understood something about each other that could not be understood by any doctor, or psychologist, or social worker.

As the days passed, I began to get back in the swing of the place. One regular spot on our schedule was the recreation area on the top floor. It was the roof but with fenced in and covered areas. There were ping-pong tables and a few stationary bikes. There was also a large open space, kind of like a basketball court without the nets. One of the nurses would escort some predetermined bunch of us up there, and we would peddle the bikes or play some ping-pong. There had been a table in the attic of the house I grew up in, and I could handle myself pretty well with a ping-pong paddle.

"He's the pro," the therapist joked. I used to keep rallies going with the other player. Just hit the ball back and forth. On this particular day, there were two student nurses visiting the floor. They were fairly unobtrusive, just hanging around, adding to their academic resume I guess, and one of them played me some ping-pong. We were just hitting the ball back and forth. I don't think we talked all that much.

But after a few rallies, she commented, "You're just here for the rest."

Maybe it was half in the form of a question, but she was getting at something. Even with the lingering effects of my recent journey, I didn't really look all that crazy. I didn't look as crazy as the average Payne Whitney patient who was being treated for lord-only-knows-what.

But I was back. Once again, I lost all sense of time. I traveled from one day to the next without any definite sense of how long this all would go on. Things might have continued like that, but once again, something happened. It usually does. This time the thing that happened, happened in arts and crafts. There's probably a more official name for it. Maybe they call it occupational therapy or something like that. But something happened there, or should I say right after I left the room, that scared me right down to my shorts.

Eight patients were seated around a large square table amusing themselves with various activities, paints, colored paper, various drawing materials. These activities may have therapeutic value. I'm sure that, handled appropriately, they can be useful. In this case, however, the dominant figure in the drama was the therapist, Ms. Banks, a single woman in her early forties. She may have been a diligent student in occupational therapy school. She probably was if she got a job at Payne Whitney. But she had completely overlooked the fact that she was interacting with human beings.

When I was readmitted to the hospital, I was interviewed by two psychiatrists, and I drew a distinction between them. One saw the patient and the doctor somewhere on the same continuum, one maybe a little crazier than the other, but both fighting the good fight to the best of their ability. I pointed out that the male doctor saw a great divide separating the doctor from the patient, a divide that which might be compared to the glass partition dividing a scientist from a community of rodents being observed for an experiment in animal behavior. Ms. Banks fell firmly on the side of the animal behavior scientist.

Her first screw-up came in her interaction with Doris, the acquaintance of mine from the lounge area downstairs, a woman who'd once had her paintings shown at a library in Bridgehampton.

"Are we going to do some painting today, Doris?" Ms. Banks inquired, a smile plastered on her face.

Doris got up and quietly walked over to the shelf containing the art supplies. She returned and dutifully began to apply the watercolors to the white paper. Some activities are undertaken at a certain time of day, or out of professional obligation. Others are conducted because they bring real meaning and joy to life. Doris was a painter. In her own life, outside of the hospital, painting was a spiritual and important thing to do. Being asked to perform this activity on the command of a stranger in a blank institutional room cut her to the quick. There was no electroshock here, no forced cold showers, merely an instructor who had chosen to overlook the fact that she was interacting with human beings, adult human beings.

"That's very nice, Doris," Ms. Banks contributed, without stopping to look at the painting. She continued to circle the room, taking notes with a black felt tip pen on her clipboard. I was seated down at the far end of the table, the end closest to the door, absentmindedly drawing with colored markers on a large sheet of newsprint. I looked over at Doris, who returned my glance. Had Ms. Banks been any more clueless, it would have been painful. Up to this point, it was just embarrassing.

Seated to my right was a young woman of some twenty-four years who was interning on the floor, a genuinely pretty girl with long, brown hair and a hopeful smile. "I heard you playing downstairs," she volunteered. "Terrific."

"Hey," I replied.

"I think it was James Taylor. 'Fire and Rain,'" she continued.

"You were right," I was warming up. "I saw him perform on the Sheep's Meadow in the Park." Words and phrases remained a challenge, but I wanted to do my best for this pretty intern.

"Absolutely, I was there. Summer of 1979."

"Could have been," I was outdoing myself.

Ms. Banks spotted us talking from across the table and strode briskly around the room.

"Would you like to participate in the activities?" She smiled at Julie.

"I think she is participating," I was tempted to reply. I filled in an area with a purple marker.

"Jordan, I think it would be very nice if you entertained us with some music. Why don't you go down and bring up that guitar of yours." This was not phrased as a question. This was clearly a command. Ms. Banks had established her authority. I could do nothing but obey.

I took the elevator down to the seventh floor and picked up my guitar in its black cardboard case, but as I was stepping back into the hallway for the return trip, trouble hit. I ran into a couple of the nurses, no one in particular – just two of the employees on the floor. For some reason, they caught my attention and slowed my progress back to arts and crafts. They made some comment. Here, you would think I might just brush by them with a glazed look on my face, but as I paused to respond to their remark, I stopped moving. I just stopped moving entirely. For that moment, it was like I was thrown back to my spot at the bottom of the footpath in Central Park.

Like in the park, I was aware of my surroundings. I was aware of the hallway and the bright white light coming down from the ceiling. I was aware of the nurses standing beside me. I just wasn't moving. I simply froze, and for a matter of moments (it was more than seconds), I didn't move a muscle. I realize how bizarre this behavior sounds. Try pulling that one on Forty-Sixth Street and Eighth Avenue. It's just not something people normally do. It is not within any accepted range of normal behavior, but standing there in the hallway of the seventh floor of Payne Whitney Psychiatric Hospital, I froze up like a statue or a large block of ice.

The two nurses were mildly alarmed. If I had continued in that position, there surely would have been immediate consequences. But for some reason, as unaccountable as the original decision to stop moving, I started moving again. I moved past the nurses, black guitar case in hand, and returned to occupational therapy. Maybe I shared a couple of tunes with my fellow patients as they engaged in other forms of creativity therapy, and in relatively short order, the period was over. We carried on, to lunch, or our medicine, or ping-pong, or group therapy, or lounging by a closed window, or whatever came next. But I did not leave that experience behind. I was badly shaken.

The heart of my concern was this: *What if it happened again? What if it happened again, and the next time I stayed frozen?* I was not particularly experienced in this form of behavior, and it seemed entirely plausible that the next time, I might continue my impersonation of a two-by-six plank of wood indefinitely.

I was also filled with misgivings about how this behavior would go over among the powers-that-be in my esteemed psychiatric hospital. This was not the way people normally behaved, there on the seventh floor. What if they decided that a patient who froze up warranted some other form of hospitalization, possibly a form of hospitalization further removed from the streets of New York and further removed from any chance of a return to my former life, a life of regular meetings with Dr. Rubin?

All of these thoughts occurred to me in relatively short order. And once again, I decided I had no choice but to take things into my own hands. My days at Payne Whitney were numbered. I would soon be moving on, and this time, I wasn't coming back. I wanted out. And I set my mind on achieving that objective, the sooner, the better, and I lost very little time. There were two elevators that left the seventh floor. The one I had used on my first escape was located behind the central door to the floor, but there was another elevator that we used to travel to the recreation area. This elevator also went down and could be used as an exit, or so I imagined. The next day, I was seated in a chair by that elevator, waiting for an opportune moment to cut out.

Much to my dismay, as I was seated there watching the elevator door, a small group of patients, led by one of our nurses, arrived at that same elevator to travel up to the recreation area on the roof. It seems I had been designated to take part in this excursion, and I was swept up in the party. I had no choice but to join them going up, instead of going down as had been my intention. So there I was amidst a group of patients from assorted floors exercising their bodies as well as their minds, in the ever-present search for better mental health.

My first attempt at escape had not gone as planned, but I remained resolved. I had frozen up once. There was nothing to say it wouldn't happen again, and the consequences could be catastrophic. I had sustained a fear of being confined in a hospital despite the fact that I had re-entered on my own, but being sent to some more secure hospital was not a thought I took lightly. At the time, these thoughts were very real, real enough to propel me forward into action once again.

My escape came at night. I had been frightened before, plenty frightened, but never like this. I lay on my bed, under a blanket and a sheet, fully clothed. My religious training had been limited, but I knew one prayer, in Hebrew and in English, and I repeated it quietly to myself.

"Shima Yisroel, adonoi elohanu, adonoi e'chod. Hear O Israel, the Lord our God. The Lord is one."

When I thought I was not due for a bed check, I got up and quietly snuck down the hall, staying as close as I could to the left-hand wall. At the corner was a small office with a light on. A man was seated at a desk with his back to the open door.

I paused, quietly collected myself, swung past the office door and through the front door of the Payne Whitney Psychiatric Hospital. The door was not locked. I was through it and out on to the landing. The elevator took me down to the ground floor and opened onto the carpeted, softly-lit receiving area. The next obstacle was the receptionist positioned behind a large desk. With skills developed through years of sneaking into the expensive seats in Yankee Stadium, I walked by her. The key was to look like you knew where you were going and to move calmly. Attribute it to my calm presence in walking across the lobby if you like. It's hard to stop someone who is moving as if absolutely nothing is wrong, and despite my inner turmoil, I think I pulled that off. I was out the front door, and back on the sidewalks of New York City.

As it turned out, I was not entirely beyond the reach of the Payne Whitney staff. Just a block and a half up Sixty-Eighth Street, off to my right, on the opposite sidewalk, were three of the nurses, returning from a nurses' night out, or a trip to the deli, or a beer at a local pub. They saw me, and I saw them.

"There goes another one," one said to the other.

I don't think that they said anything like that. The three nurses looked at me. They may have even stared a little. I kept walking. They kept walking. No one else was pulling this kind of stunt during my time in their hospital. Everyone else seemed content to be discharged through more recognized channels of the procedure. Essentially, on the streets of New York City, there was nothing they could do but watch me walk by. To that extent, I was a New Yorker. I knew how people moved around in this town.

It was dark of night, sometime after eleven o'clock. I had no home I could go to, no destination. I had nothing more than the clothes I was wearing. But with a little bit of hutzpah - that's Yiddish for *balls* - I had gained the freedom to walk the streets without the ever-present monitoring of a staff of psy-chiatric professionals, the freedom from midnight bed checks and inadequate prescriptions. Above all, the freedom from the over-arching fear that at some point I might be sent to some more draconian form of mental hospital, one where all my freedoms might be even more severely curtailed. I felt some sense of relief.

I may not have had a home to go to, but I still had cash. As with my former excursion, I chose a destination I could clearly identify and place: the St. Moritz Hotel on the corner of Sixth Avenue and Central Park South. In 1985, the St. Moritz was still one of the landmark hotels in New York City, both for its prime location and its excellent service. But my decision to spend the night there was based largely on the fact that I knew exactly where it was. I wouldn't get confused.

The receptionist saw I was going to pay cash. This may have compensated for the fact that I had no luggage and probably looked like hell.

"A gentleman like you will be using room service," she remarked.

I left a two-hundred-dollar cash deposit to cover the cost of my Corn Flakes and toast. She was satisfied and gave me the electronic key to a room on one of the upper floors.

Like the Plaza down the block, the St. Moritz catered to the well-off tourist who comes to New York City to see a Broadway show in the theater district and ride in the horse-drawn carriages parked across the street. For me it was a place to rest my head and try to figure out what came next. I knew what I had left behind. I really had no idea what was to come.

I didn't sleep that night. I was planning a new life. This time, those plans involved buying a pick-up truck and driving out west. I had an idea that it was easier to get ahold of a pickup truck in one of the outer boroughs, Brooklyn or Queens or someplace like that. That is what I planned to do.

Chapter Sixteen

You Need Forty Bucks? – 1985

Sometime in the small hours of that night, alone in my hotel room in the St. Moritz Hotel, I got another idea.

Why not call Rubin?

It made perfect sense. It was the most sensible idea I had had in a long time, although up until then, it had not occurred to me. I took it one step further. *Better not call Rubin in the middle of the night*, I thought to myself. I decided I would wait until daybreak. And that's just what I did. I lay on my back on the bedspread of the king-size bed, and I waited for dawn. There was no equivocation or back talk. Frankly, I couldn't have handled the confusion. I had a new course of action.

I remained awake as if I had drunk too much coffee before bed, enough to keep your mind from settling down into sleep. When there was some light coming through the window, or when the neon lights in the clock radio reached six-thirty, I would make the call. That was all. The rest would just have to take care of itself. I couldn't be bothered right now.

Rubin said two things in that phone conversation that have stayed with me. He answered the phone, groggy with sleep.

"Hello?" he said, a rasp in his voice. I told him who was calling, and he asked the question, "How did you make it back?" Maybe he was still half asleep, or maybe he was asking the big question: How did you make it back from the distant reaches of your mind?

Rubin knew the broad strokes. He knew, at least in general terms, what befalls a patient who cuts his medication and is hospitalized. He knew, at least in general terms, the horror I had experienced in setting off on my own. So he asked, "How did you make it back?"

I don't know whether he expected an answer. I didn't supply one, but it struck me as a broad philosophical question at the time. He followed my silence with some welcome news:

"We can start right where we left off." He was more fully awake and made this statement with simple conviction.

From that moment on, I was back under Rubin's care. Like my choice to get in my father's car and drive to New York City from Ithaca just sixteen months before, it was a moment of surrender, of choosing to place someone else's judgment ahead of my own, and it was certainly a choice I have never regretted.

It is a decision of this kind that makes all future progress possible. The decision may be brought on by a cumulative disgust with a failed lifestyle, an overwhelming amount of emotional pain, or even a fear of eternal damnation, but without an active choice on the part of the patient, the best efforts of the most skilled will be for naught. I wanted back in. I wanted what Rubin had to offer. This stage of the temper tantrum had passed. Whatever might lie ahead, I wanted him walking by my side.

I was going in to see Rubin that afternoon, but first there was business to attend to.

With the new day, I traveled back to my former residence at the S.R.O. It was a big step down from the St. Moritz, but I was hopeful I would find what I was looking for. Surely, I could have returned there after checking out of Payne Whitney, but the thought never crossed my mind. The S.R.O. was associated with a protracted nightmare and self-imposed imprisonment. It had nothing to do with new beginnings. There, amidst the clothes and papers scattered on the floor of that darkened back room was a bottle of lithium capsules. I hadn't flushed all of them away. Dr. Henry Jekyll should only have been so lucky. Payne Whitney had begun administering the drug, but still, it was helpful to have a supply until I could be reunited with my doctor.

My next stop was William Greenberg's Bakery on Madison Avenue. Greenberg's had a unique form of advertising. He fanned the smell of butter and sugar out through their front door of his small shop. Every pedestrian was reminded, as they walked by, that Mr. Greenberg, or one of his sons, was cooking up some terrific pastry inside. I went in and bought a mid-sized apple pie. I was on my way to Rubin's office, and for once I wasn't concerned about arriving on time. It's not every day that one of his patients returns from an adventure of the likes I had seen. Rubin stood up and turned to face the front door as I entered. I saw a saw a look of relief pass over his face. There was no indication of serious physical injury, no blood-stained sling over my right arm. I took my seat in the black leather armchair behind the closed door of Rubin's office.

"I cleared out the afternoon," was one of the first things he said. If arriving late was unheard of, Rubin clearing out the afternoon was positively historic. He just didn't do things like that. But, as I said, it isn't every day he has a patient come back from such a far-flung journey.

We broke bread, as the saying goes. We dug in and ate some apple pie. We enjoyed at least a few delicious bites of Mr. Greenberg's creation. Rubin then cleared the floor for me to tell my story. He provided the opportunity for me to talk. But actually, I wasn't interested. I never did get around to spilling all this stuff. In general, we were more interested in the current events of the past week than in stories from the past, however interesting or adventurous. If Rubin reads this, it will be the first time he hears about what happened to me during those weeks.

I was back. The first session would be followed by another, and then another. Rubin knew he could set things right, and I was prepared to do my part. In that first session, as always, Rubin was not one to dwell on the dark side of things.

"You need forty bucks?" He said.

I shook my head.

Whether Rubin knew it or not, my bank account was still healthy. Had I chosen to, I could also have gone back to the S.R.O. His question was more significant for its tone than for its actual meaning. Sure, I'd hit a rough patch, but Rubin's question was saying, "Life goes on. Isn't there a hotel in this town that will put you up for the night?"

He was not going to moan over any hard luck or belabor the difficult times I had been through. There are two myths promulgated by the Hollywood movie business. First, that all you need to do to remedy a problem is to articulate it, and second, that a kiss signaling a monogamous relationship solves all problems. We knew these were both false. I'd get better through hard work, not through rehashing the past. In the meantime, I was to up and have at it.

Chapter Seventeen

The Small Blue Book – 1985

I spent a few nights in the McBurney YMCA before I found a suitable sublet near my school. I found a compatible room-mate who didn't ask a lot of questions, and that spring, I re-enrolled at Columbia for two more classes. But my stay at Payne Whitney was not simply forgotten. Over time, I figured out what the old guy was talking about when he mentioned "going back to meeting." I figured out that he was referring to Alcoholics Anonymous, and I figured out how to get to a meeting myself.

I was not alcoholic. I had never had any difficulties with substance abuse, cocaine, nothing. All the drugs in my head were manufactured internally, by my own anger. Still, Mr. McEnery had seen the worst, the darkest of the dark. He didn't need to talk about it, I knew. Yet, his presence was one of unbounded good fellowship and compassion. Couldn't the man listen as no one I'd ever known could listen? He clearly was on to something, and I wanted it. So I wasn't a drunk. There had to be ways around that minor inconvenience.

One sunny Sunday morning, I went to a meeting in Washington Heights, and when it was over, another old guy came up to me and said, "You working? We've got a meeting every morning at seven o'clock."

His simple, compassionate statement has stayed with me always. These men don't take out ads in the New York Times. I had found one in Payne Whitney, and I found another in Washington Heights. It gave me a goal to strive for – I was ready to take "certain steps" – a goal I never would have known anything about had I not gotten myself temporarily locked up. I did find the Big Book, on an upper floor of the Flatiron Building, where AA had its New York office. I stumbled in, paid my five dollars, and walked away with the masterpiece of clear thinking and simple writing. No one asked me any questions. If they don't want the occasional non-alcoholic showing up, they should stop sending field reps to the major in-patient psychiatric hospitals. I think that simple statement should serve to silence all of those who might say shouldn't be writing about this in the first place.

The Big Book says, "The grouch and the brainstorm were not for us. They may be the dubious luxury of normal men, but for the alcoholic these things are poison."

Replace "alcoholic" with "card-carrying severe obsessive-compulsive," and the Big Book was speaking directly to me. My suspicions were confirmed some weeks later when I handed Rubin the book in session. He handled it with a reverence normally reserved for firstborn male children or the Torah itself.

MUDDLING THROUGH

Chapter Eighteen

Above Cayuga's Waters – 1986

We did get back in the swing. I had a place to live near the Columbia campus and with my regular visits to Rubin's Park Avenue office, I was able to complete fifteen credits, the maximum Cornell would accept from an off-campus institution. If I wanted the original degree, I would simply have to go back to Ithaca to complete the remaining courses. I still considered Cornell as my alma mater. I'd done the first three years in Ithaca, and if going back was what was necessary to graduate, I was game. Rubin seemed to think this was possible. As for myself and my family, we placed our trust in him.

There, of all places, I ran into Sloan Townsand. It was autumn of 1986. She might have had some idea that I was enrolled at Cornell, but the likelihood that I would still be there some six years later must have been remote. For my part, I knew nothing at all. I had certainly never considered the possibility that she would be enrolled as a first-year law student at Cornell. My first sight of her walking up the path leading up to Annabel Taylor Hall hit me hard, like a large bucket of cold ice water, with both the water and the bucket. She saw me about the same time.

"Would you believe in a love at first sight?"

Such is the line from the Beatles classic. That is the way it had been with me and Townsand some eight years before, on another bucolic academic campus: Phillips Andover Academy in Massachusetts. I had been on my way to lacrosse practice with the J.V. lacrosse team, when, in much the same way as at Colombia, I had seen her walking down a hill, alone, with a softball jersey on. The shirt had yellow sleeves which appeared bright in the afternoon sun and contrasted with her dark, black hair. That was pretty much it for me. I saw that beautiful girl with large sparkling eyes, and I was done for. I'm not saying there weren't high points. There were. By two years later, however, it had turned into the kind of misery only a severe obsessive-compulsive can generate.

I was walking towards her. She stood still in front of the law school. There was no turning back. There was no place else to go. Though my illness and the shock of the new environment had deprived me of the capacity to articulate sentences, I was about to come face to face with the very woman that had been on my mind every day for the past eight years. I'd written songs about her, rehashed all the painful details of the split countless times, and recalled the weeks we spent together like jewels shimmering in a dark night.

We had been cast members in a production of *Our Town*, which in the Andover style, had been taken on the road. We had spent two weeks traveling through England, performing at two different British public schools, the English equivalent of our private schools, and spending five days in London attending the theater. Such was the life of an Andover student.

It was in London, walking home from the pub one night in the rain, that I lost it completely. For a time, my feelings were reciprocated. She came back to campus one evening and left me a funny note. She threw pebbles against the window of my third floor Foxcroft dormitory. It was spring, when under any circumstances, that campus is a little intoxicating. Walking with Townsand by my side through a pine needle carpeted forest, I was way, way too immersed in a feeling that was not sustainable.

Sloan agreed to go to the senior prom with me. She told her best friend that I was the only one she would go with, and I asked her, but she broke it off before the dance. I now realize that, as a fledgling severe obsessive-compulsive, I could well have been a little frightening. But that wisdom and perspective came some twenty years later. Faced with Sloan Townsand in late August 1986, I was entirely defenseless.

Cornell is at its best during those last few days of summer break, all of its natural wonder and the free time to enjoy it. The gorge is filled with students, swimming and jumping off the rocks into the clear, clean water. On the Arts Quad, the grass is dotted with sunbathers. In Collegetown, undergraduates amble about carrying posters and newly purchased kitchenware back to their apartments. The onslaught of academic pressure that awaits is left for the future. Cornell without classes is a wonderful thing. I wish I could say I was able to partake in this general feeling of goodwill. I wasn't. My world was far more dark and dire.

I approached Sloan Townsand and she stepped forward to greet me. From there, it was all downhill.

"Jordan!" Sloan exclaimed.

I would have liked to reply. I would have paid good money to reply. I simply was not able to do so.

Sloan picked up the slack. "I'm a student in the law school! Isn't that crazy?"

Still, she got nothing. Standing there in a white dress, a green shoulder bag over one shoulder, I knew who I was dealing with here.

Sloan continued to expand on her decision to attend law school. She explained her progression from UCLA to Berkeley and finally here to Ithaca. I contributed very little but let my eyes wander to the students passing by and the traditional ivy on the law school building behind her. To my left, at the bottom of Cascadilla Gorge, the waters rushed by below. My failure to participate became conspicuous. A look of distress crossed Sloan's face. I moved on.

The human capacity to forget pain is an evolutionary advance that, in my opinion, should be ranked with the opposable thumb. Emotional pain is not easily calibrated, but that late August afternoon, as I wandered down the hill toward one of Cornell's infamous bridges, I reached levels of pain I had never before encountered. It was bone-crunching pain, like being leveled by a speeding truck and left by the side of the road.

In the meantime, I was trying to put together a life. Upon arriving in Ithaca, the week before, with my carefully packed four pieces of luggage, I had temporarily lodged myself in the first-floor lounge of the house I had lived in during my final two years in that city. It was a large, old, turquoise building that had been the sight of my darkest days, the final months leading up to my emotional breakdown. The associations were not good.

Still, I needed someplace to plant myself until I could find more permanent quarters. I had left New York with a blind optimism that everything would work out. That is more or less the way I functioned under all conditions. When there a next step to be taken, I had taken it. Undoubtedly, however, spending nights alone in that lounge set me back. I lay there on that prickly sofa and looked at the yellowing wallpaper with the repeated figure of a buxom woman on a swing, and couldn't help but be taken back to the days when everything was coming apart and I had no idea what to do about it.

With that same unbridled optimism, I entered the off-campus housing office on the lower level of the student union. A current member of the house where I was crashing had doubted my ability to find a place to live. She seemed to think it was tough, next to impossible. Determined to prove her wrong, I acted quickly. I saw a notice for a room in a fraternity on North Campus, walked up there, and took it on sight. The next day, I lugged my stuff up there and moved in.

As fraternities go, Acacia was of the kinder, gentler variety. For one thing, it was not called by three consecutive Greek letters, as almost all the others are. It was a fraternity in that all the members were young men who lived together in a large building, but it lacked the swagger, the panache. As I recall, there were no fraternity parties during the five weeks I lived there. Nor was there a steady stream of female students coming at night or leaving in the morning. There was no relationship with a sister sorority. There was simply a bunch of guys living together. On the surface, it had promise.

My room was on the first floor, down a quiet side corridor. The fraternity was not fully enrolled, and they rented out the remaining rooms for extra cash. To the extent that a boarder chose to associate with the fraternity, he or she was certainly a second-class citizen, however well-defined his position might be. For the sum I paid in rent, I was also entitled to share meals with the members. This, in fact, had been the primary selling point. I shared all this news with my parents to much approbation. Hopes were high. I was on my way.

The first great challenge of the excursion, besides walking across campus and carrying on a conversation, was the lack of telephone service. I had managed to get hold of a simple brown phone, but there was no way to hook it up in my room. The local phone company promised to come out and connect it, but I was told it could be days. This feeling of isolation caused me a great deal of anxiety. Little did I realize how much trouble that simple phone was to cause once it was hooked up. In the meantime, I relied on the pay phone in the student union. It was from here that I had informed my parents how swimmingly everything was going.

It was my fourth night at the fraternity. I had managed to register for a full load of classes, which any reasonable appraisal of the situation would have deemed absurd. If I could complete the fifteen credits, I would get my degree. I would be a Cornell graduate. This was the long-sought holy grail toward which I so aspired. For better or for worse, the next day, classes would begin. I had spoken with Rubin from campus. The simple fact that I was stumbling around like a blind, drunk person must have been discussed, but I was putting on a brave front. In the still, quiet night, in the northern environs of Cornell University, all the confidence had left the building. I was left with nothing but uncertainty and fear, uncertainty about what lay ahead (obsessives deal very poorly with uncertainty) and a pervasive sense of fear, in all likelihood accentuated by the fact that two of the rooms in my hallway had been taken by women. We never conversed. They even seemed nice enough, but they were there. None of this was good, and with absolutely no one to talk to it all became that much worse.

My phone had not yet been connected. Had it been, I would have called Dr. Rubin. We had a long tradition of him accepting calls after hours under unusual circumstances. I considered this such an instance. I lay on the bed staring straight in front of me, trying to find a way to establish some kind of composure. The thoughts running through my head came relentlessly, one after another: the resentments, the worries, the fears. I knew I was expected to function the next day, to interact with fellow students and professors. How this was going to happen escaped me entirely.

The next morning was the first day of the fall semester. Twelve thousand students and the faculty to instruct them were poised to engage in the academic exercise that is Cornell University, "where any person might find instruction in any subject." Such had been the vision of Ezra Cornell, the university's founder. When his partner, Andrew Dickson White, had asked him how he planned to accommodate so many people, Ezra had responded, "Wait until you see where I'm going to put it."

The story, no doubt apocryphal, is intended to make fun of Cornell's location in the hinterland of Western New York State. It all seems to have worked out fine, with a healthy student body studying everything from meats in the agriculture college to Russian literature in the arts and sciences college, from computer graphics in the engineering college to hotel management in the school by that name. All of them had come together, and this was the first day of class. By some convoluted sense of logic, I thought I could join them.

My first class was set to meet at eleven-fifteen. The one I had selected was to cover the origins of the novel, a topic well within the liberal arts tradition that was appropriate for a Cornell history major. I entered the classroom well in advance of eleven-fifteen and took a seat in the second row. The other students filtered in and took their seats in the sloping bank of chairs, each with a small desk attached, and together we awaited the appearance of our instructor.

The young man came in through one of the doors near the front of the room at the bottom of the inclined slope of chairs and began to unpack a black briefcase which contained a paperback book and some notes on loose pieces of white paper. He proceeded to share with the class his views on Samuel Richardson's *Pamela* which, based on the title of the course I had signed up for, I knew was an early novel. I can assure you that is all that got through. I sat in my chair with the L-shaped wooden desk in the front. On the desk was a red spiral notebook with a picture of a bear etched in black on the front. There was a medium blue ballpoint pen beside it, but very little note-taking was going on. I was too frightened.

Fear had been, I suppose, a way of life for some time now. Here it had proceeded to the point of paralysis. The instructor was giving it a good shot. He was youthful and engaging. He smiled. He acknowledged that this was not the most accessible area of literary study, but he wanted to open it to us in the best way he knew how. I was aware that the students all around me were busily taking notes, absorbing information that would be of use to them for a paper or a final exam. As far as I was concerned, another day was drifting listlessly by. The idea that I would gain insight into Richardson or *Pamela* made about as much sense as the idea of water being absorbed by a rock, a cold, hard slab of concrete. I remained in my chair until the class ended. I got up and walked out.

I did have one academic connection left over from my undergraduate days. My advisor, a kind man named Henry Simpson, was still on the staff of the history department, and he had tried to be helpful. I had gone to see him some days before. Professor Simpson had seen great potential in me back in the day. As head of the history department, he had taken me on as his advisee and had admitted me to the Honors Prose Seminar. In my constant quest for perfection, I consistently handed my papers in late, losing the half grade I might have gained by rewriting my notes in the wee hours of the morning, certainly an early warning of the severe O.C.D. When I came back to campus, Professor Simpson was still eager to guide my academic progression.

I had shown up at his fourth-floor office during the registration period. He had been rotated out of his position as department chairman and relegated to a more modest office in McGraw Hall. Professor Simpson knew I was coming back to try and complete my degree, so it was not a complete surprise when my distraught face, topped disheveled hair, appeared at his doorway. It was not office hours, which would have been the appropriate time for a visit, but it was the week of registration, and I needed guidance in selecting my courses.

"Hello, Jordan."

Professor Simpson looked up from a book he had been reading and greeted me cordially. It was all downhill from there. As with my interaction with Sloan Townsend, I just didn't have it. The upshot of our visit, however, was that I was now enrolled in a seminar with a leading light of the department whose most recent book had won a Pulitzer. It was to this elite grouping of scholars that, on that first day of classes, I next proceeded. The way was paved before me. The history faculty had welcomed me. Even the Pulitzer Prize winner greeted me cordially.

As should come as no surprise, however, I was unable to appreciate this class either. I was seated at a large, white table with twelve other honors students. I knew very well that our instructor was laying out the nuts and bolts of the course. I even had the syllabus in front of me. Unfortunately, my mind was somewhere else entirely. One of the female students in the early novels course had said hello to me on our way out. I spent the better part of the history seminar preoccupied with the fact that I hadn't responded, and how our inevitable next encounter might proceed. The rest of the time, I was worrying about a fly that was buzzing around the room.

Chapter Nineteen

Like the U.S. Cavalry – 1986

My brown plastic phone was now making and receiving calls. It was one of the old-fashioned kind, narrow and elongated, with the white buttons set in the middle of the handpiece. You would think this would provide some form of relief, but in actuality, it turned into a form of extreme torture.

I invariably made my weekly call to begin the session at exactly the right moment. Dr. Rubin had accommodated himself to my class schedule, and at eleven o'clock on Wednesday morning, he was fully prepared to speak with me. The problem wasn't the beginning of the call, it was the end. Psychiatry is a form of medicine very much wedded to the clock. Sessions begin at an appointed time and end a certain time. The patient soon learns to suspend his anguish when the endpoint is reached, to get up and walk out to face the day. He may hope to resume the train of thought next time, but when time is up, time is up. The therapist, too, has this in mind and doubtless makes a good-faith effort to prepare his patient for that eventuality, that the session will close and he will have to walk out the door.

The terrible problem I faced among the apple orchards of Western New York State was that a phone therapy session lacked a clearly defined ending. On Park Avenue, when the session ended, I walked out through no less than three doors, each of which closed behind me. I passed a uniformed doorman and became integrated into the street life of a big city. No matter how much I might long to have the last word, going back was in no way practical. The doorman was that intimidating, and the three doors were closed. In my boarder's room on a side corridor of the Acadia fraternity house, nothing was so clearly defined. The session might have come to an end according to the four red digits on my clock radio, but the possibility of adding just one more addendum required nothing more than redialing the number, pushing eleven small buttons. Sessions had grown strident. Rubin was very aware that I was foundering, and in his eagerness to help me, he had a tendency to take the bull by the horns. I had a tendency to react badly. It was trouble all round.

Dr. Rubin back in the day, kept a full schedule, one patient after the next, from early morning through the evening, the hours before nine and after five being most sought after. The point is, all the time in his day was allocated to one patient or another. During a crisis, he did what he had to do; Dr. Rubin, however, did not have time to allow one session to overflow into another. When I started to do this, he was forced to convey, as tactfully as possible, that my behavior was not acceptable. But when my stubbornness persisted, he made himself very clear. My reaction to such an unwelcome reprimand was to "beat myself up," a losing tactic I had employed from way back. Yes, it made me miserable, but it didn't stop me from compulsively making highly inappropriate calls.

There were two other actors in this sad affair. I was in touch with my parents by phone, and they, too, were aware that I was foundering badly. They let me know that they would like to come up and see me, and as I posed no strong objection, they flew into the Ithaca airport. They rented a car and drove to campus. I was supposed to meet them on the steps in front of Willard Straight Hall. As usual, I was late. On campus I had been, at least once, brought to a complete halt in front of a signpost, unable to decide whether to pass it on the left or the right. Proceeding in a straight line from the outer reaches of North Campus to the student union still posed all kinds of problems.

"We weren't sure you'd show up," my mother said.

Together, we walked back through the Arts Quad, past the architecture building, and along the road that led past the fraternity houses. The tone of the visit was resolutely positive, both on the part of myself and my parents. I really didn't have it in me to go in any other direction. I remained resolved to complete the credits and return to New York City victorious. Yes, there was an air of unreality to the proceedings. Attribute it, if you like, to the Jewish emphasis on higher education. We were, all of us, so enamored of the Ivy League degree that we overlooked the reality all around us.

Whether or not my parents were reassured when they left, I couldn't say. The phone contact with Dr. Rubin remained a constant scraping on a raw wound. The obsessive's tendency is always to "go back" one more time, and try as I might, I couldn't seem to refrain from calling again once the session was over. Dr. Rubin would bark at me, and I would suffer. To very little avail, I tried wearing a homemade wire ring to remind myself not to call. It didn't work. I was floundering in the water, gasping for air, and going under.

It did very little for my view of myself to hear Dr. Rubin declare, "I have to decide if I'm going to treat twenty people or one person."

In an effort to stem the obsessive thinking, Dr. Rubin resorted to an extreme measure. As a regular part of his practice, he was intimately aware of the work being done on the new frontiers of medical research. Not only did he have a comprehensive understanding of the human brain, he kept up to date on the latest developments in new medications. Dr. Rubin was aware of a new drug that he felt held promise for my condition. As things had taken on a desperate tenor, he decided to try it. The fact that the drug had not yet been approved for use in this country did not dissuade him. He had a supply smuggled in from Canada and gave it to my parents to mail to me.

To tell you the truth, I was hopeful. I lay on the floor in the corridor outside my room. It was mid-afternoon and there was no one else around as I opened the brown cardboard box, carefully wrapped and taped. Inside was an orange translucent pill bottle similar to the countless others I had had before. This one, however, had no label. Inside the bottle was a collection of small, round, white pills. I trusted Rubin on this one. He had said two at bedtime. New drugs were always an adventure. The amoxapine had brought with it dreams of unfettered flight. On a date still to come, I was to experience the release, the joy of my first week on Zoloft. There was an outside chance this new drug, brought in clandestinely from north of the border, could help. It was not to be.

Well into October, I ran into Townsend again, and hard as it may seem to believe, it was worse than the first time. I was exiting the athletic complex, a stone structure consistent in architectural design with so many other Cornell buildings. It opened onto the back of Barton Hall, a huge cavernous space for indoor athletic activity. The Grateful Dead had performed there in the spring of my freshman year, and a friend had tried to give me a ticket. I had refused on principle, in what only could have been seen as an early resistance to joining anything. By October of 1986, some six years later, my unusual brain chemistry had taken the tendency to pathological extremes.

There she was, going in as I was coming out. Sloan Townsend had not been entirely dissuaded. She still thought there was an opportunity for conversation.

"Jordan!" Once again, she greeted me warmly.

I arrested my descent down the steps, caught by her dark eyes. My own showed a combination of fear and distress. I was even less capable of carrying on a conversation than last time. The woman who had been in my thoughts day and night for six years was standing on the lower level of the stairway beside me, and I couldn't talk. Sloan forged bravely ahead. She expounded on her law school experience and all that had drawn her to that profession. I don't doubt that there was some form of a smile on my face. I turned and descended the steps and walked away. Sloan did not try and stop me.

I crossed campus, skirting the uphill side of the Arts Quad and passing in front of the building where I was still showing up for my class on the early novel. I was in a place that I had never been before. The pain was that intense, and this was coming from a guy who knew something about pain. I headed for the shoreline of Beebe Lake, found a rock by the water, and sat. I rank that afternoon as the single most painful experience of my life. The pain is not with me now. I do not relive it by recalling it. I simply remember sitting alone on a large rock, the trees rising around the perimeter of the lake assuming their autumn regalia, the water flowing off to my right, over the small falls and down toward Cayuga Lake. At times like this, it is advisable to continue breathing.

I had taken to wandering around the fields up there around Acadia. I was deep in my thoughts, under the mistaken impression that I could think my way out of the hole I was in, when in fact it was the thinking that was digging the hole deeper. The phone therapy wasn't working. I was very much alone. It was on such an afternoon that I gathered a large bouquet of wildflowers, dried and in the full array of fall colors. I'd been sitting on a hillside and had acted spontaneously.

On my way back to the fraternity in time for dinner, one of the brothers, who had seen me around, put his hand on my shoulder. His simple act brings a tear to my eye, a reminder of the power of human contact. The cook put my dried flowers in a vase at the center of the table, and the fraternity president publicly commended my civic gesture.

Things were going from bad to worse. When I wasn't lying alone on the floor of my unkempt room, I was outside wandering around. Rubin sensed trouble. With a finely-honed sense of the life of a severe obsessive-compulsive and manic-depressive developed over thirty years of practice, he saw danger on the horizon and closing fast. He told my parents to get their asses up there, and like the U.S. cavalry, they appeared at my door. My venture to return to the Ivy League institution out there among the Finger Lakes of Western New York was not a success. My parents carted me back to the city, badly shaken and talking a blue streak. I had a room to return to after the turn of the year, and in the meantime, I found a sublet on Columbus Avenue.

It was a tough spell for Rubin and me. On some level, I felt that he had endorsed a course of action that had turned out so badly. On top of that, I saw no way to work toward my objective: my degree. At first, I tried to argue that I should go back up and try and complete fifty percent of my coursework, which would give me the right to take "incompletes" I could finish in the city.

"I won't be responsible for you," was Dr. Rubin's response to this idea.

He never used those words again. He had never used them before. But during those first couple of weeks back in the city, Dr. Rubin had something positive to contribute as well. He told me my parents had come in to see him and he repeated something he had said to them.

"He's going to feel like a failure, but he deserves a medal." That is what he said.

Chapter Twenty

My Beautiful Launderette – 1986

The title of this Chapter was also the title of an independent, low-budget movie that came out sometime in the 1980s. For me, it has an even greater resonance because I recall it as the name of an actual laundromat that operated for some months on Columbus Avenue at about the same time. I patronized this establishment while in a state of almost complete emotional disarray. I was living for a few months in a small rented room three blocks to the south, also on Columbus Avenue. As I recall, I was paying the woman who had the lease on the apartment two hundred dollars a month.

I don't know why that laundromat holds such a place in my memory. It could be, in part, the romance of the place. The proprietor had had a vision, and he had seen it through, which is not often the case with laundromats. Ice-cream parlors and candy shops, yes; cafés, frequently; laundromats, no. But this guy had been so taken with that movie that he had sought to recreate its central locale on the Upper West Side of Manhattan. Speaking strictly for myself, I would have to say he succeeded. There was a ready supply of coffee and tea made available free of charge to the patrons. The walls were decorated with prints. When he opened his doors, which I believe was shortly before I moved into the neighborhood, everything was clean and modern. Even the metal carts were decorated. There was music. As best as I can recall it was songs in French. Finally, and certainly not least, there was the proprietor. He wasn't too busy to say hello to the newest customers as well as those who had been coming in for a while. He actually has a role to play in this story.

I said I was in a state of "emotional disarray." The term requires further elaboration. In point of fact, I had been in emotional disarray since the summer I had been carted down from Ithaca for the first time and begun treatment for an emotional breakdown brought on by two faulty genes: one that inclined me toward manic depression, the other that inclined me toward severe obsessive-compulsive disorder. I was twenty-one at the time and both had had the opportunity to flourish into the fullest and most grotesque reality. I had hit bottom.

Two years had passed, with much progress certainly, but with my more recent experience trying to complete an Ivy League degree, I had taken a considerable step back. My time in Ithaca had knocked the stuffing right out of me. What was going on inside my head, only my psychiatrist could say for sure. It wasn't pretty. I was showing up at my father's fledging publishing business weekdays and walking back to the Upper West Side to save money on car fare. You might say that, apart from my psychiatrist, I was very much alone.

Still, clean clothes were a necessity, even for a guy as mixed up as I was at the time. True to form, I kept a regular schedule in this domestic activity. I did my laundry every Saturday morning, and the only place in the neighborhood with a working washer and dryer was My Beautiful Launderette. Once again, the pattern held true.

Women go for the individual, the man walking his own path. The problem may be that this man is singularly unable to have another person beside him. That takes me back to one Saturday morning in early November when I was over at the laundromat doing the wash. My clothes were in the dryer, and I was seated on one side with a book on French grammar open on my lap. My ever-present conviction that time was best spent educating myself had not been dampened by the recent fiasco in Ithaca. I integrated very little, but the book also served the purpose of discouraging conversation. This woman was not so dissuaded. She sat in the same row, two chairs away. The chairs were plastic and turquoise.

"Would you like a coffee or tea? I'm just going over there," she said, at full volume

I must have sensed that she meant well. It wasn't just the ambiance. Anyone able to reach out like that must have been doing something right.

"I'm okay."

The very fact that I was able to replay in audible articulate words was of some note. I was rising to the occasion. The woman got up and walked over to the to the beverage counter, which I remember being right up at the front of the place, near the plate glass window overlooking Columbus Avenue. She wasn't gone long and returned with a cup of tea in a white and tan cardboard cup. She must have felt that I held promise as a conversationalist because she resumed where we had left off.

"He does a great job," she said, nodding to the young man in charge.

I was, at the same time, reaching some conclusions about my fellow patron. If I had to assume anything about her country of origin, which is always a difficult proposition in New York City, I might have assumed that she hailed from somewhere in Latin America and that she hadn't been in this city all that long. New York has a way of draining the friendliness right out of you. She had long black hair and dark eyes. Like me, she was dressed to do laundry: pale brown sweatpants and a matching hooded sweatshirt. The nice clothes were probably in the wash.

"How are you?" she said. Yet another question rarely asked on a first encounter in New York City, and never with sincerity.

I think I laughed. I know I didn't respond.

"What is your name?"

Here was a direct question that only warranted a simple reply. I felt up to it. "I'm Jordan," I said, still holding tight to my book on French grammar. There was really nowhere to go. My clothes were still in the dryer.

"I'm Louisa."

I think I smiled. My eyes wandered to the colored clothes tumbling over and over behind the circular glass window in front of me.

"Where are you from?" Louisa asked, doing more than her share to hold up one end of the conversation.

"Well..." I laughed. "I guess I'm from New York. I was away... Now I'm waiting for my room to open up. It got sublet."

It was a whole sentence, which was an indication that I was indeed outdoing myself. There was something about this Latin woman that inspired trust: a warm, straightforward presentation, a sense that she was showing all her cards and would not be easily thrown off balance by anything I might say. Add to that the fact that I was incredibly lonely, and there were the makings of a conversation.

"I lost a sublet too!" Louisa exclaimed.

I wanted to add that I'd be going back at the beginning of January, but the words didn't make it to the surface. Not even close.

"What are you reading?" she asked.

I held up the book. "I'm a student," I said with a smile. The sarcasm was also a positive sign.

"French?" she asked.

"Well…" There was nothing I could add at that particular juncture.

"I'm still learning English," Louisa laughed. It was a warm and friendly sound, like the Big Man had sent someone along to cheer me up. My dryer had stopped spinning a few minutes before, and there was a good crowd in the place, Saturday morning being to laundromats what Sunday morning is to bagel shops. I thought I should get my stuff out. I didn't have anywhere special to go, but I also didn't have anything in particular to add to our conversation, and I had a habit of leaving any social situation I was not absolutely required to sustain. I made some attempt to acknowledge Louisa as I headed out the door. She looked up and smiled.

What can I say? The week was a blur, an exquisitely painful blur. I see it in others, strangers not unlike myself in the day, wandering around this city. I'm sitting in the atrium of the Citi Corp Center, minding my own business, notebook on the table before me, when a young man comes walking by, dressed not so much for the weather as to cover his body in public. His hair is uncombed, his look distracted. He is clearly a guy with no place to go and no idea what he will do next, out walking in the big city. I know this man. He sees his psychiatrist at least once a week. For his sake, I hope it is twice. He is in a muddle with no clear idea of the route out, or even the provisional destination. I hope to God he has a place to sleep tonight that is safe and dry.

So was I in the autumn of 1986. Ronald Reagan had attained a second term in office, despite my best attempts to prevent it. The world was still in imminent danger of nuclear incineration, but Rubin had persuaded me that there was very little I could do about it. My father, however, was making a game attempt at a new business, which was lucky for me, as it gave me a place to go during the day, a destination in the morning, a reason to go outside.

The business was by any standard a quixotic endeavor. In the days before the Internet, facsimile machines enjoyed a brief period of favor. They were a way to quickly transport documents from one location to another without using the U.S. mail. In the mid-1980s, a lot of people were using them. There was, however, no easy way of getting the fax number you needed. My ever-intrepid father saw a need, a niche, an opening, his sign that there might be an opening for a new book to fill it. He decided to create a national directory of facsimile numbers.

Where such an intrepid and fearless resolve came from, I couldn't say, but I might venture to guess. There was a propensity to think big that might be attributed to the graduate work he'd done at Harvard Business School in the years directly after the Second World War. The Class of '49 had been full of men who thought big. They'd kept in touch. If there was another reason, one might suppose it was because my father too had been manic-depressive and known to go to emotional extremes, as had his brother and many others on that side of the family.

Looking back on my father's business endeavors during those early years of my illness, at times I have been prone to wonder how much he was motivated by a desire to provide support for me any way he could. I just can't get past that. Running a start-up publishing operation gave me a place to work, as I did from time to time in later years. Making sure none of his endeavors actually made it, left open the possibility that I would have to work for a living. I support this possibly outlandish supposition by pointing to the fact that, once I'd been accepted into the doctoral program in English literature at Fordham University many years later, he had no trouble starting a business that became a big success, and which continues to partially support me to this day.

Be that as it may, in the autumn of 1986, "the business," as my father's ventures were known, provided a destination when I set out on those November mornings. I know for a fact that I contributed very little. But the office was safe and dry, and the Latin woman who officiated was extremely congenial.

I had one other destination during those early weeks after the collapse in Ithaca: Dr. Rubin's office. Here, things were not quite so simple. It was a rough time for us, the worst we had experienced since our first weeks together. The phone therapy, while I was in Ithaca, had been a fiasco in every way. I had taken too much of his time, and he had reacted. His visage had taken on, in my mind's eye, a bearded, gnarled scowl, completely unlike the smiling countenance I had grown accustomed to seeing greeting me in the waiting room on Park Avenue. If I was paranoid all the time, which I was, my relationship with the good doctor had taken on the attributes of a horror movie. That is the way I had come to see him.

Still, we had to work together; there was no alternative. There were all the drugs, which, since my stay in Payne Whitney, I treated with the highest degree of respect. I knew that getting out of whack by so much as a few hours could send me completely, and I took them as prescribed. There was no question I needed his help. His advice hadn't panned out as planned. There had been a big-league screw up in which Rubin had been a significant player. He had professed that I could succeed at Cornell, which I hadn't. I was justifiably suspect about getting back on the horse; there was just no alternative.

So, from my new place over on Columbus Avenue, regularly on Monday mornings, I took the Seventy-Ninth Street cross-town bus over to the East Side, and we tried to pick up the pieces. This was not new ground for Rubin, and he shared the fact that he was resolved to make the next two months good ones, a time frame of some meaning to him as a psychiatrist. We were just not connecting, not during those first weeks back. Rubin had a name for it, a psychiatric expression for describing the state of affairs when the patient is showing up but resisting all attempt at cooperation. I don't recollect the exact expression, but I know Dr. Rubin remarked with his usual comprehensive grasp of the situation that he "always learned something," when he passed through such a difficult time.

I got through the week. The days came, and the days went. The sun rose in the east and set in the west, though those of us living on the island of Manhattan paid it very little mind. And when Saturday morning came around, I returned to My Beautiful Launderette. My hair might have grown long, and in all likelihood, I was behind on my dental checkups, but I wasn't going to wear dirty clothes. I drew the line well before that point. Whether or not Louise would be there was an open question. I was hoping she would

That Saturday, at just about nine-thirty in the morning, I set out. I might not have been fully aware of it at the time, but we severe obsessive-compulsives have our own internal clocks and calendars that keep us on time without our consciously intending it. Imagine my astonishment when I opened the follow-up report from my physician – this was many years after the morning in question – and discovered that I had managed to choose the exact same date as the year before to show up for my physical. Coincidence? Maybe. Maybe not. We do the same thing over and over, and we do it in the same way. So, that I should head off for the laundromat at the same time as the week before was really not surprising at all.

I walked north along the west side of Columbus Avenue, past the fenced-in schoolyard of the local elementary school that hosted a huge flea market on Sundays. I crossed Seventy-Ninth Street with the grounds of the American Museum of Natural History now on the eastern side of Columbus. My Beautiful Launderette was halfway up the next block.

The launderette didn't make it. Maybe it was a losing proposition to begin with. You couldn't pad the tab with expensive desserts or bring in a more upscale line of clothes for the spring season. The potential for making any real money was distinctly limited. I don't think that under any circumstances, in any of the limited number of cities where I have resided, I ever encountered a laundromat that tried to do more than offer wash and fold services to increase revenue. The location of this place, on Columbus Avenue in the '70s, put it in a high-rent district. The ambiance and the catchy name just weren't going to make much of a difference. As a patron, if only for a limited amount of time, however, appreciated what it brought to the neighborhood. The owner remembered me when I came in. He looked up from a lint tray he was scraping free of lint and said hello. I appreciated that.

I managed to get my clothes divided up and placed into two adjoining washing machines. This in itself met the criteria for a successful day. I assumed the same turquoise, plastic seat I had sat in the week before and tried to assimilate the difference between "quand" and "des que," which seemed to be two different ways the French had of saying "when." The subtleties escaped me entirely. Having a book open before me, however, could not have been more essential. Louisa walked in.

I caught my breath. Such was the effect her appearance had on me. Her black ponytail was streaked with a line of blond. It may have been there the week before, but if it had, I hadn't noticed. She walked over and sat down beside me. Evidently, there was no big rush on the laundry.

"How are you, Jordan?" she asked.

There again was that direct approach. Strangely, it did not take me long to be somewhere else. I had nothing to contribute to the conversation. The words were all three or four feet under and showed no signs of coming to the surface any time soon. Louisa turned to share my view of the spinning clothes through the small, circular windows in the center of the off-green washing machines. They matched the chairs.

"I wasn't sure when you were going back to your place," Louisa said.

"January 1ˢᵗ," I replied. The sense of what I wanted to convey was simple. It did not require elaboration, which would have been beyond me. At no time since the breakdown had I really carried a real conversation. The debacle in Ithaca had managed to make things worse.

Louisa, ever the generous laundry mate, volunteered to get coffee, and this time I went with the flow. She came back with two white and tan cups with the fold-out cardboard handles, filled with coffee and milk, volunteering one of them for me, and then attending to business, beginning the process of doing her laundry. I returned to my French grammar but could make neither heads nor tails of the parts of speech before my eyes. The book in my hand was shaking, which was a common side effect of the medication I was on. It could also have been because I was holding the book a tad too tightly.

Louisa sat down beside me, directly beside me, as in there were no seats in between us. This time, she had a conversation ready. "They blow up the balloons for the parade right over there." She nodded her head to left.

I knew what she was referring to. The Macy's Thanksgiving Day Parade began at Eighty-First Street and Central Park West. I had traditionally been out of town for the holiday, but I knew the routine. It was an Upper West Side tradition; oversized Underdog, and Big Bird, and Mickey Mouse come to life in the sky over West Seventy-Seventh Street. I detected in Louisa's comment an invitation to associate outside of the laundromat. I wanted nothing to do with it. Let me rephrase that. My ill-formed habits of many years standing had no opening for such a connection.

I laughed and got up to check on the dryer. I can't say with any certainty that I contributed anything else of substance to our interaction over the three or four additional times we did laundry concurrently. Louisa tried to be nice. She tried to be friendly. And both of us became regular customers in the eyes of Marco, the dark-haired man whose vision was My Beautiful Launderette. I didn't have the verbal skills at the time. Maybe that was it. I had no way of talking about what I was going through. Even if I did, the events of my life over the past year and a half were not conversation, as conversation is currently construed. These things were not discussed, and I didn't have anything else to fall back on. I can say that by the time I moved back to 110th Street, Dr. Rubin and I were communicating again. The day when he had had to shift rooms to find a better position for a sore leg made the difference. He was out of his element in an office he sometimes rented to another psychiatrist. He tried to prop up his right leg on a foot-stool. I saw he was hurting and I felt compassion. I just couldn't hold out any longer.

That was not the end of my association with My Beautiful Launderette. The following February, I found I had Louisa on my mind. I bought a small heart-shaped box of chocolate, after much indecision, and brought it down to Marco with a note, including my phone number, for Valentine's Day. He gave Louisa that chocolate. I know it because she called me. But there is nothing any more positive to report. Carrying on a relationship remained well above my pay grade. Still, it is nice to think that a nice man with dark black hair named Marco had made the effort to create a laundromat with charm and a funky name, and that two people almost connected there.

Chapter Twenty-One

Uptown – 1987-1994

It wasn't much of an apartment, really: One small room with an adjoining kitchen, big enough to walk into but not to sit down in. There was a bathroom and two closets. That was about it. Still, it served me well. I lived there for a solid seven years, from the spring of 1987 until the fall of 1994. At one point, Dr. Rubin informed me that I was living in poverty. I can't say I ever saw it that way. I knew it was a Dominican neighborhood. Everyone spoke Spanish, and there was no sign of money, either in the stores or in the residential buildings. I guess I was just too busy to worry about it.

One indication of the tenor of the neighborhood, above 170th Street in Washington Heights, was the courtyard of my building. I lived on the fourth floor, which was also the top floor, and the windows in both the main room and the kitchen looked down into an air shaft. If you looked up you could see some sky, but down below, early in the morning, a group of Spanish-speaking men and women would gather to divide up the flowers they had purchased wholesale into individual-sized quantities carefully loaded onto supermarket carts for sale around the city.

I picked up on the particulars of their operation from one Mexican woman who sold the flowers locally. She set up her cart regularly on Broadway between 171st in front of an optometrist's office. I learned that all the flower sellers who set out across the city hailed from the same town: Pueblo, in Mexico. But there was something more about this woman in her twenties with long, straight, very black hair. There was a gentleness about her that I came to appreciate with many in that community.

She would sit quietly by her supermarket car, filled to the point of overflowing with colorful flowers, and two young children, no more than five or six, would sit quietly beside her. There were no discipline problems here. None. I wouldn't really say there was any kind of relationship between me and this young woman. Once I bought a bunch of flowers and gave her one as a friendly gesture. She replaced it in the cart as I walked away.

Inside my building itself, most of my neighbors were from Santa Domingo. I sensed that, at some point in the not too distant past, there had been a population shift in the neighborhood. There were three old Irish women living in the building who seemed to be the vestige of what had once been a larger Irish contingent. I was aware of other such changes in the history of this city. The Grand Concourse in the Bronx had once been entirely Jewish until they all moved out to be replaced by a newer generation of immigrants. One of the Irish women lived right next door. She didn't get out much, but she came by to borrow a book every once in a while. She enjoyed my copy of Leon Uris's *Trinity*. And she made a point of saying goodbye when it came time for me to leave.

There was another Irish resident in the building, a man who did service as a volunteer doorman, even if he did so sitting down. Jimmy had put on a lot of weight and had some kind of asthmatic condition. This didn't stop him from seating himself on the top step in front of our building on St. Nicholas Avenue and greeting all who entered. Jimmy always had a friendly word, about the weather if nothing else, and I, for one, appreciated that. He dressed well. He always looked presentable, which Rubin approved of. Jimmy knew I was going to Columbia and liked to say that his union would pay for classes, that he was thinking about taking a degree at Hunter College. Jimmy, long retired, didn't make it to Hunter College. The heat and humidity of a New York summer exacerbated his breathing condition, and he passed on to that great front step in the sky.

I had another neighbor I remember fondly. She, too, was a remnant of an earlier time in the history of St. Nicholas Avenue and lived on the third floor with her grown son. On one occasion, she actually invited me into her place for a visit. This had never happened before. It was then I learned that her son was being treated for mental illness, induced by an experience with illegal drugs. I'm pretty sure she was Jewish, which might have had something to do with our connection. It could also have been the fact that I, too, was dealing with mental illness. It was noticeable back then.

I was not entirely on my own up there. During my first year in that apartment, three Cornell friends came to visit. Susan, a Julliard-trained dancer, and two guys I had shared a house with during my sophomore year in Ithaca, Brent Friedman and Frank Nast. Brent had been immortalized in my ongoing interactions with Rubin. He'd been given the nickname, "Brent with the book." The name grew out of the fact that Brent had gotten a book out of the N.Y.U. library for me when he was in law school there, and it implied that he was an important person in my life, one worth Rubin remembering.

The three of them were checking in. It was safe to say none of them had been in that part of Manhattan before. David complimented me on a wooden bookshelf I had nailed together with lumber I had purchased from a lumber yard over by the Major Deegan. He had recently joined a woodworking cooperative himself. Frank thought I had done a nice job of laying out my own space. Susan had been a support in the year I spent on 110th Street. She showed up, too. I don't know how they really took it all in. It was clear that I was under it, that all was not right with Jordan Fineman. We did not discuss my illness. I can only surmise that they knew I was a fighter, that I was getting the best possible care and that somehow, I would pull through. We had shared a group house where all eleven of us had danced in a circle to Springsteen's "Thunder Road" amidst a party of friends and neighbors, and they had shown up to see how I was doing.

The first two years up there in Washington Heights were all about Columbia, credits, and the Cornell degree. I commuted down to the 116th Street Station on the Broadway local, the 1 Train, which was an experience in itself. The only way to get to the platform was by means of an elevator. There were three of them, which took turns descending from the upper part of the station to the bowels, deep below. The elevators were made entirely of metal. They were large and moved very slowly. During the summer months, they were stiflingly hot. The train platform itself could be worse – deep underground and dimly lit by white globes. My perceptions were doubtless affected by the drugs and the severe O.C.D. On more than one occasion, I got on the train going in the wrong direction. I was that disoriented.

Such was the nature of the anger I still dealt with. Such was the obsessive rumination it bred. I still reminded myself almost continuously that anger was so dangerous. I had a mantra that was never far off:

Number one: don't get angry. It's bad for your health.

If you do, never let it show.

And always, always, always let it go.

I know Rubin and I may be in the minority on this one, but that is how I got better.

Chapter Twenty-Two

The Chance to Dance – 1987

In the fall of 1987, I had my ducks in a row. I was settled in my new place with my name on the lease. Even more importantly, the administrators of both Cornell and Columbia had come to a meeting of the minds on my academic future. I was to be allowed to complete my remaining fifteen credits as a visiting student in the Columbia School of General Studies, and should I do so, I was to be granted a Cornell degree.

This really mattered to me. I don't exactly know why, but it did. I had held on to that objective this far, and I wasn't about to give up now. That fall, I was in an introductory course in cultural anthropology. But there were other advantages to being enrolled as a Columbia student, even on a part-time basis. Not least of these was a spectacular athletic facility and a full array of recreational classes. That fall, in addition to the two academic courses in which I was enrolled, I took introductory jazz, a dance class. Let me be clear about one thing: This was my own choice. In the years to come, Rubin would strongly advocate for a wide range of creative activities which he knew would build the creativity I would need to write. The jazz, I came up with myself.

It was a choice rooted in many aspects of my earlier life. Years before, as a middle school student at the Warren Country Day School, I'd had leading roles in two musical theater productions. The summer after my freshman year at Cornell, I'd been a paid performer in a traveling children's theater company. It was one part of a summer stock theater that also had hosted a company that produced Broadway musicals. I think they did *Guys and Dolls* and *The Music Man*. All of which is to say that I'd spent time around people singing and dancing. I'd loved *A Chorus Line* and listened to the L.P. over and over.

I was not entirely new to the Columbia gym. I'd been using the pool regularly since my first days on campus. I swam thirty-six lengths exactly. I swam crawl stroke, and I swam fast. For this burgeoning habit, I have to credit the good doctor. Since our first days together in the summer of 1984, he had taken a strong position in favor of regular exercise. During that first tough year, when I lived with my father on Fifth Avenue, I had made use of the spectacular running track that skirts the circumference of the Central Park reservoir. At some point along the way, Rubin has seen fit to explain that emotions are not all in your mind. They are regulated by many parts of the body.

But the class, the jazz dance, was something new. The dance studio was located three floors below the street level, which was one level above the pool. Out of necessity born from is urban location, Columbia expanded vertically. Where Cornell didn't have to think twice about extending its reach further into the surrounding apple orchards, Columbia did not have that luxury. Every square yard of surface area was likely to be contested and fought over by students, faculty, and neighborhood alliances. They compensated by drilling further into the earth.

The first day I got an idea what dance class involved. I had literally never been in one before. The back wall, opposite the door, was all mirrored. This was so that you could see what unusual things you were trying to do with your body. And they were strange things indeed. The class began with an extensive stretching routine, including a rigorous workout of the abdominal muscles. The preparatory exercises included sets of push-ups, one of the few parts of the program where I had an advantage over my classmates who were all female. All of this had been done to the beat of a vigorous recorded soundtrack. It was at this point, however, that the dancing part kicked in. Our leader stood in front of the class and began guiding us through an extensive series of leg movements, all of which were completely new to me. I did my best to keep up.

It was here that I first began to realize what a remarkable dance instructor I had stumbled upon. The leg movements are each intended to serve a purpose. They are the building blocks that will, over time, go into making up the carefully stylized choreography of the jazz dance itself. What might at first appear to be nothing more than the extension of the calf and the pointing of the toe actually has a broader significance for the aspiring dancer. Under these circumstances, it would have been the most natural thing in the world for the instructor to correct the students, of whom I was certainly the most in need of correction. From the very start, however, this teacher only said positive things. If I seemed to be getting it right, if only to a slight degree, she complimented me. It was the same for everyone else in the class. The end result of her distinctive pedagogy was a remarkably positive environment.

But that was just the warmup. Each class built toward a dance routine. Our leader shared with us a series of steps she had worked out beforehand. She broke the routine down into segments, each a few measures long and set to the tape she turned on and off. The result was a full-fledged combination in the spirit of the great Bob Fosse himself. It was all rather exciting. Exhilarating, even. The thing is, I wasn't very good at either remembering or repeating the steps.

My way of ameliorating this difficulty was to stand at the back of the class. This worked in two ways. First, it gave me a whole room full of people to copy. Second, it lessened the likelihood that anyone would notice that I really had not picked up on the sequence of the steps. I tended to begin with my left leg when the right was called for, or vice-versa. This difficulty might be attributed to a childhood history of dyslexia, which I had been treated for but had never taken too seriously. Here, too, however, our instructor gave off a thoroughly positive vibe, and I'm not referring to the upbeat music she selected. She never criticized or corrected. She only said positive things to reinforce the steps we were doing right. It worked for me.

The combination of the spirited soundtrack, the vigorous physical activity, and the intense concentration taken together had a marvelous effect on my emotional state of mind. I recall sitting on a wooden bench in the locker room, two levels above, feeling terribly intense pain, which was, in fact, my experience day in and day out, only to find that forty-five minutes later, after dance class, I was actually quite refreshed. There was no other experience during those early years that had quite the same effect.

This propensity toward dance, I am proud to recall, had roots in my family history. My paternal grandmother, who I called Nana Pearl, loved to dance. I remember her moving around the dance floor, guided by my father, at my sister Anne's wedding. She must have been pushing ninety at the time, and the simple fact that she was dancing at her granddaughter's wedding was of great significance to her.

"I'm dancing…I'm dancing," I heard her say, partially to herself, as my father led her near my table adjacent to the dance floor.

But Nana Pearl was not content to wait around for weddings and bar mitzvahs for the chance to dance. Rumor had it, and I for one believe them to be true, that Nana Pearl, in the final stage of a full and active life, paid a young man to take her dancing at Roseland. What can I say? She loved to dance.

The connection to my grandmother did not occur to me at the time. I was just doing something I wanted to do. I was committed to that class. My parents, at the time, were living in their beautiful apartment on the eleventh floor of a building directly across the street from the Metropolitan Museum of Art. I returned periodically as a dinner guest. I used to sit with my family around their designer glass table and eat the food brought in from gourmet shops on Madison Avenue. But even at these significant occasions, I remained loyal to my jazz dance class. I left before dessert was served so as not be late. My father might have appeared surprised that I had chosen to study dance. In hindsight, however, I think he was very proud.

The funny thing was that, despite my dyslexia and my inability to remember the combinations of steps, I had an aptitude for jazz, a talent of sorts. This might have been due to a characteristic my psychiatrist had called to my attention. He once stated during those first couple of years, "You can burn a city or light a city. It takes the same amount of energy."

Rubin was responding to one of my angry outbursts and implying that my energy might be put to constructive purposes.

I can only suppose that some of that energy came through in my dancing. I know this because one of my classmates told me that the instructor had complimented me. The dance teacher had said that I had what it took to be a professional dancer. I let this go right by. I never saw myself going down that road.

While I never pursued dance as a profession, the instructor's kind words, as relayed by my classmate, reinforced a longstanding belief that I had a stage presence. Doubtless, the hours I put in at the dance studio, both in that first class and subsequently, served me well when, many years later, I tried my hand at stand-up comedy. There was something about being aware of my body and the way it appeared to others that carried over. But let's give that first dance teacher all the credit. She was really on to something in the way she taught.

I did go back for one more dance course at Columbia the next semester, and any number of individual classes at two commercial operations in the city: Steps and The Broadway Dance Center. I still stood in the rear line, and I was never very good at learning the routines. But I had fun. I can honestly state that walking up Broadway after a class at Steps, a container of O.J. in my hand, was the only time I was happy during those tough first four years.

Chapter Twenty-Three

Signs of Progress – 1988-1994

I did eventually complete the necessary credits for the Cornell degree. Semester by semester, two courses at a time, I commuted from Washington Heights to the Columbia campus on the 1 Train, accessed from the 168th Street Station deep below ground. I knew what I was working toward. And when everything was completed and all the forms were signed, with a great sense of gratitude and relief, I returned to Ithaca for the formal graduation ceremony, only four years delayed by my illness. My parents were there. The obligatory photograph was taken: them standing on either side of me, attired in the equally obligatory black gown and tasseled hat. It was indeed a proud day.

With that landmark behind me, I got the idea firmly lodged in my head that I would make an independent living – an idea in no way supported by reality. As a history major and an upper-middle-class Jew, the most logical choice was the legal profession. I acknowledged that I wasn't quite ready for law school, but I was filled with enthusiasm about the prospect of working as a paralegal. I had the Cornell degree and a couple of decent changes of formal attire.

I well knew that the first step was to take the LSAT, to add that all-important score to my resume. I also well knew that a course offered by the Stanley Kaplan Test Prep School was in order to secure an acceptable number.

The course went surprisingly well. I didn't have to talk to anyone, and I was pretty good at taking the repeated practice test. I bought a wooden butcher block table and installed an air conditioner in my fourth-floor studio apartment and sat there taking practice test after practice test. There is an element of my cultural heritage that prepared me for this process. I recall I was eating a lot of frozen blintzes at the time. I cooked them in a pan.

My LSAT score was outstanding, and, equipped with all the necessary paraphernalia, I began to look for work.

My venture into the marketplace was, by any objective standard, not a success. Over the next five years, I secured and lost four paralegal jobs, each with a substantial starting salary and benefits. Betwixt and between, I lost two jobs in telephone sales and was let go from a regular position with a temp agency. I will spare you the gruesome details. It wasn't pretty. Looking back, I wonder how I survived that ordeal at all.

There are, however, two positive things I can say about this misadventure. First, it got me out of the apartment and into the company of others on a regular basis, two habits that were essential for a recovering severe obsessive-compulsive. Second, the federal government took pity on me, and, when I settled into a life of regular part-time work and graduate school, the Social Security Administration saw fit to send me a check at the beginning of the month.

Chapter Twenty-Four

No Flavor for His Fare — 1989

There is one other component to this account that does not exactly fit the narrative. That very first summer after Stanley Kaplan but before my first paralegal interview, I took two months to return to work as a camp counselor at a summer camp in the Adirondacks.

Dr. Rubin considered it the highlight of that summer. He didn't place too much stock in the whole Camp Ojibway experience. He was, however, pleased as punch that I had lost my virginity. I was twenty-seven years old the summer I returned to the camp I had attended as a child. I was head canoeing instructor and a counselor in the Cubs' Den, the building that housed the youngest campers. Wendy Crisp was an assistant in the kitchen. The circumstances could not have been more opportune. Our relationship, such as it was, continued into one more long weekend at my apartment in Washington Heights, the area of Northern Manhattan where I lived. After that, I never saw her again. Dr. Rubin was the doctor. He was the one with the medical degree and the thirty years of practice in psychiatry. He was convinced I came out ahead.

You need some background here, some context. Camp Ojibway is a summer camp for boys situated amidst the splendor of New York State's Adirondack Mountains. Specifically, it is positioned on the shore of Spruce Lake, a pristine body of water with two small islands and pine trees around the edge. The physical plant of the camp could not be better: the cabins on the hillside above the lake, the ground a carpeting of soft, brown pine needles. In one of the more spiritual exercises of the camp, the entire community gathered for a campfire in a glade looking out over the water at sunset, and shared commendations. The lake itself was surrounded by low-lying peaks, mountains now only an echo of the mighty peaks they once were. The Adirondacks, in geologic terms, are an old mountain range. Camp Ojibway, too, was mellowed by time.

The summer I returned, it was 1989, the camp was still under the direction of the man who had been orchestrating affairs for thirty years. George Bellows had taken the reigns from his father, who had founded the camp, I believe in the 1920s. Here, too, there is a story to be told. George had watched me grow and develop over the six years I was a camper. He had written a recommendation that had something to do with my acceptance to Phillips Andover Academy. For some indeterminate number of years, even before he hired me to run the canoeing program, we had exchanged Christmas cards. But George Bellows is not the topic of this story. Neither is his kind wife, Lacy, or his two daughters and one son, all of whom were involved in the running of Camp Ojibway. The person who interests me is his niece, Wendy Crisp, an assistant in the kitchen

On the grounds of Camp Ojibway itself, I did quite well. The odd part was that in an entirely male environment, I did

O.K. Apart from the kitchen staff, on a day-to-day basis there were very few women or girls of any age around, and I functioned. I don't know what exactly this says about the nature of my illness, but maybe someone should write it up.

The troubling part was that Camp Ojibway had a sister camp down at the other end of the lake. Camp Bluebells had been founded at the same time, I believe, and functioned autonomously in most respects. The two camps were, however, linked. Both the boys and girls took riding lessons at the same facility, and there were intermittent co-ed activities. The camps joined together every two weeks for an evening of entertainment produced and performed entirely by the campers. There were socials and dances as well.

For me, the nerve-wracking part of the week was after-hours. It had been a tradition of some long-standing that once the campers were placed securely in their beds, with one counselor in each section left behind to man the fort, the collected male and female staff would go out, usually to a local bar.

It was here that my true colors came shining through. I just wasn't very good at the bar thing, no matter how congenial the female members of the gathering might have been.

"This is the fun part..."An intuitive member of the girl's staff tried to remind me when she found me at the far end of the bar, alone with my Diet Coke.

However, week in and week out at Camp Ojibway, I was thriving. On his year-end review, George wrote that I "ran a spirited canoeing program." I'd like to think that was true. I saw the twelve canoes lying neatly aligned on the dock as a means of building self-esteem. I tried my level best to create tasks and levels of achievement the campers could attain and feel good about themselves. In a first for the Ojibway canoe program, I laid out a row of slalom markers, empty Clorox bottles anchored with rocks on the lake floor, to liven up the basics of canoe paddling. I knew enough to teach the basics and had the help of the waterfront director for the most advanced paddlers. I enjoyed myself, and I think many of the campers did too.

There were other parts of Camp Ojibway life that agreed with me. I worked on the skits that the youngest campers performed at the bi-weekly concerts and played guitar in the all-male singing group. I helped supervise the dining room table to which I was assigned. In general, I felt myself a positive part of that community. George spelled this out for me in no uncertain terms. The camp administrators had organized an all-camp scavenger hunt that involved the individual cabins making their way around the grounds in search of clues.

George gave me no particular responsibility. He simply wanted me to walk around. I know these instructions could be open to interpretation. There was no indication that I was any kind of authority figure. I had to conclude that the camp director felt my presence might do some good.

Meanwhile, the male counselors and the female counselors were pairing off. At least two pairs mated for life. I know it for a fact, not only from Facebook but also from the camp bulletins that George still edits that get sent out once every year or two. I was in the room the night Penny and Bart met. Penny approached me first, but at the time I wasn't biting. George Jr., the camp director's son, and his partner Jen had already known each other. They were both steeped in Adirondack Camps tradition, seemed destined for each other, and were braced for the long haul.

I showed up at these inter-camp social gatherings when I felt compelled to do so. But the Big Man seemed to have other plans for me that summer. There was another young lady flying well below the radar. That would be Wendy Crisp, who I will make an effort to describe. Wendy stood about five feet eight inches tall, just slightly shorter than myself. She had been blessed with a head of long, rich, red hair, which hung down below her shoulders. Her eyes were deep green. She smiled and laughed readily, but when seated in the company of others maintained a dignified reserve. Wendy, it would seem, had a better perspective on Adirondack Camps than I did. She knew it was all make-believe. But the two of us were very much in it together, she by birth and long association, and me by the fact that I had attended for six summers and attained all the camp's highest accolades, both as a sailor and an outdoorsman. We were both products of the Adirondack Camps and steeped in its tradition as well. Though she was around my age, Wendy was divorced. She had three children.

When I later introduced the subject of Wendy to Rubin in session, she earned his highest accolade: a "nice person." He was tipped off by the fact that when her youngest son was resistant to going into the lodge for lunch, Wendy didn't force the matter. She appreciated the fact that I picked him up, put him on my shoulders, and carried him in.

The friendship between Wendy and myself grew slowly over the course of that summer. At no time did I consciously set out to win her. I thought about the growth of our relationship not at all. As long as I was down at the Camp Ojibway end of the lake, I was a going concern. I was tremendously fit. I'd been in shape at the beginning of the summer, but I'd found that paddling a canoe four or five hours a day did wonders for my upper body as well. I was busy. Maybe that was it. There was always something to do, which left very little time for my longstanding practice of rumination.

I saw Wendy behind the serving counter in the Lodge, the long, entirely wooden building where we gathered three times a day, as a camp, to eat. But I had no agenda. None.

Still, there must have been something in the air, some subconscious, electrical connection developing. I recall one evening meal in particular when this became apparent. This was well into the summer. It was during the evening meal when a tall counselor from the senior section and I were called on to pitch in. The dessert that evening was ice cream, and the kitchen staff required a couple of counselors to scoop the stuff out of the gallon containers and into the individual bowls to be served to the campers and staff. I had plenty of upper body strength for the task. So, Kevin and I were back there, kind of over to one side, scooping away, when Wendy swings by with a toss of her long, red hair, and a smile with her white teeth, and we greet each other.

"You sly dog..." Kevin said as he kept on scooping. I find this humorous.

When the Ojibway staff did not go out at night, we sometimes congregated in the back of the lodge. The sense of camp history was palpable. Lining the walls, above head level and extending up toward the ceiling, were rows of initial boards, green painted planks on which the campers from each year had painstakingly carved their initials, lifting off the coating of paint, and leaving the white of the board below. Tradition held that with each passing year of attendance the camper would be entitled to a larger emblem.

But there were other signs of camp history: a plaque with the names of the winners of the final sailing race of the season between the campers of the highest rank. My name appeared there. Off to one side, tucked amongst the books on Adirondack history, hiking, and camp craft, was a more modern photograph of a space shuttle taking flight from Florida or Texas. George never liked to brag or take on airs, but the consensus seemed to be that Camp Ojibway had produced an astronaut.

On one of these nighttime gatherings, Wendy chose to join in. She seemed dressed for the occasion: nothing showy, but she was neat and attractive. Adirondack nights in early August can be cool, and she was wearing a long-sleeved green shirt, buttoned up close around the collar. The shirt had shades of brown and seemed to have been chosen with care. She looked strikingly beautiful, seated there talking quietly with one of the other Ojibway counselors. I was seated on the opposite side of the room, in front of a large topographical map of a section of the High Peak Region toward which the camp would be sending expeditions in the coming weeks. I didn't speak with Wendy. Conversation was still not my strong point. That is what severe obsessive-compulsive disorder can do to you.

But, day-to-day life at camp continued. The campers who weren't out on extended trips continued to make their way to swimming and archery, to shop and tennis. The grounds may have maintained a simple, rugged exterior, but there was no shortage of things to do. There was a swim at the end of the morning and the afternoon, and even the opportunity for an idyllic sunset sail after dinner. Wendy and I were both a part of this community, and as necessity would have it, our paths continued to cross. She may have spent more time around the lodge, but it was simply inevitable that we would see each other from time to time. And as we did, our rapport increased. I don't think we spoke all that much. If we did, I don't remember what we spoke about, though I do remember on one occasion another male counselor remarking on the connection between us.

We agreed to spend a day off together. Conversation must have been involved because, at the appointed time, we were both at the wooden bench just up the hill from the lodge. It was ten o'clock on a Saturday morning, and it was bright and sunny. We had plans. Wendy and I were going to spend a day together. She had a truck, her kids were all appropriately cared for, and I had my day off in front of me. As we started to walk up the dirt road that led up to the camp parking lot, and the Northway beyond, George's son, who handled much of the upkeep of the physical plant, called after us.

"Have fun, kids!"

He was walking with Kurt, the tall, lank assistant director, his Irish Setter beside him. We passed out of sight around the bend. We were on our own.

Wendy must have made the plans. I didn't know my way around up there. She, on the other hand, lived year-round in the small city of Plattsburgh, which was within easy driving distance of the camp. This, however, was not our first stop. Wendy drove us to a state park. As I recall it, there was a grassy hillside dotted with picnickers overlooking a lake.

This is where the relationship started to get steamy, and as describing the steamier part of relationships is not my style, I intend to give it short shrift. Let's just say we rolled around on the grass a little, quite oblivious to the men and women around us. I assume there were children as well. In one of the more humorous moments of the story, the collected parkgoers gave us a healthy round of applause when we got up to leave. I never knew quite how to interpret that.

As Wendy and I were walking back to the parking lot, the day's activities took a minor twist. Wendy Crisp was making a beginning as a jeweler. She had taken to creating beaded earrings. She is still at it, as I know from her website, and I can now state with certainty that she is darn good. She is an artist. That Saturday morning, she was just getting started, but in our youthful roll in the grass, one of her blue, beaded earrings had come off. Returning to look for it would involve reentering the scene from which we had just made a grand exit, but my fearlessness in doing to scored me some additional points. We went back and found the earring in the grass.

From that point on, it would seem, our tracks were laid before us. The train had a full head of steam, coal in the caboose, and a downhill stretch heading into the distance. It was Wendy's house, and there was nobody else home. I might pause to interject at this particular juncture that I still had no agenda. No conscious plan of what might come next. We were two people, very much on our own. Hormones were certainly involved. What Wendy thought was happening I really couldn't say. In more recent years I've taken to thinking I can intuit other people's intentions. But even looking back, I have no clue. Would it be fair to say that someone must have had an agenda?

I did get in her car and drive to a local pharmacy for a condom. Wendy tried to reassure me that, given the day, the point in her cycle, it wasn't necessary. I really didn't understand these things, but I wasn't about to take any chances. Then, I suppose, it happened: my "first time," to use an overly employed cliché. I will spare the reader the details. I didn't know what I was doing, but Wendy had it all under control. She had laid a mattress on the floor of her kitchen and lay down on it. The rest seemed to take care of itself. I was twenty-seven years old, and according to many cultural traditions, Wendy "made me a man." We returned to camp in time for dinner.

The summer was winding down by this point. We were together just one more time on the Camp Ojibway grounds:

a whole night spent together in a bed in an empty cabin normally reserved for senior staff. It was the last night I ever spent at that camp. The next day, I boarded the chartered bus with the other campers and counselors bound for New York. George made a point of sitting next to me for part of the ride down. I considered this an honor. I don't recall the details, but we discussed the season that had passed. By any measure of the circumstances, George had shown his true colors in hiring me that summer. He knew I was deep in psychotherapy, and he knew I was taking an array of psychiatric medications. The man, however, had his own set of considerations in putting together a staff. Over the course of many years, he had reached his own conclusions on the kind of person most apt to have a positive influence on the campers. By those standards, I must have measured up. I can say that at the end of the summer he had no cause for regret.

Wendy and I were in touch. We had discussed the possibility of her coming to New York for a visit. And within a month's time, she did. She came down on a Friday and stayed through the following Monday. Upon my return from camp, I had gotten myself hired as a paralegal. It was the first of four such jobs I would hold in the next five years. Those combined with three others that came and went, made seven jobs lost. But in September of 1989, I was still the optimistic entry-level paralegal, looking to work for a couple of years in the field before going on to law school. It all sounded so positive. The significant fact, strategically overlooked in the interviews, was that I was also a severe obsessive-compulsive.

Wendy and I spoke on the phone, and I was there to meet her when she stepped off the bus on the upper level of the Port Authority Bus Terminal. She looked fine. How else can I express it? She wore an Indian-style jacket with buttons down the front. Her long red hair was parted in the middle and combed evenly to either side. It was flat and smooth and reflected the white neon of the Port Authority lighting as she walked through the gate. We embraced. Dr. Rubin had forewarned that there would be a sexual weekend ahead. Looking at Wendy that afternoon, it wasn't hard to see why. I led her down to the A Train, and together we traveled up to my studio apartment in Washington Heights. We spent the next two and a half days together in my apartment, up at Ft. Tryon Park by the Cloisters, and on Saturday afternoon in the city. Wendy was showing an increased commitment to her earrings, and we went to look at a jewelry shop she thought might sell them. There was plenty of sex.

By Sunday night, it would have been apparent to any objective observer that something more serious was taking place. During an interlude when we came up for air, Wendy sat on the floor with her back resting against the radiator cover below the living room window. The living room was also the bedroom, and it looked down into the airshaft from four stories above. It was clear by her face that she was dissatisfied with the way things were progressing. We did not have a discussion, and, in probably the most callous moment of my then young life, I chose to brush past it. I brought her back to the bus on Monday, returning the way we had come, by way of the A Train, and we parted ways. I never saw her again. In fact, I was inclined to keep in touch and repeat a similar kind of weekend. Dr. Rubin put a stop to it.

"She might have ideas of washing floors to put you through law school," he declared.

Call it ignorance, or subconscious blinders, but I had managed to overlook the reality that Wendy might have longer-term expectations.

Wendy lived more than five hours away in upstate New York. I was floundering around in New York City, trying to hold a job. To my credit, I was left with the distinct idea that my diligence in completing my Cornell degree had inspired her to go back and get her own B.A. in French at S.U.N.Y. Plattsburgh. To this day, I do think she did so. We completely lost track of each other, though I did maintain relations with the camp. I was on their mailing list to receive the alumni bulletins, and George and I continued to exchange Christmas cards for quite some time. And so it remained for a solid seventeen years.

Such is the nature of the Internet, that old connections can be renewed with little forethought or planning. It was an autumn evening in 2006. I had completed two master's degrees and was trying my hand at being a writer, still very much under the guidance of Dr. Lawrence Rubin. That cool overcast night, I found myself sitting alone in a Warren park, not far from my sister Louise's house. I was due over there for dinner and had some time to kill. There was a chill in the air, and it was drizzling slightly. I took out my Blackberry, inspired by I know not what, and punched Wendy Crisp's name into the Google search engine, and as should come of no surprise, she was there.

Wendy had her own website devoted entirely to the sale of her original earrings, her works of art. The blue, beaded earrings looked similar to the one we had gone back to find on that grassy hillside all those years before, but they were more sophisticated. There was a page on the website for contacting the artist. I wrote, "I apologize." And I signed my name.

I think it was appropriate. I think it has made me feel better. The A.A. Big Book, which had been my guide since before my summer at the Adirondack Camps, is all about clearing out the past wreckage of a misspent life and living with the world in terms of openness and honesty. The Steps provide specific guidelines on how to do this. I believe my brief apology was in accord with their Ninth Step.

Wendy did not write back. In more recent times I have seen that she is a going concern on Facebook marketing and selling her jewelry. I think she is motivated by a desire to bring joy to others with her original art. She offers to make earrings on demand for a particular color dress, or wedding, or occasion. It is her way of reaching out to others and trying to spread some happiness. That is the way it seems to me. I have not made any further attempt to connect. We are separate individuals. I also realize that I have no idea how Wendy looks back on that summer. It might have prompted her to complete her undergraduate degree, but even about that, I can't be certain. By apologizing I "swept off my side of the sidewalk," for I believe that an objective analysis of the circumstances would determine that I had been selfish.

I am most inclined to judge my behavior toward Wendy Crisp harshly when I consider it from my father's point of view. He always taught me to treat "young ladies," with the highest degree of respect. But the Big Book, too, has sound advice on sexual matters. It advises the alcoholic not to act in a manner that is "selfish, dishonest, or inconsiderate."

As with all questions, A.A. suggests that important questions be left in the hands of recovering alcoholics' Higher Power: "Counsel with other people is often desirable, but we let God be the final judge." The book advises against taking matters to extremes: "One school would allow man no flavor for his fare and the other would have us on a straight pepper diet." It reassures members that "We all have sex problems. We'd hardly be human if we didn't." Clearly, there is a place for healthy sexual relations, in all of this for, our "sex powers were God-given and therefore good, neither to be used lightly or selfishly nor to be despised and loathed." These are some of the sensible points the Big Book makes.

I can say that I was in Dr. Rubin's hands during the summer and early fall of 1989 and that he knew enough to put an end to it when he did. I look back on that experience wistfully. On a daily basis, it troubles me not, as my Ninth Step has cleared the slate. I can only hope that Wendy Crisp knows a similar amount of peace. I believe she does.

Chapter Twenty-Five

The Microfiche Room – 1994-2004

What can I say? For more than ten years, I was the microfiche assistant at the Fordham Law Library, on Sixty-Eighth Street just west of Ninth Avenue. The principle benefit of this position was that, for the most part, I was left alone. The Microfiche Room was hidden away on the second floor of the library, immediately to the right upon exiting the elevator. The thing is, despite the generous amount of microfiche and microfilm it contained, this room played no vital role in the life of the law school. Even in the '90s, much of the collection was available online. As for the rest of it, there just wasn't much call for any of it. In the later part of the fall semester, we had a rush, as the first-year law students participated in an exercise in legal research. Most never came back.

But the reality was the Microfiche Room existed, and someone had to staff it. On a daily basis, new microfiche and rolls of microfilm were delivered to the law library, and someone had to file them. Someone had to be on hand to be of assistance when the occasional student or professor showed up. The Microfiche Room was, for better or for worse, a component of the Fordham Law Library under the supervision of the reference librarian who had selected me to work there. Whatever it may or may not have done for the legal community, it did an awful lot for me, if it provided nothing more than a place to go.

My experience as microfiche assistant was characterized by nothing so much as regularity. I worked fourteen hours a week: five hours on two weekday evenings and four hours on Saturday afternoon. I ate dinner at the same deli at the same time, a Korean deli on Broadway between Sixty-Second and Sixty-Third Streets, and I caught the same Liberty Lines Express Bus back to Warren. This regularity persisted even when it was in no way called for. The library followed the academic calendar. During the Christmas holidays, the students were away, and the place was dead. I mean a ghost town. Nothing was going on. But my supervisor did not object, and I came in for my regular hours.

When I first pulled into the Microfiche Room, it was not usable. It was here I made a real contribution. I mean the dark interior room was in a state of complete disarray. Frankly, no one could have found anything. Nobody even tried. Working very much on my own during those solitary hours, with nothing but the humming of the cooling system to keep me company, I established some sense of order. More importantly, I created a basic index of the collection. I was at my best working alone, and the index made it possible for students and faculty to determine whether or not we owned a particular legal journal or set of cases, and which cabinet it was in. Believe it or not, before I was there, no such index existed.

But all of this was largely beside the point. There was one, and only one, reason I succeeded at the Fordham Law Library, that was my supervisor, Lenora Williams, the head reference librarian. I don't think I would be in any way remiss if I was to point out that Lenora was not the easiest person to get along with, so I get some of the credit as well. It was a successful relationship in both directions, and it lasted. It stood the test of time. I think it would also be fair to say that, outside of my doctor and my father, no single person made a greater contribution to my recovery than Lenora.

It was my first week as a microfiche assistant. I'd been up in the room alone, in the quiet space, which in itself could take my mind to distinctive places, when I got the idea that I needed a book from the stacks on the main level. I came charging out of the elevator at full throttle, barging ahead past the circulation desk and the reference area, where Lenora was standing. What might have been a red flag to another, lesser supervisor might have been a red flag, to Lenora was a call to action.

"He's got to be stopped," she said quietly to no one in particular. She'd faced down water cannons in southern towns. She wasn't about to be thrown by an out-of-control severe obsessive-compulsive.

From that point on, Lenora used our interactions as opportunities to get me under control. She would reprimand me for my carelessness. She never tired of telling me to "slow down." And when I took the overly forward step of walking into the dean's office on a matter not worthy of his secretary's attention, she laid into me completely. I never heard Dr. Rubin concur, but it seems to me there was a lot of good parenting going on here. My father, in one of his few admonitions, advised me to stay with her.

Much of the time, there wasn't a whole lot to do up there in the Microfiche Room. My first responsibility was to file the newly arrived microfiche and rolls of microfilm. This required a certain amount of attention to detail, but when I was alone with just the radio playing, I was up to it. During the downtime, I was there if anyone needed assistance in using the collection. This did happen from time to time. I found, however, that on occasion there was something about the privacy and the seclusion of the Microfiche Room that invited personal conversation.

A brief description of the infamous room is in order. There was very little color. All around the perimeter of the large rectangular space were five-foot-high gray metal cabinets, each with ten wide horizontal drawers. Some of the cabinets were older. These, too, were metal, but they were in an off-shade of yellow. In addition to those against the walls, there were cabinets in the center of the room as well, with enough space to walk around them on all sides. The Microfiche Room was nothing if not functional.

The other featured attraction were the readers themselves. There were three that usually worked, and two just for show. One of the newer ones had Internet capability; There was a way to send out prints directly online, but we never got it working. In the front left-hand corner was a desk for the microfiche assistant, with a computer that did have an active Internet connection and various indexes that were rarely used. The room needed to be kept cool on account of the fiche, so there was an ever-present hum of the cooling system. I did have co-workers on and off over the years, but much of the time, I was up there alone.

Still, there was something about this nondescript room with no windows that seemed to cause law students, otherwise actively engaged in pursuing a career, to stop and talk about personal matters. I suppose there was something about the microfiche attendant that contributed as well. On a number of occasions, one of those students, seated at one of the working microfiche machines, paused to speak with me about a subject that had nothing to do with completing their assignment. One young man opened up about his marriage. He had married a beautiful Latin woman, the daughter of a newspaper publisher. He voiced his regrets that she shared none of his professional aspirations, but consoled himself with the thought that Sunday, a quiet more private time, was a good day of the week for them. Another first-year student told me that after graduating from Skidmore College, he had worked in construction. A young woman from Texas conveyed the fact that she was gay.

The routine lasted after work as well. I invariably caught the same bus back to Warren. The Warren-bound bus arrived promptly at eight o'clock at the picturesque bus stop across the way from the grand plaza of the Lincoln Center for the Performing Arts. In winter, there was a Christmas tree, and in summer there was outdoor dancing. I did not partake. What with all my regular patronage of the Liberty Lines express bus service and my invariably courteous interactions with the bus drivers, I became something of a known commodity. One of the drivers went so far as to inform me that I had been nominated for "passenger of the year," a distinction voted upon by the drivers. I didn't win. Still, the nomination must say something about my concerted effort to remain cheerful. This demeanor, at least on certain occasions, was appreciated.

Once the bus arrived in Warren, which it inevitably did shortly after nine, my structured routine continued. Variation involved choice, which was never my strong point. I had a membership in the Warren Y.M.H.A., the Young Men's Hebrew Association, which was located, conveniently, just two blocks from my place. It was there I proceeded. I closed the place at ten o'clock, which left forty-five minutes for a workout or a swim. There were familiar faces at the Y, many of them Jewish.

I don't think I ever had a conversation, but I relied on the exchange of words with the elderly woman who staffed the front desk, upon paring. From there I walked the quiet tree-lined streets back to my apartment, where I meditated for thirty minutes. The meditation was a constant every night for ten years. I went to bed at eleven.

There was one week during my period of employment at the law library that stands out, and not for any reason directly connected to microfiche or microfilm. In a single week, I learned that three of my female friends had gotten married. One was Susan, the Julliard-trained modern dancer, with whom I had remained in distant contact since we both moved to New York shy of receiving a Cornell degree. The other two dated even further back and had been supportive during the early days of my illness. Lauren had been a year ahead of me at Cornell, and Tracy had been a fellow camp counselor at the Cultural Arts Day Camp of the Warren Y.M.H.A. In some quiet and unstated way, I had relied on all three.

That week, a truth that had been shared by an anthropology professor at Columbia hit home. Marriage is both marrying one member of the opposite sex and moving away from all the others. My relationship with the three female friends had never been sexual. Still, in a very real sense, when they became joined to their spouse, they were lost to me. And I felt it. Lauren had always been in the loop; From the time she advised me on which member of the history department to select as my academic advisor to the whole night we stayed up in her Collegetown apartment preparing for an English exam. I brought her a gift when I returned from my summer working in Alaska, and I spent a final evening in New York with her and her two best friends before she flew off to Israel. Lauren knew what I was up to every step of the way and in a dignified and respectful manner, supported me, even when I called her hysterical, upon first finding myself situated in a studio apartment in an alien environment.

That week, Lauren returned my call. It had been some time since we had last spoken, and she was excited to hear from me. But that was the last time. She had married a guy she knew from high school, and in due course they had children. They traded in their Brooklyn apartment for a home in New Jersey, and Lauren was reduced to a name on my Facebook list. I suppose Facebook is better than nothing. Still, there is something lifeless and anonymous about a Facebook friendship. A friendship that had once been alive and vibrant sits on a shelf along with a hundred and fifty-nine others, level and the same.

There was another component to my days of no small significance. Two evenings a week, I showed up at Hunter College on East 68th Street and attended classes in the graduate school. First, I completed a master's degree in American history. What Hunter gained in terms of flexibility and affordability, it lacked in ease of administrative detail. But I weathered the fine print and got the degree. At the same time, I took the undergraduate courses in literature necessary to be accepted into the MA program in English Lit. I completed this as well. My endeavors could be completed without undue social interaction, and I was blessed with two outstanding and highly qualified academic advisors.

I was trying to hold a job, and at times the grip was tenuous. Lenora rode me as hard as she reasonably could, given the fact that there was very little to actually do and I was being paid eight dollars an hour. She did her level best to teach me that there was a chain of command in the law library. There was the dean. There was the library director. There were supervisors, and that in this hierarchy, I was but one small part. When I got excited, she told me to "slow down." When I handed in work with a careless error, she strongly reprimanded me and sent me back to do it again. I went from week to week with a constant apprehension that I would be let go.

To tell you the truth, I don't really recall what Dr. Rubin was doing all through my ten-year journey through my employment at the Fordham Law Library. We were seeing each other twice a week, and there was the ever-present task of trying to find the appropriate mix of medications. One morning stands out. Dr. Rubin appeared at the door to the waiting room right on time for our eleven-fifteen Monday morning session. He invited me into the office. Our first task on mornings like this one was to discuss my reaction to a new drug. It had been spectacular.

"What did you think of the Zoloft?" Dr. Rubin asked, watching me intently. He probably knew more about it than I did just by looking at me, but he very much wanted my reaction as well.

"I like this drug…a breath of clean, fresh air. Hopefulness… Release… I'm walking up Madison Avenue just north of 79th Street, and I get the feeling that we've got a shot. We've really got a shot here."

"Good," Dr. Rubin said, satisfied with what he'd heard. "How have you been?"

I was getting ready to move on. I had been accepted into a doctoral program in English at the Fordham Rose Hill Campus.

It was also during my ten years of employment at the Fordham Law Library that my abiding interest in the twelve-step program of Alcoholics Anonymous had the chance to gestate and grow. Dr. Rubin approved. He knew that there was much there that could serve me well, and I attended any number of open meetings, mostly of A.A. and O.A. (Overeaters Anonymous), the two fellowships where I found the richest repository of experience. It is remarkable how many churches on the Upper West Side leave their basement doors open. I made a game effort to join a fellowship called Emotions Anonymous, where I thought I might actually belong, but found both its philosophy and its membership not to my liking. This was a blow I took hard. Over time, however, I came to peace with the simple consolation of the Big Book itself and Dr. Rubin's extraordinary understanding of its inner workings.

Lest I come across too much as a loner, I might add that those ten years of stable part-time employment were enlivened by a steady friendship with a young woman native to mainland China. Shu and I were, in fact, good friends. I ably assisted in her successful application to the doctoral program in finance at N.Y.U. and when that program concluded proofread her dissertation. For her part, she hung in there through the many ups and downs – the changes in medication and mood swings – with great constancy. We went together to countless movies on Saturday nights, and she joined my family for one Thanksgiving dinner, to say nothing of our ski weekend in the Berkshires at the home of my aunt and uncle and all those meals at Chinese restaurants. The friendship was platonic and lasted until she left town with her new husband to take up a teaching position at the University of Iowa.

SELF-EXPRESSION

Chapter Twenty-Six

Woodlawn – 1997

"The only way out of the cave is through the mouth of the dragon."

I wrote that. It has a Zen-like quality, I think. I wrote it while swimming lengths at the Lehman College pool, Lehman College being a part of the City University system here in New York City, which is where most of this took place. This was the summer of 1999, while I was enrolled as a graduate student in Hunter College, a sister school. Lehman College had a huge pool, actually Olympic in size or bigger. The joke was, you swim for about twenty minutes. Then you get to the other side. So, as I was making my way up and down this pool, at a slow but steady crawl, I was thinking about speaking openly about some of the dark days, about living through mental illness. There are still all kinds of taboos about this subject. Maybe there are good reasons for this, but if there are, I, for the life of me, don't know what they are. They may stem in part from the perception that people don't get better, and for most of human history, that may have been true. Fortunately, for me, that is no longer the case. Psychiatry may not have brought humanity past the age of armed conflict, but it has made huge advances in dealing with severe obsessive-compulsive disorder, even when that condition has psychotic tendencies. It just has. Deal with it.

So there I was, swimming up and down this enormous swimming pool, thinking about what it would mean to go public: to publish or speak publicly about my condition and recovery, as my incredibly capable doctor had implied I might, and the whole idea terrified me. That's when I came up with the statement in quotations above. Somewhere around lap seven, I realized there was no other way, that I really had no choice in the matter. There was only one way out of the cave, one entrance, and if I perceived some kind of dragon standing there, I was just going to have to walk past him, or through his mouth if that was necessary. The funny thing is, I've been at this for a while now, and it turned out it wasn't much of a dragon at all; it was papier mâché, glue, and feathers. When I walked right up to him, he fell right over. No fire, no loud, ugly noises, no violently beating wings, nothing.

On that particular day, I didn't head back to the apartment. I took the 4 Train one more stop, outwards, to the end of that line to the Woodlawn Cemetery, which is known as the final resting place of public figures and luminaries from every walk of life, though at the time I couldn't have named them. I hadn't thought through this trip; I just went, as I was accustomed to doing. The entrance to this renowned resting place was a short walk away along a quiet street, just a couple of hundred yards from the Woodlawn subway station. As I descended the stairs from the elevated, I knew I was in a part of the Bronx I knew nothing about. Warren, too, was part of the Bronx, but it was far removed. The huge expanse of Van Cortlandt Park, with its golf course, was visible off to the left.

The cemetery was hard to miss. It was surrounded by an eight-foot-high gray wall. I made my way along the perimeter until I reached the front gate. It was wide open and welcoming to the living as well as the deceased. A broad asphalt driveway led up to a guardhouse, and one of those barricades that go up and down to let the cars through. It was down, and there were no cars going through. As I approached the guardhouse, the man in charge, a Hispanic of medium height in a blue uniform, stepped out. He was there to greet me. It seems the Woodlawn Cemetery understands its place in American culture, and they had a brochure all printed up to guide visitors to the points of general interest. The security guard had a pile in his hand, and he was smiling.

"Hi," I said as I approached. I accompanied the greeting with an abbreviated wave of my right hand.

The security guard stepped forward and extended his right arm with a brochure at the end of it. "You going to look around?" he asked.

This man enjoyed his work. Couldn't say why exactly. Maybe it was the chance to spend so much time outdoors. Maybe it was the chance to assist visitors. Every day, he came to work at a place where others only came in limousines and black clothes, unless they were like me and had no idea why they had come at all.

"Thanks," I said, as I took the brochure from him. I hadn't been expecting such assistance. To me, it all looked like green grass and tombstones.

"Guess I'll just walk around," I said.

The security guard, having accomplished his task, left me to make my way.

I was still struggling with the same problem: how to come up with the guts to talk publicly about a subject nobody else discussed at all, not even among family. I was trying to figure out where I could come up with the courage to stand up before a darkened room of amateur comics and tell jokes that would make it quite clear I knew what I was talking about, as my doctor had also recommended, to write first-hand accounts about an experience with mental illness that would be reviewed by strangers on the Internet. The prospect was daunting, to say the least. The opposing reality was that this was what Dr. Rubin wanted, what he felt was necessary for my continued recovery. I wasn't in the habit of contradicting the man.

So I started walking around. The cemetery had been laid out with care by a landscape architect who knew his business. It might have been Frederick Law Olmstead, the man primarily responsible for Central Park. I'm not sure, but I think so. I walked here and there, consulting the brochure but not paying too much attention to the points of historical interest, the famous people and dignitaries there interred. I was just letting my mind wander, as was my habit, "thinking too much" being the primary distinguishing quality of the severe obsessive-compulsive. And what gradually sank in, as I ambled over those grassy hills, was that, quite regardless of what I chose to write, and regardless of what I chose to say, this is where I was going to wind up: under a grassy hill just like this one. There was no denying this reality, this fact, this incontrovertible truth. And somehow, with that realization came a feeling of liberation.

Kind of like, "What the fuck?"

Excuse the profanity, but it was kind of like that. What could the funny looks or sideways glances really matter? If this is what I had to do, I would just do it. It would have no bearing on my resting place, six feet under. There was no consideration of an afterlife. There was little thought given to the effect my speaking out might have, positive or otherwise. It was more of a realization that, in the grand scheme of things, it really didn't matter.

The Woodlawn Cemetery played its role for me that April afternoon. I never went back. Neither have I spent time walking in any other cemeteries. But my resolve has at no time been shaken. Rather, there has been a progression toward more and more openness, primarily in print and on the Internet after an initial, if abbreviated, career as an amateur stand-up comic. Each time I took it a little further, owned the experience as my own a little more, spoke a little more forcefully. I have signed a series of op-ed pieces in the Warren Press with my own name, and every one of my Facebook friends who is paying any attention at all knows that I have been hospitalized for mental illness.

Two aspects of this progression strike me in particular. First, that I wouldn't have been able to do this had if I not staked out a broad swath of independence. Granted, that had its roots in a protracted period of severe mental illness, which can incline a guy to spend time alone. But, since I've gotten my feet more or less on the ground, I have not been overly inclined to reengage in any pre-established peer group. Some of them still exist: friends from grade school who announce Christmas get-togethers on Facebook that I could have chosen to attend or at least acknowledge, peer groups in graduate school (I was a fully enrolled member of a doctoral program). There have been others. Staying outside these ready-made environments comes with a price: feelings of isolation, the loss of social interaction. At the same time, I question how those things go together with speaking out about a prolonged period of mental illness. They have more to do with Friday night dinners and Karaoke parties. The tendency, I believe, becomes to fit in, and talking openly about mental illness just doesn't help one fit in.

The second aspect of the progression that comes to mind is that, even without the Friday night dinners and the Karaoke parties, I have become ever more comfortable in my own skin. There must be all kinds of clichés that express this idea. Doubtless, they appeared on Salada teabags back in the day. Something about being true to yourself, not being afraid to stand up as your own person, not going along with the crowd for its own sake. It is probably covered in Bartlett's Quotations and in those novels assigned in the doctoral program, some of which I actually read. But I am more at peace in a way that I would not be had I chosen to run away from the most significant part of my life to date. And I hold on to the hope that, if I can get enough traction, get my balance, and hold steady, others might accept me on those terms as well.

Chapter Twenty-Seven

Stand-Up – 1999

In my abbreviated career as a stand-up comic, one night stands out. It began with a taxi ride to the New York Comedy Club, which, in the early summer of 1999, stood on Twenty-Fourth Street over by Second Avenue. I believe it still does. For some reason, which presently escapes me, I was running late. I was also more than a little nervous. I was scheduled to perform that evening before a full room of spectators, considerably more than the seven or eight who usually show up at the weekly open mics. These would not be fellow performers. They would be strangers who had paid admission, and there would be a lot of them. I was scared.

I was studying American history at the time, as a graduate student at Hunter, and I had chanced upon a history book that described in detail the events of D-Day, June 6th, 1944. In one section, the historian recounts the experience of one soldier with a decidedly sunny outlook. He was slotted in to take part in the initial landing on the beaches of Normandy. His responsibility was to cross the beach and go straight up the cliffs into the German machine guns. They were expecting something like eighty percent casualties. Two days before the landing, the soldier was called into his commander's office and reprimanded for trying to send a letter to a girl he knew in Paris. Had the letter been intercepted, it could have given away details of the landing. This poor sucker was trying to arrange a date for a night out with his girlfriend in Paris after the attack.

Something about this engaging story resonated on that July evening as my taxi cab made its way down Second Avenue, stopping at far too many of the traffic lights. I'd been at this for a couple of years, at various open mics around the city: Stand-Up New York on West Seventy-Eighth Street, The Ha Comedy Club when it was way over by Ninth Avenue, The Boston Comedy Club, ironically named and standing on Third Street in the Village, and the New York Comedy Club itself.

This was an honest way to learn a trade. You paid three dollars for the privilege of standing alone in a white spotlight before the assembled comics, for five minutes. The stated objective was to make them laugh. This is harder than it seems. For one thing, the other performers were thinking about their coming five minutes on stage. For another, they had very little interest in encouraging the competition. That is the way it seemed to me, anyway.

Still, my performance had improved over time. I can say no one else was trying to do what I was trying to do. I was looking for laughs in some combination of my own experience in recovering from mental illness and Rubin's insightful remarks. It was distinctive. I was fond of pointing out the futility of anger, though the bits frequently lacked an effective punchline. If I was looking for an affirmation, I found it in the fact that the other comics were paying attention. Once I had

had some experience, I found I could hold the room and that, when I concluded, I received a heartfelt round of applause. The laughs were a plus and were very welcome.

There was one master of ceremonies at Stand-Up New York who was particularly encouraging and gave me a thunderous introduction when I had been away for some time. Had it amounted to nothing more than this, it would have stood out as a memorable and wonderful experience.

I did, however, take the additional step of signing up to perform in the "bringer." "Bringers" were looked down upon by the regulars at the open mics, decidedly so. A paid employee would stand in the dark, narrow entranceway that led back to the performance area at the New York Comedy Club and try and approach the performers. The entranceway doubled as the bar, where we were at liberty to receive a free soft drink, should we so desire. This guy's job was to convince the comics that it would be in their self-interest to bring four friends or family members as fully paying guests to an evening showcase. In return, the performer would be entitled to perform for a full ten minutes before a full room of men and women who were drinking alcohol.

This had a certain allure. I think the reason the open-mic regulars looked down on the entire process had something to do with the club sponging off the comics. It was generally agreed that you could improve and learn your craft by coming out at five o'clock and performing for the other comics. There might not be all that much of a response, but it was still possible to read the room, to determine what was working and what wasn't. The open mic was a well-established institution in the world of stand-up comedy, the route countless comics, including all of the greats, had taken when they were starting out. The bringer was seen as a way for the club to make money.

For some reason, I signed up. In his pitch, the club employee liked to point out that there would be an agent in the audience, though I had little thought of becoming a professional. Another enticement was that one act from the showcase would be guaranteed a spot in a regular Friday night show. I don't think it was that, either. Maybe I just wanted to see what it would be like to perform before a full house. That could have been it. At the time, the only people I could bring to this bringer were family members. My mother and father agreed to show up, as did my older sister, Louise, and one of her old friends. Everything was in place for my big night.

So there I was, making my way in fits and starts down Second Avenue in the back seat of a yellow cab, and I knew fear. I can't say I'd never been frightened before. The night I made my second unauthorized exit from the Payne Whitney Psychiatric Hospital had been bad, too. The cab let me off on the corner of Twenty-Forth Street, and I walked the half block up the north side of that side street to the door of the club. The next thing I clearly remember is sitting in the waiting area off to one side of the stage. The performance took place in the larger of the two rooms of the club. The open mics were often held in a smaller room on the side of the building. That is where I did my first performance. If it hadn't been for a wonderful master of ceremonies sitting right in front and cheering me on, I don't know if I ever would have come back. The rest of the comics were reading the paper and chatting among themselves.

The night of the bringer, things were different. I'd had two or three years, on and off, to perfect my act. You might think this would confer a degree of confidence. Sitting over there in the holding pen, it did not. It was a darkened area to the right of the stage shielded entirely from the audience. Through the front of the curtained space, we could look out toward the elevated platform with the microphone. We – and by that, I mean myself and the five other comics – were not conversing. We just sat there and waited our turn. I was prepared in that I knew the words, the lines, the bits I wanted to share. I was confident I wouldn't forget what I wanted to say. It was all material I had been doing at the open mics. I had selected my best ten minutes – the ones that had worked or had at least kept the room quiet and attentive. That night, I sat quietly and awaited my turn.

Much of the humor among my cohorts tended toward the raunchier side of the spectrum, not suitable, you might say, for younger audiences. There was plenty of sex and off-color references. Don't get me wrong; this did elicit an audience reaction. There were funny people there, all of whom had the guts to stand up in front of a room full of people they didn't know and try to make them laugh, a noble calling by any standard. I can say that my material stood out. It was different. I heard my name called and proceeded out through the front of the dark, curtained-off area into the light.

I remember very little of the actual performance. I remember the white light in a pool around me and the glare in my eyes. I remember that there was a full room of people before me and that they were all looking at me. I didn't forget the words. I proceeded from one bit to the next, and I think I did it well, as well as I had ever done. And I remember that the audience was listening to me. I held their attention. Whether or not there had been any real laughs, I couldn't say. When I concluded, they applauded a real, solid applause.

As the M.C. stepped to the stage and took the microphone from me, he said, "Jordan Fineman! Let him hear it!" And I did. I did hear it.

I returned from whence I had come, numb to the world and floating in a very good place.

That was not the end of my stand-up career. I kept writing new material and taking it out to open mics, particularly at Stand-Up New York. I kept listening to CDs as well: Jackie Mason and Margaret Cho, and the bedrock: Mel Brooks and Carl Reiner's "The 2000-Year-Old Man," as well as the early Bob Newhart and Woody Allen, and Bill Cosby. But I reached a point where the stuff I wanted to perform was too edgy for even that crowd. I tried a bit about my time in Payne Whitney and my friend, the M.C., let me know I was over the line. The part about getting taken from Central Park in the back of an ambulance tipped him off.

I might have stopped anyway. I was writing autobiographical fiction. That is what really mattered. I am convinced that is why Rubin had wanted to take on the stand-up comedy in the first place. With his encyclopedic knowledge of writers and their development, he had foreseen that trying my hand as a comic would contribute to the way I sounded as a writer. He gets full credit for that. I really don't think there is another analyst in New York or anywhere else who would have had that insight and been able to implement it.

The fact of the matter is that Dr. Rubin had me undertaking a whole range of similarly intended activities. I purchased blank canvases and acrylic paints at Arts Student League and painted impressionistic landscapes. I bought loose scraps of fabric in the garment district and sewed collages. For a solid two years, I studied ceramics with a wonderful instructor at the West Side Y. I bought Japanese ingredients at the Sunrise Market on East Ninth Street and tried to cook Japanese food. I think that is about the sum of it, if you don't include the video editing, which I studied in the computer laboratory at the Rose Hill campus of Fordham University, where I was enrolled as a graduate student in English literature pursuing a doctoral degree, and the guitar, which had been a regular part of my day for a lifetime.

There is very little question in my mind that all of these creative activities together made it possible for me to start writing. I fully buy into Dr. Rubin's stated contention that creativity pursued in any one field of artistic endeavor has ancillary benefits in all the others. Creativity is a capacity that can be increased in many ways.

About a related matter, however, I am not nearly so certain. I could swear that during our final years together, Dr. Rubin was laying the groundwork for a future career that would actually advance in many directions. He seemed to imply that I would be a performer, that I would tread the boards before well-heeled crowds in major theaters, that I would take my video-editing skills on to directing movies, as he did in fact, have me write two screenplays. He went so far as to convey the idea that I might work toward a doctorate in American history at Columbia University, building upon the master's degree I already had.

My regular meetings with this esteemed man were brought to an end. Dr. Rubin was approaching retirement, and my family wanted to see me situated in a more sustainable situation. Given my propensity to soar to unhealthy heights and swerve into the psychotic, there is very little momentum toward these extracurricular activities at Warren Mental Health, where I now receive my care. Strange as it may seem, however, I am growing to accept this eventuality.

It was Dr. Rubin himself who encouraged me to look toward the wisdom of the ancient Greeks for insight, and it was in that culture that the myth of Icarus and Daedalus originated.

In that story, a young son is granted the gift of flight, necessary to escape from imprisonment on an island. He is warned by his father, however, not to fly too high, as the sun would melt his wings, and he would crash into the sea. Icarus, the son, however, becomes overly excited. He finds the ability to fly so new and intoxicating, that he ignores his father's warning and flies too close to the sun. His wings do, in fact, melt, and he perishes in the water below.

I look toward that story when I am prone to wonder what might have happened had I remained with Rubin. I take consolation in the wonderful gift I have of being able to set words on paper, and I am thankful that, to date, I have not followed the temptation to reach higher. With a healthy sense of moderation, I am still airborne.

But even if the stand-up comedy has no immediate successor, it stands alone, in memory with shining distinction. It was a wonderful, if trying, set of experiences. I brought me into contact on a regular basis with a distinctive group of guys and gave me the chance to hear their stories. It provided an underappreciated view of this city I call home. It made me braver, and in the end, it gave me what passes for a writer's voice.

Chapter Twenty-Eight

Imko – 2000, 2001

During the fall of 2000, as the United States was entering a period of political instability brought on by the hotly contested results of the presidential election, I made a friend. I have been given to believe that friendships do not often begin quite this way. Imko and I met on the uptown Broadway Local, the 1 Train, at Seventy-Ninth Street. By the time we got off the train at 238th Street, we had accepted each other as compadres, fellow travelers, friends.

I had made a start with things Japanese before we met. Here, as in most everything else, I was following Dr. Rubin's suggestions. He rarely came right out and told me what to do, but he had a way of making himself clear. In those formative months, I stopped into a French café in the West Village and came into session singing the praises of a cute French waitress, Dr. Rubin made it very clear I was headed in the wrong direction. He well understood how those pathways diverge in a "yellow wood." How one thing leads to another.

From the point of a distant perspective, I think I can understand why he was so interested in my immersion in

Japanese culture. It is a complex and multifaceted crystal with many sides and many angles, but I know for certain he was interested in quieting my rampaging thought process. From the very beginning, he saw the Japanese emphasis on meditation and creating a quiet mind as integral to this effort. I would have to surmise that he felt the Japanese' alternate views on human sexuality would also work out to my benefit.

By the time of our first subway ride together, Imko stood out as someone I would like to get to know. I'd been spending time in the Japanese part of town, around East Ninth Street, and had mastered and memorized a number of phrases in Japanese. It was a clumsy way of making an introduction, and thus far I had succeeded in interacting only with women who were paid to do so: workers behind counters who were selling me food. What was different about Imko? I really don't know. Maybe it was something in the stars, or in the hour of our birth, or in our own adopted view of the world. For whatever reason, by the end of our forty-five-minute trip it was like we were the oldest of friends. Caught up in conversation, I failed to get off at my regular stop, 231st Street and Broadway. I rode the train one stop further, and we both got off at 238th Street. We exchanged phone numbers on the elevated platform and parted ways.

Within forty-five minutes, we were talking on the phone, not because we were compulsive or scared or lonely, just because it was the right thing to do. Thus began a close association that lasted through the fall and into the winter. We did all kinds of things together. For starters, we took a hiking trip through Harriman State Park, a scenic wonder forty-five minutes north of the city. This turned into an adventure when the bus that was supposed to take us back sped by on a darkened country road. The clocks had shifted back the weekend before, bringing on the evening darkness earlier than expected, and it was a flag stop. In the dark of the evening, the bus went right by. To make matters worse, it had grown cold, colder than I had expected. I was feeling like a heel of a date when a state police car came along, and, seeing two hikers standing by the road, stopped to pick us up.

I was distressed, thinking about the stressful situation I had created for a nice Japanese girl. It was nowhere written in the Camp Ojibway guidebook that a day's hiking trip was supposed to end with a ride in the back of a state police patrol car. I am happy to report, however, that Imko seemed to enjoy the whole thing. The conscientious state trooper brought us to a train station in the next town, which had connecting service to Penn Station, from which the 1 Train returned us safely to Warren. It had been an adventure, and no doubt brought us closer.

From there on, we saw each other regularly. Imko came to the law library to see where I worked, late on a Saturday afternoon. Afterward, we walked through Riverside Park, above Seventy-Second Street. I didn't take it as a compliment at the time, but my hard-working Japanese friend gave me a hard time for only working part-time. I suppose this might be taken as an indication that I passed for normal. We attended a New York Giants football game with two tickets contributed by a family friend who also drove us there and back. I have to say, I found the military flyover and vehement cheering of the crowd not entirely to my taste. We took a boat cruise with Shu who was now a doctoral candidate in Finance at N.Y.U. at the time. And any number of times, Imko spent the evening at my apartment. We seemed to always get the same bus driver on the Number 10 Bus when I brought her home.

There were other shared endeavors. We played squash at the Warren Y.M.H.A., and one night, Imko slept over. She passed the night on the couch with me on my bed in the bedroom. We tried to meet up for the Rockefeller Center tree lighting but failed to connect. We passed an afternoon at Rolling Hills, a public garden in my neighborhood, again with my friend Shu. All of this, however, was a preamble for our grand adventure. We took a trip to Washington D.C. and Philadelphia. I don't think about this nearly as much as I should. It provides a clear indication that with the right person, I am entirely capable of sustaining a prolonged period of intimacy and interaction. If I did it all those many years ago – and by any standard of measurement, I am healthier now – what could really be the big deal?

We made our plans. We would travel down to the capital by bus and spend two nights in a D.C. youth hostel. From there we would travel to Philadelphia for a brief visit before returning to New York. We were both looking forward to the trip. There was an undercurrent to our preparation, a point of conversation that was never too far off the table. Imko had not made up her mind about one extremely important matter. She wasn't sure whether or not she would return to Japan. I had picked up on the fact that there was a lot of tension between her and her mother. There was also the ever-present reality that women in Japan hold a distinctly second-class status. I wasn't trying to solve Imko's dilemma. It was just something we both knew she was dealing with.

On the morning of our scheduled departure, we had decided to meet up on the platform of the ever-present Broadway Local, the 1 Train headed south. It seems to me we spent an awful lot of time on that train, with me putting my arm around Imko's shoulder when we were seated in front of the side window and there was room to squeeze it in. In honor of the occasion of our departure, I had purchased a small, red, glass box. I had seen Imko admire it in a store we had visited, and it was consistent with her desire to open an accessories shop someday. She used the word "accessories," for small items like that box, though I had never heard the term used in exactly that way before. We took the train to Times Square and walked over to the Port Authority for the bus ride to D.C.

Imko and I both grew from the time we spent together. If we hadn't, it wouldn't have been much of a friendship. I have, to this day, two handwritten notes in a cardboard box in my closet testifying to Imko's appreciation of my company. I never wrote it down, but I have to believe she too knows how much I valued her spending time with me. That said, I think it appropriate to add that Imko had, at times, a tendency to be a little persnickety. We arrived in Washington in the late afternoon and, as should come as no surprise when a severe obsessive-compulsive and a young woman not conversant in English were traveling together, we had a little trouble finding the youth hostel. I can honestly say that if Imko got frustrated with me, I was nothing but patient. This might be attributed in large measure to Dr. Rubin's recurrent admonitions on the danger of expressing anger or irritation, and an even larger measure to my father's example on the appropriate way to treat a young lady.

We arrived at the Washington D.C. youth hostel in time to receive our American Youth Hostel sheets and settle in for the night. We had big plans for the next day. We were going to take in the sights. A Japanese woman and a Jewish man were going to absorb a full day of American history. When I came downstairs that morning, Imko kvetched at me for being late. True to form in our evolving relationship, I patiently explained that there had been a logjam in the men's bathroom and, in good spirits, we set out.

It was a memorable day for us, one of many we shared together. We traipsed around The Mall, Imko snapping pictures, and me carrying the knapsack filled with an ever-increasing collection of brochures. A highlight of the excursion was our visit to the Holocaust Museum, a memorial that seemed to hold resonance for both of us. For me, the connection was obvious: My entire extended family, the ones who hadn't immigrated to America, had been wiped out. The ones who had immigrated spoke very little about the ones who had remained in Romania and Hungary, but the facts were clear. Most of the Jews, all the people who looked like me, had been exterminated.

Imko's connection was not so clear. I attribute a good part of my connection with Japanese women (and there were quite a few others after Imko left) to the fact that there is no anti-Semitism among the Japanese. I don't know exactly why this is. It could be because it is a Buddhist culture. We saw an exhibit in D.C. that documented the fact that, unlike most of the countries of the world, Japan welcomed the Eastern European Jews fleeing the Nazis.

But something else happened during our visit to the Holocaust Museum. We passed the entrance to a public restroom, and I said, with what passed for humor, "That is where you go to throw up."

Imko reprimanded me for making a joke on such hallowed ground.

"How do you think the Jews survived all this?" I asked her. "It was just that kind of humor that has kept the Jews going."

We passed through the exhibit, which really wasn't easy to look at, and out onto the grassy mall in front. Another set of brochures had been added to the collection in my knapsack, and Imko had taken a few more photos. I chose to elaborate on one of Dr. Rubin's favorite themes, the therapeutic power of laughing at yourself. He had brought it up on our first day together, and never tired of repeating it. Imko was an appreciative audience.

I said some other things that morning which Imko took to heart as well. I spoke about anger and how if you're angry at other people you will be just as angry at yourself. I may have even said something about forgiveness being its opposite. It wasn't a long discussion. We had places to go and things to see. But in the context of her ongoing struggle with her mother, I think some of it hit home. So, we kept on walking around. We saw some American art and a collection of airplanes at the Smithsonian Air & Space Museum. I took quiet pleasure in seeing the Wright brothers' first airplane, which flew for less than a minute in its first trial. Dr. Rubin liked to celebrate my small victories by drawing a parallel to the first flight. I had shown it could be done. From there on out it was only a matter of refinement and improvement.

Our trip back to the city involved a stopover in Philadelphia. We didn't stay overnight but only got off the bus for a few hours to look at the Liberty Bell and the nearby historic sites. Imko took a creative shot with herself walking in imitation of a statue on a rooftop. Coming out of Philadelphia, we made out in the back of the bus. Back in New York, there was a routine to attend to. I had my work in the law library and classes to attend to. The presidential election, which was supposed to be decided by the early morning of the first Wednesday in November, was stretching on unresolved. Imko was also attending classes at The International Center on West Twenty-Third Street, and we hung out with some of her friends from there at night.

Through all of this, a question was still unresolved. Imko had not decided whether or not she would return to Japan. The

decision was made, late one evening, in front of the Metropolitan Museum of Art. We were walking arm in arm in front of
the fountains at Eightieth Street. It was dark and quiet. There
was no water in the fountain. Up ahead, an older woman stood
alone waiting for the Fifth Avenue Bus. All of a sudden, Imko
pulled up short and grabbed my right arm, "My mother – she
will grow old!" she cried.

I believe that at that moment, Imko decided she would
fly back to Japan and make the best life she could.

Our days together dwindled. I visited her in her Bronx
apartment one night as she was packing, and, uncertain about
how I had conducted myself in a relationship in flux, I called
Dr. Rubin from a pay phone on the street.

"You did well," he reassured me, choosing his words carefully.

On the morning of her flight, I was not so well-collected.
I was supposed to meet up with her for the taxi ride to Kennedy Airport, but I arrived without the one thing I was supposed to bring: a book that was to serve as a present for one
of her female mentors. I left her to travel to the airport alone
while I returned for the book. Believe it or not, I showed up at
the airport still without that darn book. I was thoroughly flum-
moxed. Imko was not. She was calm and collected, her luggage
checked and her carry-on piece in order. We said good-bye at
the gate.

"You're the greatest man I ever knew…" she stated.

I watched her walk down the passageway toward the gate
until she was out of sight. She did not look back. Alone, I
made my way to the subway for the return trip to Warren.

Imko and I did a good job of staying in touch, which
is not an easy thing to do when two people are separated by
a continent, an ocean, and numerous time zones. She called

the day after 9/11, and I spoke with her when she was in the hospital the morning after giving birth to her daughter. When I traveled to Japan, she looked out for me in Osaka and Kobe. I cannot, however, claim that we are in touch today, not even on Facebook.

Dr. Rubin's explanation for this turn of events was simple enough. "She has a jealous husband," he commented when a card I had sent was returned.

Such, I imagine, is the way of the world. I can state, however, that without Imko's companionship and friendship, none of the rest of it would have even been possible. The chaos that was to follow in two years' time is not on her account. More than anything else, it was brought on by the three-week vacation I took to Japan in 2002, which was a huge success in many ways but left me with some unfortunate residual effects.

Chapter Twenty-Nine

A Walk by the River – 2002

Back in the height of summer, 2002, there was drama – high drama – in the Bronx, with a police escort and an ambulance ride. Whether or not my experience as a comic directly contributed to this adventure is an open question, though my recent trip abroad almost certainly did. Whether or not it has made me a writer is another.

Ambulances are not uncommon around here. Most of the time, however, they are arriving at one of the assisted living centers or over at the Home for the Aged, a venerable institution by the river, established to cater to the wealthy Jews from Manhattan's Upper East Side in their waning years. These ambulances rush past my apartment at all hours of the day and night with their sirens wailing. On this occasion, I was inside. There was no big rush. I don't think they turned on the sound effects. Still, on balance, I'd say I'd prefer to be an outside observer. On the day in question, unfortunately, I was not.

There are many chemically induced medical conditions that require more than a good sponsor and strict attention to

The Steps. There is an entire pharmacological industry that treats mental illness, and it is improving all the time. There is a lot of money in it. The overwhelming majority of these illnesses do not require hospitalization. The patient consults with a psychiatrist, goes up to the pharmacy counter, fills his or her prescription and takes it home, with some misgivings at first, no doubt. Still, that's how it works. It is only on the rare occasion that those medications must be given inside a hospital, a psychiatric hospital. That has happened to me on two occasions. The first time, it was actually because I screwed up taking the medications on the outside. That was the story of a neurotic misbehaving during his psychiatrist's vacation. It had nothing to do with the psychotic. The second hospitalization is the one I want to address: a stay in the Westchester Psychiatric Hospital, which had everything to do with the psychotic. It was there that for the first time I was put on Zyprexa, the latest generation of anti-psychotic medications. I'd like to say there was a lot of love as well. Maybe there was a little of each.

For some days, I had been gradually descending into madness. There's an outdated term; "madness" sounds positively nineteenth century. These days, everything has a precise, clinical description. I think the doctors would say I was moving into a psychotic episode. Strange things had been happening with increasing intensity for a few days, as I fell more and more "into character," as I began to believe I was actually a character I had written about and portrayed in a stand-up act. Gradually, I went from writing about this shmuck to believing I was him.

He, and by that I mean P.W., is a harmless guy. He's a comic figure, really: bashful around women, unable to hold a job for more than a few weeks because of his intense shyness. In my writing, P.W. is prone to say wise and interesting things, but no one takes him too seriously. I had even played him on the stage of amateur nights at a comedy clubs. There, he fit right in. This is the character I thought I had become. All my writing had autobiographical roots, so P.W. was in some ways an exaggerated form of myself, but I still was taking on a different persona.

Along the way, I came to believe in other things that were far removed from reality. I looked out at the red light on top of a large building visible from my bedroom window and endowed it with supernatural meaning. I began seeing the everyday occurrences of daily life in terms of the grand issues of Good and Evil. The talk radio hosts on the local sports radio station were somehow allied with Good. Go figure that one.

I began cleaning my apartment in the middle of the night, making repeated visits to the garbage chute in the hall. I'd been battling severe obsessive-compulsive disorder for a good twenty years. I just had never had a psychotic episode before. There was no time when I was not fully accountable for my actions. Severe obsessive-compulsive disorder and bipolar disorder can make you very miserable, but the world was always stable around me. I always knew who I was and had no doubts about my sensations. This time, things had taken a darker turn. I didn't even have anything in the bathroom cabinet that could have helped. These changes don't take place instantaneously. During the early stages, certainly, there is ample opportunity to note them, to discover a new dimension growing inside from your healthy self, and to take appropriate remedial steps. On this occasion, I lacked that perspective.

On that August day in 2002, I walked out of my apartment building and along the sidewalk of the thoroughfare that runs out front with only one shoe on, the other being dragged by its laces. I was thirsty. I now know that dehydration makes psychosis worse. I did not know this at the time. I made my way along Warren Avenue, past the adjoining set of six-story brick buildings in the summer heat. I passed the bus stop where people were waiting for the bus, people who may have known me on better days. I made the choice to veer to the right into the tree-lined residential area of one family homes, but the trees provided little relief. I was going under.

Having arrived at the gate of the Rolling Hills botanical gardens, I acted in a manner that may have been consistent with the character of P.W. but was in no way something Jordan Fineman would have done, not even on a hot summer's afternoon. I rang the buzzer by the side delivery entrance and asked for a glass of water. You laugh? I hope so. Otherwise, the rest of this is going to sound pretty strange.

I don't know exactly how this went over in the administrative offices. I suspect it may have been the first time alarm bells were sounded. But, consistent with the service-oriented nature of the non-profit institution, the director arrived at the gate with a water bottle in her hand. She saw a man around forty in a loose-fitting white baggy t-shirt with a washed out print on the front, wearing only one sneaker. His jeans were worn through in the right knee. His hair was copious and un-brushed. We did not converse.

From there, I headed straight downhill toward the Hudson River, one of the landmarks of the community. It seems I had a destination in mind. I walked down the potholed scarred pavement of 254th Street on a weekday afternoon. There was no one else around. At the foot of the hill was the Warren Train Station, one stop on the Metro-North railway headed up toward Poughkeepsie. I walked up the stairs to the overpass above the train tracks, still with just one shoe on. On the far side was terrain with which I was intimately familiar. From the southbound platform, I jumped down to the dirt borderline of the river itself. Thick undergrowth grew by the rocks that abutted the water. I made my way south through an opening in the weeds and onto what passed for a beach in the northwest Bronx. Then I did something I have never been fully able to explain. I slipped out of my clothes and into the water. I fully submerged myself. Dr. Rubin, with his encyclopedic knowledge of the many religious traditions, called it a rite of baptism.

The water may have temporarily cooled me, but it did little to improve my state of mind. I put my clothes back on, this time lacing both sneakers, and began to make my way north along the water's edge. I paused to sit on one of the rocks with the water of the Hudson sloshing around below my feet. To my right was a flock of geese. But on that August afternoon, they assumed an aura of mythic proportions to me, like messengers from some avian land, far away or above. Lodged in the rocks, but within arm's reach, was a small plastic bottle half-filled with river water. This too, I assumed had been left for me by a divine power, and I drank it to assuage my thirst. It was a hot day.

I continued along the eastern bank of the Hudson River. On the opposite shore were the Palisades cliffs, geologically significant rock formations running vertically from the line of green trees above to the water below. They appeared remote through the haze and humidity. I approached the next outpost on the Metro-North rail line, the Ludlow station. Here again, I did something to draw attention to myself as a man having a breakdown, a psychotic episode, a descent into madness, call it what you will. Under the overhang of the otherwise deserted southbound station, I saw a metallic pipe protruding from the side wall. Beneath the pipe on the right-hand side was a metal chain. I pulled on the chain and water came running out of the pipe. This was just what I needed, cold water that had not been contaminated by the many impurities of the Hudson River and the remains of someone's three-week-old Gatorade. I lay down on the ground, pulled the chain and let the cool water run over my face and head.

I wasn't interested in taking a train. Instead, I began to walk south, back along the train tracks to the Warren Station. It was then I first noticed the three policemen who were to set the future course of events in motion. They were walking quietly towards me, two men and a woman. I approached them as well.

Their greeting was friendly. "How are you doing?" one of the policemen asked.

I was aware that things had taken a serious turn. The "men in blue" were on the scene. I did not answer the policeman's greeting but kept walking along the dirt that divided the southbound track from an abandoned track no longer in use. The three policemen fell in line and began walking beside me.

At this point, P.W. did exactly what P.W. was inclined to do. Without directly acknowledging the presence of the officers, he (that would be me) began proclaiming his credentials to the hillside at healthy decibel levels.

"Abraham Fineman, my father, Harvard Business School, Class of 1949... Jordan Fineman, Phillips Andover Academy, Class of 1980... Cornell University Class of 1984... Candice Fineman, Harvard Kennedy School... Louise Fineman, Harvard Business School... Anne Fineman, Brown University."

The policemen walked affably by my side. I was moving in the direction they wanted, toward the Warren station and the help that awaited. We arrived at a patch of shade beside a particularly large bush. Here, I was inclined to stop. The policemen did not immediately force the matter.

"What's your name?" one of the men asked.

"P.W.," I answered without reservation.

"I'm J.T.," the woman, a young, svelte African American, answered.

"I'm A.J.," The man who had asked the original question answered as well.

"I'm G.S." The third policeman completed the introductions.

Remembering these events all these years later still brings a tear to my eye. Do they teach that in police officer school, or were these guys just really good?

The fact remained that they had business to attend to. They had an ambulance waiting. "Why don't we head up to the station?" The first policeman asked respectfully.

I wasn't inclined to move. I was appreciating the shade, and I told him so.

"Better move out of this hot sun," the second man said.

I still wasn't moving.

"Bet we could find something to drink," the woman said.

Still no go. With a stubbornness completely out of character to Jordan Fineman, P.W. had become a problem. He had resolved not to cooperate. The police officers, kind as they had proven themselves, understood that action had to be taken. Much as Jordan Fineman might shudder at the thought, these two strong policemen picked P.W. up and carried him the remaining distance to the Warren station, up the stairs, across the overpass, and into the ambulance waiting on the other side. P.W. did not fight. He did not resist. He simply remained limp.

I say I believed I was this character. That is not completely true. There was some part of my consciousness that was still Jordan, and that part knew what was going on and, frankly, was terrified. The ambulance attendant, some kind of E.M.T., treated me kindly as well, and with him, I was more cooperative. I lay down in the back of the vehicle and let him secure me.

That was the last I saw of the police officers. They had done a first-rate job. Things had gotten a little stressful when I wouldn't go along with them, but on balance I couldn't have asked for a better rescue team. I had been in deep trouble, and the three police officers had taken the first step toward setting things right. If love is "wanting to make another person happy," as Dr. Rubin has proposed, then these three police officers performed a loving act that day.

I rode in the back of the ambulance with the attendant by my side and no siren blaring. Together we made the short trip to the psychiatric emergency room of the Allen Pavilion of the Columbia Presbyterian Hospital. The Allen Pavilion is a kind of annex that serves the far northern regions of Manhattan. The ambulance pulled up to the unloading area, and I was wheeled inside.

So, there I was in the receiving area of the psychiatric emergency room of the Allen Pavilion of the Columbian Presbyterian Hospital. One of the first things I did was step into the small bathroom and throw up. I didn't think this one through at the time, but in hindsight I can see that it was my body rejecting the unconventional means of hydration I had employed while walking beside the river. I had had the bizarre idea that the small plastic bottles lodged among the rocks (I'd drunk more than one) had been placed there by some divine power for my benefit. Actually, they had been sitting there for days, if not weeks, and were filled with river water, rainwater, and the remains of someone else's beverage, and were entirely unfit for human consumption, I threw up the whole lot.

Then it was back onto the dolly, where I was to remain until I could be transported to some more permanent facility.

Unfortunately, I am compelled to report that, during my brief stay in the emergency room, I again did not cooperate. Maybe it was because I had yet to receive any Zyprexa, I really don't know, but I did not do exactly what they wanted. The burly male attendant wanted me to lie down. I wouldn't. I refused. I felt I was compelled to play some part, a part I knew was not in my own self-interest. He pushed me down. It wasn't that big a deal I guess, but at the time, on top of everything else, it was quite upsetting.

I have no recollection whatsoever of speaking with the doctors at this psychiatric way station. They must, however, have learned the names of my parents or other family members, possibly with the help of the police officers and my digressions while walking by the river, because from there on out, things were taken out of my hands. Arrangements were made. I was provided for. On this occasion, unlike my previous hospitalization for screwing up the medication, everything, I believe, was done right. The psychiatric emergency system worked. That August afternoon, I was in no condition to take care of myself, or fend for myself, or really do much of anything for myself. I needed help, and I got it.

I was loaded in the back of another ambulance and taken to my more permanent accommodations in the bucolic surroundings of Westchester County. There are reasons they locate these kinds of places in the countryside, amidst the trees and the grass. When, years later, things got rough again, I tried to replicate the experience on my own by spending time in the Rolling Hills Gardens, not outside the gate, and in Pine Hills, a green and quiet town in the Hudson Valley. Granted, some hospitals are right in the heart of Manhattan, so I suppose it isn't always possible, but on balance, I believe it is preferable. There is something about being in nature that is good for the mind. It has healing qualities. I have a distinct recollection of lying in the back of the ambulance as the vehicle drove up the long driveway that led up to the hospital and looking out the rear window at the trees passing overhead.

I suppose I should try and say something about my state of mind during all this, this being a first-person account, but that is not easily accomplished. Rubin asked me to write him a longhand account of what I was experiencing at the hospital. He may even have it filed away somewhere – who knows? From my current perspective, those thoughts are not easily recreated. Nor would I want to, to be honest. The whole thing was so dark and twisted and distorted. I still believed I was someone I was not. I believed I was this character, this P.W. By this point, I was no longer uncooperative. I was doing what I was told and going with the program, at this point, not a twelve-step program. The fact of the matter was, I had absolutely no idea what was going on. I was very mixed up.

They gave me my own room and started me on the Zyprexa. My doctor had been informed of my whereabouts, as had my parents, my sister Louise, and my brother-in-law. My doctor knew, like the last time around, that these things happen. He put in a lot of extra hours on the phone, speaking with my family and with me in the hospital, to make sure things proceeded as they should, but this whole thing didn't throw him.

The Westchester Psychiatric Hospital was entirely situated on one floor. It was not well lit, at least that is the way I re-member it. I had my own room, small and rectangular with white walls. At one end of the room, opposite the door, was a large window that looked out on something green. There was a single bed along one wall and a large closet. There was also a dresser where I had the vague idea it would be necessary to hide my writing from the authorities who would search the room. In retrospect, I do not believe any such searches took place.

All the necessary functions of daily life were provided. I remember that breakfast cereal was provided at a central table, along with orange juice, milk, and plastic bowls and cups for consuming them. There were bathrooms, but here the details remain vague. Personally, I was still in another time and place. Call it the Twilight Zone if you like. I didn't watch the show all that many times, but it might come close.

I do have a specific recollection of the central meeting room, where at periodic intervals, once a day, or once every few days, all the patients on the floor would gather to be interviewed by one of the senior doctors in turn. This doctor was a woman, and she was good. In a few sentences, she would speak with each of us to determine how we were doing, and at the end of the session she would decide what our medication levels were to be. I think she did a great job. They had me on twenty milligrams of Zyprexa, which is an extremely high dose, and, day by day, it did its thing. It brought me back to this planet. It returned a sense of reality, of what was really going on in this world around me.

I took the medicine. I did everything I was asked to do. I would like to say at this point that my behavior throughout my stay at the Westchester Psychiatric Hospital, unlike my behavior during the heart of the crisis, was exemplary, just as cooperative and courteous as could be. I got along fine with the doctors and the other patients and did everything as it should be done.

The front door was locked. I never went and tried it myself, but I'm quite certain it was, and I remained aware of this fact. There was a loss of freedom here. Clearly, there were sufficient reasons for this. Some of the other patients might have wanted to walk out; I don't know. Speaking for myself, I had no desire to confront the system in any way, but others might not have been so stable. I'm sure the precaution had to be taken. I was constrained, and despite the outdoor exercise and the amiable nurses, that was ever-present. Beyond that, there isn't a whole lot I can say. I suppose it is a built-in human defense mechanism that we are endowed with the ability to put these experiences behind us. On a day-to-day basis, I think about that time not at all. A city bus I take regularly drives directly in front of the Allen Pavilion, and the thought sometimes crosses my mind: "I'd rather be out here than in there."

That's all it amounts to.

I had a support team during this process: my parents, my older sister Louise, and her husband, Craig. They, too, did a great job. They brought me my clothes and kept in close contact with Rubin as I progressed. My father tied up some of the loose ends I had left back in the city. Evidently, there had been some unnecessary phone calls, only vaguely recalled, to business organizations, that would have left me with unwanted obligations. My father, too, took this in stride. He seemed to have an innate understanding of exactly what was going on. It could have stemmed from his prior experience with others who had had psychotic episodes, but he knew, like my doctor, that these things happen. As with my prior hospitalization, my parents saw to it that I got the best care possible.

My stay at the Westchester Psychiatric Hospital passed in a blur. Granted, the blur took on an increasing degree of clarity as the days passed. I do recall that a portion of each day was set aside for outside activity. I had my own way of using this time. Most of the others sat together around a couple of picnic tables and chatted. I used the time for a vigorous walk. Our group of patients was let out on the grounds for half an hour or forty-five minutes. We were constrained within a limited area, but I set out nonetheless and walked around the perimeter at a good pace.

This choice may have been motivated, in part, by my long-standing aversion to chit-chat, but at the same time, I believe it did me a lot of good. It got my heart pumping and my blood circulating. It was also helpful to be moving around amidst the trees and grass and bushes of the garden. This experience stood me in good stead. It set the example for many walks to come. This, too, helps bring me back when the chemistry runs awry.

And time passed. What more is there to say? Some brilliant team of scientists had been able to isolate a composite of chemicals and locate them in a small pill. They had been able to see through all the hocus pocus and the bombast and the superstition and to recognize that there is a chemical aberration at the heart of the psychotic episode. They had been able to correct it. I may have said it before, but on balance, I feel their efforts should be amply rewarded. I don't know exactly where the profits of the pharmaceutical companies go, but if, in part, they encourage this kind of research, I for one am all for paying them handsomely. The pharmaceutical companies, the dreaded pharmaceutical companies, had developed a relatively new drug called Zyprexa, and that drug had a whole lot to do with my successful stay in that hospital.

I could say something about how I got out. After I had been in the hospital for some weeks and the twenty milligrams of Zyprexa had done their thing, it became evident to the medical authorities that it was time for me to go. I was becoming a little too normal for that crowd. I recall one conversation I had with Rubin on the phone as I was getting ready to be let go. I was frightened that it would happen again.

Rubin answered my concern in strident tones: "Some people have heart attacks, some people have strokes, you have nervous breakdowns."

Talk about laying it on the line. This comment was intended to be reassuring in that it implied that these things happen only occasionally, at long intervals, and I shouldn't worry about it happening anytime soon. To that degree, it did assuage my immediate fears.

It is also important to point out that you come out of these episodes none the worse for the wear. They have absolutely no long-term detrimental health consequences. The same cannot be said for a heart attack or a stroke, however mild. On the positive side is also the fact that the capacity to believe in things that are not real, when controlled and carefully regulated, is a big part of being a writer in the first place.

I did get out. At first, they were going to send me to an intermediate living situation. I was put in a van to be taken there, but for some reason, that fell through. And then, just like that, I was free. Yes, I use the word "free." It is a word that has a meaning for me that most of the world - those who have never been confined – never knows. I express my thankfulness for that freedom every night just before going to sleep, and I express it again when I walk outside in the morning. That simple act of walking out the front door of my building and letting the door close behind me is not taken for granted. I walk up the pathway and I know that I have my freedom. At other times of the day, I know that I have so much more.

I can write whatever I please and, for a modest sum of money, see it made available for sale on amazon.com. How many thousands have died for that freedom and how many more are struggling for it to this day in China and other places around the world? Just ask the poor sucker who placed his body in front of a line of oncoming tanks in Tiananmen Square.

I can get on a bus and travel hundreds of miles to another state, as long as I make it back in time for my next session. With a little planning, I could buy a plane ticket and fly to another country thousands of miles away and return at my leisure. I can sit, rest, and eat in my locked apartment entirely free from the fear of invasion by the police or anyone else I choose to keep out. I can search the entire World Wide Web as I so choose from the comfort of my living room. I can go to the public library or a Barnes & Noble and read any book that suits my fancy. If I go to the main Forty-Second Street branch, any book ever written. I'm old school, and libraries still hold that attraction. This is freedom.

Not all of these freedoms were directly taken away during my stay in the hospital. I had very little interest in reading books of any kind while there, but I did temporarily lose an element of my physical freedom, and I believe that single loss has given me a greater appreciation of all the others.

Gradually, I returned to my normal routines. The Fordham Law Library staff had been informed about my misfortune and had made allowances for my time away. They took me back. There are federal laws that stand beside you in situations like this.

I was also still working toward a master's degree in English literature at the City University of New York. As my adventures took place entirely during the summer, I was able to resume class in the fall. Dr. Rubin played an active role in all of this. He eased me back in. I drank a lot of water – eight twelve-ounce glasses a day. I was still quite mixed up about what I had been through and tended to reject the idea that anything had been wrong at all, but I followed Rubin's advice on that one.

It made for some interesting long-distance bus trips and some quick sprints to a public restroom.

My family continued to be supportive. My first cousin Walter called to check in, and my aunt insisted that I come over for dinner despite my own apprehensions about my capacity to carry off the social situation. And little by little, the experience began to fade into the past. The human mind is remarkable in that respect.

There is a role for the good listener in all of this, but it is not a role anyone can just step into. I have found, over many years of experience, that the great listeners are those who don't set themselves apart from the troubled person, the ones who see commonality rather than difference. The really inspired listeners are those with a twelve-step foundation, who know that your troubles are really your greatest treasure, that they are yours and yours alone, and that they hold the key to your future happiness.

They are the ones who not only listen but celebrate at the same time. They are also the ones who know that it is not really about them, but only about them in that they are servants of the Big Man upstairs. When you speak with these people, no matter how troubled you might be, you feel free and easy. You are just lucky you got one of them on the phone. I found this attitude in two remarkable men – men unlike any other I had ever known before. These old- timers seemed to be living with good humor, a joy, and an open acceptance of others unlike anything I had ever encountered. It was meeting them that, more than anything else, made me want to live by the Twelve Steps, and it is this spirit I seek to emulate to whatever degree I am able as I, too, try and work the Steps myself, even as I do so without the assistance of a group or meeting.

They are unsung heroes the men and women who sit up through the night alone in a room, waiting for the phone to ring so they can speak to a stranger they will never meet. Not all of them share such extraordinary powers of empathy. But they show up. They show up and they pick up the phone. I imagine these services exist all over the country, but the one I am most familiar with is based in Ithaca, New York. The official name of the service has the word suicide in the title, but I prefer to think of them simply as "Helpline."

There is one older woman there who I've spoken with quite a few times over the years. Names were never exchanged, but I grew to recognize her voice and manner. She worked the overnight shift, through the wee hours of the morning, dispensing her love courtesy of AT&T. Maybe she still does. It's been quite some time since I've spoken with her. Her approach is gruff, from the hip. She does not share the wonderful good humor I have come to appreciate from people who have been in program, but she shows up. She's there all through the night, and she picks up the telephone when you call. I, for one, appreciate that.

I spoke to her in the heart of the night shortly after I was let go from the Westchester Psychiatric Hospital. I was due to return to work the next afternoon and, frankly, I couldn't sleep. I got this woman on the phone and started to explain my concerns that my co-workers would have found out I had a mental illness.

She paused just a moment for emphasis: "They already know," she said.

Believe it or not, it helped. I got back to sleep, showed up for work, and everything went just fine. That's Helpline. I couldn't venture to guess how many times I've called, all told, down through the years. By the grace of God, my calls are now few and far between. Some years back, when I was in a good place, I called up, got a P.O. box, and sent them a letter of testimony. I actually did. I thought it might help them bring in grant money. They've earned it.

It's a funny business, this mental illness. I know it gets a bad rap. Just look at the newspaper headlines – always some deranged person doing something terrible and the reporters attributing it to "mental illness," or Martin Scorsese making millions on a movie called *Shutter Island* about a hospital for the criminally insane.

But I just can't believe that is the whole story. I looked it up. In 2011, the amount of money spent on anti-psychotics alone was more than twelve billion dollars. That is up there with the revenue of the National Football League. Who are all those people? Aren't most of them just poor shmucks like me trying their best to get by? Doing the best they can? Trying to make something better out of their lives? And why should that be something to be ashamed of? Isn't the brain an incredibly complex organ, governed by thousands of chemical reactions? Why is it so surprising that sometimes things can go a little haywire and need fixing? The only appropriate reaction, in my view, is gratitude that modern medicine knows how to do that.

But maybe the scare factor sells better. We humans like to get shaken up. Just take a look at the AOL homepage. I'm locked in there in a million ways. Otherwise, maybe I'd switch, or maybe not. There are thousands and thousands of pictures and stories they could choose for their lead picture and blurb, and inevitably they choose the story that makes your skin creep a little – the school teacher stalked by an old acquaintance, the unsolved sexual assault of a beautiful teen.

Those choices are not arbitrary. The administrators surely must monitor which stories get the most hits. The horror movies, Scorsese's *Shutter Island*, or countless, countless others play on the fascination with the disturbed and the twisted. The humble, confused, depressed guy plodding over to his therapist would not sell as many tickets. Don't know why, but a look at cultural history makes that quite evident.

And what about the success stories? Where are they chronicled in popular culture? The a man who sees his therapist for seven or eight years, takes his medicine, and is discharged because he has become well. It happens. I know it for a fact. The times have changed. The days of psychoanalysis are passed. We are in a new age. It's not a uniform thing. There is still variation in psychiatric practice, but the discipline has advanced enormously. Psychiatrists have at their disposal countless drugs they just didn't have twenty, even ten, years ago. And more are coming down the pipe at a steady rate. There is also resistance, I know, writers and activists who claim that the new pharmacology is a distraction, that it adds to the problem rather than fixing it. I can add to this discussion only my own experience with these new drugs, which has been overwhelmingly positive. Getting the mix right takes time, no matter how skilled the doctor. There may be periods of overmedication and minor unwanted side effects. But once the right combination of medications and dosages has been found, a normal life, or what passes for one, can be resumed. That's the way it's worked for me.

Chapter Thirty

An Apparition – 2004

I'd come together well after my psychotic episode, but in March of 2004, the psychosis took a new twist. Specifically, it took the form of the vague apparition of a large, black panther that I became aware of under certain conditions.

The first onset of the apparition came as a complete surprise. I was out walking in a local park. It's on top of a small hill and has a fenced-in dog run. It was a Saturday in spring, and there were no dogs using it. This park is dedicated to the first headmaster of a private school in the area that I had attended through the ninth grade. I had roots in these parts. It was the week after the Passover holiday, the time of year my father liked to say, that the leaves came out on the trees. You could hear the cars going by on the Henry Hudson Parkway up the block and, intermittently, the 7 or 10 local bus go by on Warren Avenue. No one else was out walking. I was making my second or third circuit around the park's circumference. I'd done twelve only three days before, and I was gunning for at least that many, or more.

It was a cool evening. I was in shorts, but I had on an old grey sweatshirt. I'd been taking walks like this for a million years. But that night, something was different. It came on ever so gradually, made its presence felt in ever so subtle a manner. I became aware of a dark presence accompanying me around the park – a kind of a cat, a panther, dark as dark could be. It really didn't register in my conscious mind at first. I was too busy counting laps and glancing down at my cell phone to monitor how many minutes had passed. As I swung around the far end of the grassy area, by the partially open gate to the dog run, something clicked. It was there. It could not be ignored. I was walking in the presence of an apparition.

This had never happened before, nothing like this. I really wasn't sure exactly how to react. On the one hand, it was disconcerting and vaguely ominous. At the same time, it did not seem to represent any immediate threat or danger. I was puzzled. Such is the nature of communication in the twenty-first century that I had options. I had my cell phone, which I had brought along primarily as a time-keeping device, and I had a doctor who had the singular quality of accepting phone calls at all hours of the day or night. He prided himself on remaining by the phone when possible. For my part, I had learned to respect his time and to remain aware that he was a resource I shared with an indeterminate number of other patients. I didn't like to bug him. I thought about it a moment longer, considered the vague but ominous black cat lurking beside me, and decided to call. I knew the number.

Dr. Rubin answered with his at home greeting. "Hello," he said, his voice falling on the second syllable.

Believe me, I'd heard it before. If he was at the office and in session, he'd invariably say, "Excuse me… This is Dr. Rubin," to let me know there was someone else in the room. Tonight, he was not occupied.

"It's Jordan Fineman," I began.

I had no idea whether he had another patient named Jordan, but I was unfailingly polite, even when I was stressed out and standing in a public park. It was, in fact, unusual for me to be calling him from outside the apartment. Cell phones hadn't been around all that long.

"Yes?" Dr. Rubin responded. I knew he was listening.

"It's strange but…I'm out walking… and there's this kind of black cat…not a real one… Just an imaginary one."

Dr. Rubin took all of this very seriously. I don't think there were any possible developments in my illness that he had not foreseen or encountered before in his practice.

"Where are you?" he asked.

"In the neighborhood, just a few blocks from my apartment," I responded. I knew Dr. Rubin had taken the bull by the horns.

"I want you to take the extra Thorazine. Can you take fifty milligrams?" he asked.

"If I go home."

Dr. Rubin's voice inspired a sense of confidence. "Go ahead. See you Monday."

And that was it. I left the small park, descending to Warren Avenue through a side route, a dirt path through the brush, and crossed at the light. I walked home past the six-story red-brick apartment houses, built by the same construction company that had built the six-story red brick building in which I resided, and took the elevator to my apartment on the sixth floor. I had the Thorazine in both twenty-five and fifty-milligram dosages, and I took two twenty-fives. They were right there in the medicine cabinet. With the filtration of the drug into my system and the passage of time, the apparition faded.

These were among my final days under the capable care of Dr. Lawrence Rubin. My mental health, from there on out, was tended to by the staff at the Warren Mental Health Association, a clinic just two blocks from my apartment.

Chapter Thirty-One

An Eighth Step – 2008

I may be overplaying the whole loner thing. At least some of this is by choice and may be attributed to an experience I had while I was still in graduate school. As that chapter also admirably illustrates how a severe obsessive can work the Steps without a meeting, I would like to include it here. It went something like this.

Reiko was sitting on the couch in front of the window. I was sitting beside her. She started to get carried away about our taking a job at a villa in Europe, and I told her I was going to marry a Jewish girl. Tears came up to my eyes as I said it. I really did not realize I had led her so far down the wrong path. Tears came to her eyes as well, and she got up to put on her sneakers and left. That was pretty much it. We'd been together for six or eight months. We struggled on for a few weeks more, but it was strictly on fumes. We were spent.

Reiko had been hurt by my actions. On this occasion, the case could be made that I didn't know what I was doing. But I was determined not to repeat the mistake.

The Big Book spells it out: "If we are sorry for what we have done, and have the honest desire to let God take us to better things, we believe we will be forgiven and will have learned our lesson. If we are not sorry, and our conduct continues to harm others, we are quite sure to drink. We are not theorizing. These are facts out of our experience."

Elsewhere in the Book, it is made clear "for us, to drink is to die."

I had determined some time back that I shared the fundamental makeup of the alcoholic, although I got drunk on my own internal chemistry, generated by anger and resentment, without the alcohol. I had also determined that, like the alcoholic, my continued life was predicated on the maintenance and growth of a spiritual experience. This matter of women and sex was infinitely grave. There was very little margin for error. I simply could not repeat the same mistake.

I knew what the Big Book suggested, and when the spirit moved in the early summer of 2008, I acted. Up until that point, my Ninth Steps had been few. The Ninth Step is when you actually make amends. That's what it's called: "making amends." This can happen in many, many ways, but essentially it's an apology, clearing your own side of the deck, coming forward and standing in a spirit of humility before the other person and explaining, if necessary, that your own mental well-being depends on living in harmony with others, that you are sorry for what you have done. Let me be clear about one other thing right now. Everything I say is my own reading of the Big Book. I am not an authority. Maybe nobody is. It's an individual thing, each person working the suggested steps in their own way. Only God is in charge.

So, then there was still the matter of Reiko. This matter weighed on me. I understand that there is a certain amount of rough-and-tumble in the relations between the sexes, but I felt I had gone over the line. I had upset her and hurt her. She had expended a large amount of her limited resources in the sincere belief that she was going to marry this confused but still lovable young man. Years went by, and I did nothing to assuage my conscience. But one morning, without any real prior warning, that changed. I got up, walked out of my apartment, and took the 1 Train down to her neighborhood in Northern Manhattan. I had the Big Book with me for moral support. I was going to apologize, to sweep off my side of the deck. I don't doubt that she was partially at fault. That was simply not relevant. My only concern was to be with my own behavior.

I got off the train at 157th Street and took the familiar walk to her building on the corner of 150th and Broadway. I really didn't know if I would find her at home. Remember, years had passed in the interim. I didn't even know if she still lived there. But I pressed on. There is another side to this story, which puts my own behavior in a somewhat better light. At the time I knew her, Reiko had fancied herself as something of a landlord. She had taken another apartment and was trying to rent out rooms to visitors from Japan. The whole enterprise had been very discouraging. On those occasions when she did actually bring in a tourist from Japan, they got one look at the neighborhood and decided to room elsewhere. Like I said, it was quite discouraging.

I had a bright idea. I realized that the City College campus of the City University of New York was in the vicinity and suggested she look there for tenants. I did more than that. I got on the phone and hooked Reiko up with the off-campus housing officer. When she called me some months after we had called it quits, she told me that she had taken four apartments in the building and was renting rooms to more than twenty students. She was in business. So, not only had I returned in kind for all the good loving I'd received, but I thought I would have a reasonable chance of tracking her down when I arrived at the building. I thought she might still be a presence there. I wasn't sure.

Years had passed – by my count, five. My memory of her apartment's location was a bit vague, but I had an idea someone in the building might be able to tell me where she lived. I also didn't know exactly how the conversation would run. I just knew that I needed to apologize. I was going to take it from there. I stood in the lobby of the building and struck up a conversation with a couple of the student-aged people who came in. Nothing. I went up to the fourth floor and considered ringing the bell of her apartment (or the apartment I thought was hers). I thought better of it. I ran into another young man who referred me to the building office. It was closed. I left.

I came to the conclusion that, for that day at least, there was just no way of speaking with her. I got back on the train and went home. This experience was discussed in my next session, and my doctor made a couple of things clear. First of all, we really didn't know if Reiko still lived in that building. She might have sold her interest and returned to Japan or moved someplace else. But there was a more important fact here. Rubin pointed out that there was no way I could initiate that conversation without raising the idea that I was interested in reinitiating the relationship. The bottom line was that it would cause further trouble.

In effect, I realized that I had taken an Eighth Step but not a Ninth Step. The Eighth Step is, and I'm paraphrasing, "We're fully prepared to make amends." I'm not getting it exactly right, but you can go look for yourself. This is followed by the Ninth Step, which says words to the effect, "made amends except where to do so would cause further harm." Did this experience make me feel better? I can state unequivocally that it did. I have been, ever since, more at peace with my relationship with Reiko. I did all I could. There was nothing more that could be done.

That was the Chapter I wanted to include, as it shows how I have, in fact, been able to work the Steps. But it also goes a long way toward explaining why I spend so much time alone. I don't want to do it again. I have clearly shown I know how to seduce a woman. But I have also been shown where such actions can lead. An overly sincere demeanor in a guy not prepared to get hitched is trouble. Until I can figure out how to conduct myself more responsibly, being alone may be the far better option.

Chapter Thirty-Two

The Warren Mental Health Association –
2010-2014

The psychotic episode had taken place on Dr. Rubin's watch. It was left to Warren Mental Health to pick up the pieces and try and hold it all together. The change from the one to the other took place in the summer of 2010, some four years ago. Marcus James is a leading light at that clinic, conveniently located just two blocks from my Warren apartment. He is my new therapist. Dr. Rubin is no longer a part of this picture. This was, indeed, a disorienting transition. Leaving Dr. Rubin was very confusing, especially at a time when I was dealing with psychotic symptoms, like an apparition in a local park. But that is the way it had to be. Forces beyond my control had called this one. My father had recently passed, compounding all of the generally disorienting conditions.

My psychiatric care has now been placed in the hands of the Warren Mental Health Association. The clinic has been in existence for more than fifty years and is highly regarded. By an odd coincidence, my father took part in the organizational meetings of the place in the late 1950s. I came in with solid associations and have found, from the very start, an organization deeply committed to the welfare of its clients. Warren Mental Health has taken some getting used to. The patient at this community mental health association comes in off the street and ascends the single flight of stairs to the association's offices. The street door opens on to a parking lot. There is no one opening it, and the interior is institutional and nondescript. All of this could not be more different than the plush entranceway to Dr. Rubin's Park Avenue building.

The patient's first obligation is to pay for the ensuing services. You pay up front. Warren Mental Health is a pay-first operation, even if there are big discounts for a Medicaid card or Medicare insurance. The agent is seated in a partially enclosed booth-like area, separated from the customers by a glass partition with a small window for the exchange of credit cards and receipts. The young woman who takes care of these transactions, like everyone else at Warren Mental Health, is a professional. She is dignified but amiable toward all. She sustains a tone of goodwill. On a Monday at eleven-fifteen there could easily be four or five other patients awaiting their appointed session with either their psychotherapist, or their psychiatrist, or even a regularly scheduled group therapy session.

On one day, shortly after I had begun attending, an older, heavy-set man with white hair was speaking in an animated tone with a middle-aged woman seated across from me in that waiting room. The man was standing, his copy of *The Daily News* folded under one arm, his loosely fitted blue denim shirt hanging from his broad shoulders. I had distractions in my lap: a notebook, a pen, a Blackberry. I tried and tune him out. Just then, the door that leads back into the offices swung open. The door is kept locked to keep out the unauthorized, but those inside are entirely free to exit. A young, nicely dressed woman sped by, a broad smile on her face.

"A happy session," I thought to myself.

But just as she passed, without further witnesses between herself and the door, her smile abruptly changed to a tearful grimace. The young lady was in pain. She exited. In the far left-hand corner of the waiting room, beyond the receptionist's booth, is an area set aside for young children: a miniature table, miniature chairs, and a bookcase with books and games. On my first visit, I'd sat in one of those chairs just to be out of the way.

A little girl was seated at the table doing a school assignment. Her mother was beside her, quizzing her and helping her along. A therapist came in through the main door, also an alternate route to the offices and greeted her, "Wanna go play?"

There is nothing threatening here, certainly nothing dangerous. It is in many senses a community in which patients support each other. It is a community I am gradually coming to feel a part of.

As the weeks have passed, I have come to believe there is therapeutic value in the waiting room itself. For one thing, for a guy who spends a great deal of time alone, it is a chance to sit in a room with other people. We are all there for the same reason, to improve our mental health, our state of mind, our outlook on the world. Some of the people sitting there do know one another from group sessions or just because they have been coming for a long time at similar times. Personally, my conversations have been few and far between, but it has had an effect on me nonetheless.

I like to think that I'm open-minded and non-judgmental about mental illness, having dealt with it myself for quite some time. This being said, however, I can't get completely around the fact that I still share some of the hang-ups of the rest of the world. Even the words "mental illness" can set off tremors of vague unease in the not so distant recesses of my mind, tremors of hospitals for the criminally insane on deserted islands or of incurably sick wives locked away in attics. I can say that, thanks to the Warren Mental Health waiting room, I've been making progress on this front as well. It is healthy for me, I believe, to sit quietly with my notebook and pen in hand, and listen to one woman tell another, "I'm doing very well. I haven't been hospitalized since 1998."

There is nothing of the caricature here, no off-color joke, or attention-grabbing headline from an Internet service provider. Just one courageous woman coming out to a mental health association she feels proud to be a member of. I am growing to share her appreciation.

Marcus James, my psychotherapist, works in close cooperation with the staff psychiatrist, who I see once a month to regulate the drugs. In actuality, she does more than this and continues to contribute in many ways, as mysterious as they are essential. But it is Marcus who I see once a week, regularly at eleven-thirty on Monday mornings and for some time now on Fridays as well. I have come to believe that there is more than one way to effectively conduct psychotherapy. There are different styles, different approaches. To tell you the truth, I don't know what Marcus is up to most of the time. I do know that as the weeks have drifted by, I have gotten better. When a dark patch has come along, and there have been a few, Marcus has seen me through to the other side, scheduling extra sessions when necessary. I have grown progressively more peaceful and content.

Marcus is a big part of this story. He deserves some space of his own, to stretch out at full length in his swivel office chair.

He should be described physically, and some attempt should be made to capture, in essence, his personality. This, I have found, is the way books are written and, let's give the man some credit here, on his watch I've been reading a lot of them. For a guy who likes to think of himself as a writer, this is a big plus. I'm not supposed to be observing him. That is his job. He observes me. Still, I have sat across a medium sized rectangular office from him for quite a number of forty-five-minute sessions, and I must have picked up something. For one thing, he is tall. I would say six feet, easy. He has blond hair, rarely carefully combed but brushed over to one side. He dresses nicely, in a Warren-Mental-Health kind of way: sport shirts, slacks. There is generally a sport jacket hanging on the inside of the office door. Marcus has soft blue eyes which do a lot of the work. When he chooses not to express an opinion on something I have said, they remain placid. Should he wish to show his approval, however, there is the slightest enlargement in the space covered by his eye sockets. An eyebrow goes up. But this is barely perceptible. He says I read too much into the nonverbal clues, but without these, there would be very little communication of any kind. Marcus frequently chooses to stay silent.

The eyes, the facial expressions, can go in other directions as well. When he hears something he really likes, he smiles. It is a beautiful smile, and I have come to love it. Marcus James has shown me, over the time that we have been together, that his judgment is sound. I rely on it. Granted, I have to rely on something, but Marcus calls it straight. I like to think he has come to appreciate my company as well. I pitch it. I show up. We are both going one hundred percent, and, over time, that ought to add up to something.

Had I been at Warren Mental Health from the beginning, I don't think I would be the proud holder of two master's degrees. I seriously doubt that I would have even graduated from Cornell. I don't doubt that these achievements have made me a happier person. They constitute real accomplishments and have enriched my daily life. The work with words helped make we a writer. But where does it end? Isn't there something to be said for simple contentment? How many diplomas is enough? How many books? How many five-star reviews? How many likes? Are all these things supposed to impress someone? And do they really care?

I see this kind of thinking originating in my discussions with Marcus James. I don't question the fact that he is committed to his profession and that he is darn good at it. I also have the impression that he works hard, on a consistent basis, to get better. Marcus makes the point that performing, performing for others, can be a way of hiding myself. He has made this point many times by shutting down, in session, when I go off on some excited tangent that is supposed to be funny or interesting. It seems that he would rather have me just talk, just communicate directly. Marcus James is trying his level best to bring me into connection with the world around me.

Chapter Thirty-Three

In Front of the Infirmary – 2012

I was working with Marcus and Dr. Pavlova, but there were still all kinds of problems. It wasn't always an apparition of the panther. It was more a general feeling of being "not in control." This is a little hard to pin down, but it is most uncomfortable. In the past it had only come on late in the evening. The idea that I would have to deal with it on a cool early spring afternoon in the city had not even occurred to me.

I was mid-block between Nineteenth Street and Eighteenth Street, passing in front of the New York Eye and Ear Infirmary, when the wires went down. The green and red banner hanging behind me informed me that the infirmary had been founded in 1820. This information was not helpful to me at the time. I stood still and tried to gauge how bad things were. Whatever kind of high I had been on after the weightlifting was gone. I had recently come from the gym. This had never happened to me outside of the apartment before, let alone on the sidewalk of a downtown street.

There was no apparition – not yet anyway. The panther might have been lurking somewhere off in the evening fog, if there had been any evening fog, but as this was about one o'clock on a Tuesday afternoon, that was not actually a possibility. My primary sensation was that I was no longer fully in control. I was no longer calling the shots, or maybe I should say the system I used to call the shots was out of service, for how long I didn't have any idea. To make matters that much worse, I had an aching fear that a Darkness, a power contrary to my own self-interest might step in and start calling the shots for me. Had I been in my apartment and had it been anywhere close to nighttime, I would have taken the maximum permissible dosage of Thorazine, gotten in bed and laid still. Lying down on the sidewalk in front of the New York Eye and Ear Infirmary was out of the question.

I thought things through quickly. I needed to take Thorazine, as much as possible. I carried a small, metallic pillbox in my front right-hand pocket for just such occasions. I reached my right hand into my jeans pocket and felt it. There was some relief in that. I took it out, still warm in the cool March air. There was a picture of Elvis holding a guitar on the front. The pillbox was in the shape of a guitar with Elvis' signature up by the tuning pegs. I ran through these things periodically, using them up until they didn't close right. I stood still and opened the box. A pedestrian passed in front of me but paid me no mind. His eyes were fixated on the next block, straight in front of him. Where was his head? What kind of drugs was he on? Everyone manufactures these things internally, you know, whether they are being treated by a psychiatrist or not.

There, underneath Elvis' snide smile, I saw what I wanted: a cornucopia of pharmacology designed to see me through any event day or night, lithium in three hundred milligrams and one hundred and fifty milligram sizes, the Zoloft generic, sertraline, and yes, the Thorazine in one hundred and twenty-five milligram dosages. I was still standing. My feet were anchored in my running shoes, which were clearly pressing into the sidewalk. At the same time, I was floating. I was aware of a pressure building behind my eyes. I knew it well enough. It was like the rising wind on a hot summer's afternoon foretelling a coming thunderstorm. I was no longer fully in control. I was frightened.

So far that day, I'd taken fifty milligrams of the drug. I could safely go for another hundred. I was poised. I was alert. I knew I was in some danger. How much, I wasn't sure. This was, in truth, uncharted waters. I removed one of the larger brown pills from the box. It was covered with the white dusting of an old broken lithium capsule. I popped it in my mouth, sucked in my cheeks, and extended my tongue five times to generate some saliva in my mouth, and got the pill down. It left a bitter taste on the back of my mouth. The drug was in my system. I decided to return to my Warren apartment as quickly and directly as possible with as few distractions and detours as possible. I just didn't trust myself. There was something that I did not understand going on.

I crossed Second Avenue at the corner of Nineteenth Street and passed alongside a deli, or what passes for a deli in New York. It is the kind of place that will make you a sandwich but brings in most of its revenue from cold drinks and Lotto sales. I thought about going in to get a Diet Snapple, sixteen ounces of liquid. I had long known that staying hydrated in these situations is a plus, but I didn't trust myself to pull off the interaction. I continued west along Nineteenth Street toward Third Avenue. I have walked the streets of New York in a wide variety of altered states of consciousness from the overmedicated to the drug-deprived. I've walked the streets of the Upper West Side after going cold turkey off six powerful drugs and sitting alone in an empty apartment for four days, which was as good as a walk into a waiting ambulance. This walk was different.

I must ask your forgiveness if I do not meticulously recreate my emotional state on that day. I am just not strong enough to do so. Were I to re-experience that day in all its fearful confusion, I am afraid I might again risk my health, and, even in the name of a good story, this does not really appeal to me. Even at the time of this writing, some two years after the events in question, I can still doubt my sanity.

I made it down the block. I arrived at the corner of Nineteenth Street and Third Avenue, which was one block closer to my destination, the Fourteenth Street subway station in Union Square. I believed I would arrive there, but I wasn't completely certain. I continued to place one foot in front of the other. That I could do. I didn't think the whole thing through, but if questioned I would have explained that I had turned my life and my will over to the care of a Loving God, and to the spirit of my loving father, that under normal conditions these two guiding forces led me through the day. I would have explained that something had gone wrong, something that I attributed to psychosis and that, as things presently stood, a power of Darkness as represented by the black panther which was in charge.

Before this gets too much spookier and I lose it completely here in front of my laptop, let me say that I found a way out of this mess without the assistance of an ambulance or trained medical personnel. I did arrive back at my Warren apartment. My actual behavior did not become proxy to any kind of dark or destructive power as I feared it might. And on the course of that homeward journey, I learned something, or maybe it would be more accurate to say I experienced something I had only known once before. I did make it onto the uptown 4 Train, and once there, I did the only thing I knew how to do. I sat still, made eye contact with no one, and tried to think loving thoughts. Believe it or not, it worked. This unusual choice of thought pattern had been the recommendation of a psychiatric social worker named Jim Davison, who I met with for a few months upon first arriving at Warren Mental Health, before being transferred to Marcus James. It had been his insight that thinking loving thoughts might, in some way, decrease the need for extra Thorazine and even be helpful in a pinch. I originally found this theory a little outlandish, but left with no other recourse I gave it a try. It was entirely consistent with Dr. Rubin's more general emphasis on the positive emotions. It was here I went on that subway ride.

I don't think this subway car was appreciably different from any other on the number 4 line, or the number 1, or any other line on the New York City subway system. But for me it was. First, I tried to think loving thoughts about the guy immediately to my right. He was coming home from the gym and had his gym bag between his legs. He had showered, and his hair was still wet. Oddly enough, he wasn't listening to an iPod. Maybe he was coming down off an endorphin high and didn't need the music. I wasn't trying to get in his head. I wasn't trying to mess with him at all. I did consciously try to cultivate loving feelings toward him as a fellow New Yorker. For me, this was not a game. I was fighting for my sanity. And it helped. A little. The tension eased.

To my neighbor's right, standing against the closed subway doors in the middle of the car, were two young women, maybe in their early twenties, speaking to each other. I couldn't make out what they were saying. I didn't really want to know. I didn't look at them at all, but I knew they were there off to the right, one on either side of the polished metal pole, holding on as the train rolled on the tracks. And I wanted to love them, too. They, too, were here, in the same car as me. They were fellow New Yorkers going in the same direction. I had no idea where they were bound. I would never know. It didn't matter. We were fellow subway riders, on the same subway car. So was the young mother with a toddler between her legs seated across from me. So was the young man standing in the doorway checking his iPhone. So was the old guy asleep beside the young mother. I wanted to love them all. It was important that I love them all.

And by the time the automated train announcer on the 4 Train announced the Fordham Road stop, the stop before Bedford Park where I was to get off, I did feel a sense of love and kinship for the other riders on my car. Some had gotten off before me. I'd made eye contact with none, but they had been there for me to love. By the time I got up to get off the train, I wasn't afraid anymore. I knew what I would do. I would get on the 10 Bus and ride it the rest of the way to 256th Street. I would walk to my apartment. I was no longer afraid of the black panther. The panther had left the building. There had been too much Love around.

But what confirmed the experience for me was something Dr. Rubin had said years before, long before I had ever had any psychotic symptoms. I had described to him having an experience on a subway car, very much like the one I'd had on the uptown 4 Train, the experience of feeling a sense of loving kinship for everyone else on the train, and Dr. Rubin had said, "When you feel that way all the time, you will know you are well." The man aimed high.

This came to mind on the homeward-bound bus ride. We had been sitting in that same office, me in the black swivel

armchair in one corner, Dr. Rubin front and center in is ergo-
nomically designed chair, leaning backward below the swirling
tapestry in shades of yellow and orange. The office was quiet.
It was winter, and the air conditioner wasn't on. The sounds of
Park Avenue did not make it back as far as the interior space.

"There's no limit, you know." Dr. Rubin said. "Once love
starts flowing, it can flow like Niagara Falls."

It had been a good session. My outburst early on had
faded. We were both seeing the humor in the whole thing. It
was just about time for me to bundle up and head back out
into the cold. I had my marching orders. I was to attend to
business. We shook hands as had become a habit at the end
of session.

"Thanks," I said.

"See you next time." Dr. Rubin said as he held my eye for
just a moment.

I passed through the door.

Chapter Thirty-Four

Getting it Straight – 2012

Let's give Marcus James some credit for this one. Some four years into our work together, he has broken through one of my most persistent illusions. I had been living with a delusion, and it goes beyond the early-morning confusion upon waking from a realistic dream. I had been completely convinced that my former psychiatrist, the esteemed Lawrence Rubin, had been concurrently treating Natalie Portman and that he had been long in the process of bringing the two of us together in marriage. I no longer believe this to be the case.

I know now that with a bright and creative mind and a chemical imbalance for which I am being medicated, I have selectively heard and arranged information. I have focused on minute details that support my position while resolutely disregarding the preponderance of evidence that does not. Even now, the clarity that I have achieved is unstable, fleeting, easily dissipated like an image seen through the front windshield of a speeding car on a rainy night. Still, I've got it right. I'm convinced of it.

Marcus had been watching all of this unfold. He's got perspective. For one thing, he read Rubin's report and met personally with the intervening therapist who spoke with Rubin on the phone. They are professionals. They have ways of communicating these kinds of things. As the months have gone by, he made no explicit attempt to alter my perspective. When the issue of Natalie Portman came up, as it did in the context of my current relationships, and always with an undercurrent of doubt on my part, Marcus went right along. Now that I have come to the point of classifying these views as delusional, he is not so circumspect. He has endorsed my newfound understanding and seems more interested in what role it played for me while I was a believer.

"Delusions last as long as they are necessary."

That was his comment, or words to that effect. This could be why he made no premature attempt to dispense with it.

I haven't been able to pin down exactly what that role was, except that it made me feel good about myself at a time when I didn't have much else going right. Maybe things have changed now. Among many other things, my literary agent supports my most recent literary endeavors. Granted, this is not quite equivalent to marrying Natalie Portman, but maybe in my psyche, it is playing that role. Go figure.

I don't know exactly why, but this aspect of my illness embarrasses me more than any other. I've admitted to some pretty off-the-charts stuff without flinching, but this one still gets to me. Maybe it is the word "delusion" itself. It is thrown around with such scorn and derision. Maybe, and I hesitate to even write the word, because it is often associated with violence. But where is the big surprise here? All aspects of mental illness are thrown around with scorn and derision and associated with violence. That seems to be mental illness' place in modern society, to be thrown around with scorn and derision and associated with violence. This has simply got to change.

If I was so far off base about a movie star, and I'm convinced I was, what else could I be misinterpreting? I have to consider this reality. I sat in Rubin's small office, month after month, and consistently misinterpreted what I was seeing and hearing. I read into the doctor's facial expressions and body language things that just weren't there. Even now, I find that hard to fully accept, but I do. I got this one wrong.

A delusion may be defined as a persistent belief in opposition to the facts. That is exactly what I had. So, what is going on at Warren Mental Health? How often have I sat across the room from Marcus and misinterpreted what he might or might not have been trying to convey? Kind of makes me want to take a step back, take a deep breath, and not jump to any rash conclusions. Such may always be a good policy.

While I hesitate to reintroduce the subject in any way, there has been one ancillary benefit to my Natalie Portman delusion. During the time I was so encumbered, I noted that the movie star was a committed vegetarian. In an effort to move closer to her, I adopted the lifestyle. Well, it has been at least five years now, and I am still at it, cooking with tofu and everything. This has brought with it the fact that my cholesterol readings remain ridiculously low, a fact measurable with a number, always comforting to an obsessive. When matched with the regular daily exercise habits instilled in me very early on by Dr. Rubin and sustained religiously ever since, physically I'm in great shape. This is an ever-present source of satisfaction.

But what about the big picture, all of the compounded beliefs that I seem to believe make it possible for me to move "intuitively" through my day? Aren't these suspect as well? There is no doubting the fact that if I go into the bathroom and open the mirrored front of the cabinet above the sink, the shelves are lined with dark orange pill bottles and that they all contain pills. They may be now shipped in by mail order, but they are there none the less, staring back at me, big time stuff: the infamous Thorazine, Zyprexa, Abilify. Who am I to claim that I am a competent witness on such matters of behavior and intuition? How do I know it isn't all just craziness?

There must be a strong undercurrent of doubt behind my belief system that relies on a Higher Power. This I acknowledge. I can only add that without the ability to form decisions in this manner, I would be spending twelve hours a day sitting in the stacks of some library, a time span broken by regularly scheduled breaks, or a comparable amount of time walking back and forth between either end of the block out front. That is where I was before all this began. That is where I would return. The system I have adopted, which does involve a strong element of the intuitive, and of doubt, is undoubtedly superior.

Chapter Thirty-Five

Montefiore Dental – 2012

I've been receiving my dental care at a clinic at the Montefiore Hospital on the other side of the Bronx. I get there in one bus ride that begins just a block from my house and lets me off in front of the hospital. The same 10 Bus that brings me to and from the 4 Train. The care has been excellent. I got into trouble during the first three or four years after my breakdown. Frankly, I was too disorganized emotionally to show up for a dental appointment. Dr. Rubin was on the lookout for every aspect of my overall health, but about this there was just nothing he could do. The end result, all these years later, is that some extra visits to the dentist are required. For the most part, they have been a positive experience.

The aspect of all this that interests me was my return trip on the 10 Bus. It was November 2012. I boarded, as was my custom, at a stop on East Gun Hill Road down the block from the clinic. I didn't have long to wait. These buses run pretty frequently during the afternoon. The number 10 arrives largely empty of passengers, so I assume it's near the beginning of the route. I stepped up the two large steps into the bus and inserted my reduced fare metro card. I did not choose to acknowledge the bus driver. I'm confident the acknowledgment would not have been returned. From there, I walked to the middle of the bus and took a seat next to the window along the left-hand side. I was seated in a row of double seats, so there was an empty place beside me. I knew the bus would be filling up. It always did.

I was coming back home at around three o'clock, which meant that the local schools were just starting to let out. As the bus turned left on Jerome Avenue and headed toward Lehman College, it started to fill up. I figured I'd be sharing the double seat with a junior high school student with a backpack, which would have been fine with me. The bus pulled up to a stop below the elevated 6 Train. Across the street was an entrance to Van Cortlandt Park, which seems to spread out with enormous width and breadth across this borough. I was minding my own business, looking out the window, thinking relatively peaceful thoughts, as I recall, when a guy slid into the seat beside me. I was neither pleased nor displeased. It was bound to happen. As it turned out, I was in for much, much more.

I don't remember exactly how the conversation started. I think it had to do with him apologizing for bumping into me as he reinserted his wallet into his rear left-hand pocket. I obligingly responded that it was no problem at all in a spirit of good cheer, and we were off. It turns out that in his own way, he was a professional well accustomed to striking up conversations with strangers. I, too, had experience in that line of work.

We did indeed have more than that in common. We had both been hospitalized for mental illness. Exactly how we worked our way into this sensitive area, I couldn't say. I know he said something about spending some time "upstate." In certain contexts, this refers to spending time in a state penitentiary. In this case, it did not. I picked up on what he meant when he referred to the institution as "Ssaint something." Penitentiaries are not named after saints. There was also something in his manner that conveyed that he had been through the wringer.

I didn't chime in right away. I let him keep talking, as he did in his slightly disjointed, slightly spaced-out kind of way. I learned that he had been a student at Bronx Science, one of the three best public schools in the city, for a couple of semesters and that he had left on account of "the stress." Details were not provided. I further learned that he had been married and that he had a daughter. I learned that the marriage had ended when he was at his worst. He had earlier explained that the hospitalization had been voluntary, but things must have been bad. He was on his way to visit a cousin on a visit of goodwill, and he explained that he was inclined to strike up conversations with old people on buses. He made a passing reference to God. In many ways, he struck me as a thoughtful and goodhearted man.

The bus crossed Broadway, the dividing line between Warren and the rest of the Bronx, and started up the hill. At this point I felt inclined to pitch in. This was just the kind of fellow sufferer I would meet if I ever managed to get involved with a Twelve Step program for people with mental illness.

"I had some rough times, too," I said, looking over at my seatmate.

He left it alone, out of the kind of respect born of experience.

The bus was passing below the Century apartment building, which had been around a while, but not as long as me. I remembered when it had been built. They had originally placed a series of signs along the inclined road below, introducing motorists to the rental office at strategically chosen intervals, an advertising brochure that unfolded gradually as the motor vehicle sped south. The signs had been defaced. One of them was gone.

"I was in a hospital, too," two undercover spies connecting in the lower level of a parking lot in Eastern Europe during the heart of the Cold War.

"You look normal," the guy said.

I did look normal. I was aware of that. I fully believed I owed that to the Steps, but there was no time to go into that. My seatmate had already missed his stop, but just by one. He got up to leave, and we parted on friendly terms, each of us off to negotiate, as best we could, through a world where open acknowledgment of our personal reality was not acceptable.

Chapter Thirty-Six

Vinney's – 2013

There is a landmark in northern Warren which has not yet been mentioned. The physical layout is relevant; so is the food, which is much better than a first look at the premises might indicate. On the day in question, however, Vinny's was much more than a sum of those parts. On a summer's afternoon in 2013, a small Italian restaurant, little more than a pizza place, had the power to heal.

Vinny's is located on top of a hill, two blocks north of the Greenwood Shopping Center. Vinny's stands alone. Its nearest neighbor is Mount Saint Margret's College, a small institution of higher learning just south of the Yonkers line. Mount Saint Margret's boasts a sprawling green campus extending down to the shores of the river. Vinny's is across the street. The mood of the restaurant is determined largely by its windows. The whole of the western and southern walls are comprised of plate glass. For the most part, this is a big plus. The only drawback being that during the afternoon, the sun can tend to make things a little warm. The customers don't complain. Vinney's has a positive vibe in that way.

The windows do provide a lot of light, at least during the daytime when I am usually there. The theme is carried over into the interior decorating. The ceiling is painted with a blue sky and white clouds. To tell you the truth, I don't think many people bother to look. The interior left-hand wall is weathered red brick and features a large, flat-screen TV which is usually playing sports or ESPN. The sound is generally off. Quite conspicuously, the soundtrack of the restaurant is W.C.B.S. F.M., a New York radio station which plays songs from the 70s and 80s. The oldies station is playing my songs. I'm not proud. A glass counter runs across the back of the room, from which the pizza is served. Here, there is real creativity at play. The pizza with cream spinach is a specialty of the house I've never seen anywhere else. It is really good. There are other specialty pizzas as well as the traditional cheese and Sicilian. The surprising part is the full Italian menu they keep on a back burner in the kitchen. When someone comes in to ask for the eggplant parmesan, or even the fresh fish, they are ready to serve.

When I walked in there that July afternoon, I was "out of my fucking mind." That is an expression I have coined. It describes a particular state I find myself in from time to time. I'm not sure how it matches up with the more clinical terminology found in the literature. To me, it means that I would be better off lying still on my bed. It means that I don't completely trust myself to act in my own self-interest. I would never go online when I am "out of my fucking mind." I would go further and say that all forms of conversation are a bad idea. Still, there I was, sitting in Vinny's eating a slice and drinking a Diet Coke.

I decided to experiment. No one was going to put me on the spot. There were no surprises here. I put the theory of loving thoughts to the test. I got results. I was seated in the front on the right, near the door. I used to sit on the left, but recently this had been my seat of choice. It was two-thirty on a Tuesday afternoon. School was not yet back in session, and a crew of four neighborhood boys was enjoying their summer vacation with some pizza. They were beside the flat-screen TV, but they weren't watching it. A family of three was seated by the counter. Judging by the example of his parents, the kid was up against it in the weight department. Two brothers own and run the restaurant. One was behind the counter. The other was seated by the drink cooler hunched over his iPhone. I started in.

I began with Petro. That was the name of the owner with the phone. I just decided that I would send loving feelings his way. I don't think he was aware of what I was doing. He gave no indication that he was at the time. I looked over at him in his white T-shirt and red baseball cap and wished him well in every way I knew how. I did the same with Gino, the other owner, who was behind the counter stretching out the dough to make a pizza. Fleetwood Mac was advising the assembled to not stop thinking about tomorrow, and Gino was tossing the dough lightly in the air to the beat. I loved him, too, which was even easier to do because we got along.

I kept at it. I loved the whole store and everybody in it. We were all human beings doing the best we could. I loved the sky painted on the ceiling. I loved the spinach pizza. I loved the sound of the W.C.B.S. radio filling the room. I loved my freedom and the fact that I was able to enjoy it in this way. For all intents and purposes, I was just a guy with a notebook sitting in a seat to one side. To think that anyone was aware of what I was doing is to open grounds for suspicion. But I was aware. I was aware that my own state of mind had changed. It had. I was no longer "out of my fucking mind." Don't ask me how this had happened, but as I dumped my paper plate and plastic soda bottle in their respective trash cans and went to pay for my food, everything was O.K. by me. I was better.

Chapter Thirty-Seven

A Local Physician – 2014

Dr. Michael Bloom is one of the best doctors in New York. This fact was proclaimed from eight different *New York Magazine* covers displayed on the wall of his office waiting room. Frankly, I was impressed. There was little about either the location or the interior decorating that would have led one to this conclusion. I had wound up there because the office is just a few blocks from my apartment, and Dr. Bloom is on a list of doctors that accept my Aetna Medicare insurance card. Still, for the first fourteen years of my residence in northern Warren, I saw him very little. My psychiatric care was being taken care of by Dr. Rubin, who was also well-qualified to treat any minor problems that might arise with my physical health. Thankfully, there were very few.

There was an added advantage in looking toward my psychiatrist for the care of my body. It was frequently the case that on those occasions when I thought there was something wrong with me physically, the problem actually originated in my mind. Dr. Rubin was eminently qualified to make this discernment and call it to my attention. I grew to accept his judgment on calls of this kind. I grew to accept that there were times when I was fully convinced that I had a pain in my foot (it could have been anywhere) when in reality, the signal for that pain originated in my mind. I thought there was a pain coming from my foot when actually my foot was just fine. This thought process has a funky name: hypochondriacal tendencies. I always got a kick out of the sound of that first word.

Despite the excellent care I have been receiving here in Warren, I do miss what Rubin brought to the table in situations like that. Neither Warren Mental Health nor Dr. Bloom has quite the same authority in such ambiguous situations.

On the day I went into my physician's office, I was to learn that my hyperactive thyroid had returned to normal, that I wouldn't have to take a pill with radioactive qualities or be subject to yet another regimen of medications. Dr. Bloom had cured me without necessitating those more drastic measures. It was good news all round.

I was first in line for the afternoon session, which begins at one o'clock on Mondays. I'd already had a busy morning, an eleven-fifteen session with Marcus, and the intervening time at Dunkin' Donuts. I can only say that I had given everything I had to my failed attempts to hold a full-time job. It was brutal, but without that experience I know I would not be at home spending forty minutes during the middle of the day at a side table in Dunkin' Donuts. In the midst of those five years and seven lost jobs, I assisted my father in launching an Internet business that has been helping to support me ever since. In his company, I was actually able to be of service.

I arrived at the doctor's office right on time. I was eminently familiar with the walk over there, past the 99¢ store, the Verizon outlet, and the hole in the wall that passed for a coffee shop. I had no trouble timing my entrance. I took a seat and removed my Kindle from my black shoulder bag. Checking in was hardly necessary, as I had been going over there frequently over the past couple of months. The receptionist knew all about by my insurance information. She did, however, provide a friendly greeting. I opened the Kindle to my copy of *Anna Karenina* and started to read. I knew I was going to be seen promptly, but it was a habit of mine.

The medical assistant appeared at the doorway that led back into the examination rooms. She called me by my last name.

"Mr. Fineman?"

I replaced the Kindle into the black cardboard case it had been shipped in and stowed it in my bag and I went to join her. We dispensed with the formality of the weigh-in, as I check my weight regularly at home, another quantity measurable with a number, and I let her know it was not necessary. Once inside the small rectangular examination room, however, she did check my pulse and blood pressure. I had yet to internalize what those numbers meant, unlike the cholesterol count, with which I was very familiar. She left me alone to await the doctor. I felt an obligation to observe my surroundings. I knew that, as a writer, this was my job, and I set to it.

I'd spent time in all four waiting rooms on prior visits, and I wouldn't say I had any preference. This was the smallest, with a shaded window on the back wall behind the elevated platform on which I was seated and would be examined shortly. To my left, also on the back wall, was a photograph of a boy, about age seven or eight, smiling and looking into the eyes of an infant. I thought I saw a similarity between the kid and my doctor, but I had never raised the question. I really had never asked him any personal questions, though I was not shy about sharing details of my own life. There was a small sink built into the corner of the room to the right of the door, and a signed print that represented a couple walking, though it was abstract. The shelves above the sink were stocked with the essentials: bandages, cotton balls, cotton swabs, and small bottles of what I assumed was rubbing alcohol.

The doctor pulled the door back and entered, his silver, metallic notebook computer in hand. But, much to my surprise, he did not enter alone. He was trailed by a young woman in her mid-twenties wearing the white jacket that indicated she, too, was a doctor, or, as it turned out, a doctor in training.

"Hi, Dr. Bloom," I began the conversation.

We shook hands. He then introduced the trainee. "Joreen is observing for the day."

Joreen and I did not exchange pleasantries, but I tried to make her feel welcome.

Dr. Bloom seated himself on the purple vinyl stool, which matched the lavender color of the room's paint job. "So," the doctor began, "the last set of numbers were very good. You were back within range."

"That's great," I responded.

"I think we can cut out the medication entirely. Would you like to take another blood test today to confirm?"

This was a pattern with Dr. Bloom. On all kinds of questions that you might think he was in the best position to judge, he'd leave it up to me. I can only assume that this had something to do with the Albert Einstein Medical School choosing to send its students to him for training.

Joreen so far had contributed very little, apart from gracing our consultation with her good looks and accommodating smile. Her blue eyes looked out from beneath her overhanging black bangs as she leaned back against the side wall, not wanting to intrude on the doctor-patient conversation. At this point, however, the consultation took another unexpected turn. Dr. Bloom got up to leave. He had been summoned by one of his assistants, and he chose to close the door on the way out, leaving the medical student and myself alone in close quarters.

Thankfully, it was a good day for me. I felt on top of my game and ready to field my position. I also had very little doubt that Dr. Bloom's decision to leave the two of us alone was not entirely random. He may have been a highly regarded doctor, but he was also an educator. I sort of felt that he wanted me to interact with this young lady. Whether he felt I was to gain from the interaction as well, I wasn't so sure.

"Which medical school are you at?" This ground had not yet been covered.

"Einstein... It's my first year." I wasn't at all sure how this young woman felt about being left alone with me. I wanted to share my own pedigree. This had turned into an intimate conversation, and under those conditions I liked the other person to know I was a Cornell grad. Goodness knows I'd worked hard enough for the distinction. I also had the general idea that Cornell was a feeder school to her program.

"I went to Cornell..." I conveyed the information, and Joreen brightened.

"Yeah... I went to the University of Pittsburgh."

There was no sign of any medical personnel coming to break up what we had going.

"They send you out to doctors' offices?" I asked.

"It's kind of a rotation. I'm starting off with family practitioners. What do you do?"

It had come around to that, and I had a pretty good idea where it would wind up. "I'm a writer," I said with what passed for conviction.

"Oh…" This brought the medical student up a little short.

"I have an agent and an editor." I still felt it necessary to justify my career choice.

"What do you write about?" she asked.

Here it was, the interaction Dr. Bloom had, no doubt, been counting on.

"About the recovery from mental illness." I can say with confidence that, sitting there in my smart, blue button-down shirt and army green cargo pants, I looked like a good advertisement for the cause.

Joreen had nothing to add. She, like many others, didn't know quite what to make of a guy who stated openly that he was writing about mental illness. Maybe it had yet to be covered in the medical school curriculum.

"You're a psychologist?" she offered tentatively.

"Actually, it's based on my own experience."

Joreen had no idea where to go with this. She appeared flabbergasted. "But then people would know," she said. She was concerned. She was upset.

"The books were written as novels," I tried to soften the blow.

Just about then, Dr. Bloom came back in the room. "So," he said. "You've gotten acquainted."

Joreen did not make eye contact with either Dr. Bloom or myself. I was left wondering how far over the line I had been treading if this twenty-something medical student was so clearly affected.

Dr. Bloom was prepared to wrap things up, as was I. The thyroid condition had been successfully treated. There was no question of perception there, and I knew I didn't need any other health complications. He and Joreen prepared to leave the room. He was going to send his assistant in for one final blood test.

I never saw Joreen again. For all I know, she is now an observer at an oncology wing of a major hospital or maybe even a psyche ward. I'd like to think that our relatively normal conversation affected her positively. As a physician of any stripe, she is sure to encounter patients with mental illness. Maybe she will be more inclined to associate them with Cornell grads, or writers, or guys in blue button-down, long-sleeved shirts.

Chapter Thirty-Eight

The Payoff – 2014

This morning was supposed to be about editing the manuscript, getting down to the nuts and bolts of following my agent's instructions and putting it together. Something has intervened. There is a more pressing reality. My overall mental health requires a different course of action. I woke up with my head in a big mess. I was experiencing angry, degrading thoughts, and I wasn't completely sure which side was up.

On mornings like this, there is only one time-proven remedy, to systematically prepare my breakfast: pouring the O.J. immediately after putting the boiling water in the ceramic cup with coffee and cinnamon in it and eating it in a spirit of gratitude. This ritual is followed by the greatest part of each day, when I sit down to write. If the words and the sentences follow, nine times out of ten, I'm all better.

Rubin predicted this course of events oh so many years ago, when he said of the writing, "That is what keeps you sane."

What can I say? It would seem he was entirely correct. To tell you the truth, I understand the process not at all. It just seems to be very good for my head. The really screwy part is that I would have to ascribe this capacity, in large measure, to the time I went completely bonkers and walked through the neighborhood with one sneaker on, and the other being dragged along the sidewalk. I wound up on the banks of the Hudson River, our local natural wonder, where I promptly disrobed and submerged myself. Yes, I was experiencing a psychotic episode. Still, my learned psychiatrist later described my independent course of action as a "rite of baptism." Another event I understand not at all.

The psychotic episode proceeded as I have been given to believe these things do. Three kind police officers saw to it that I was brought to appropriate medical assistance, and with the passage of time, and twenty milligrams of Zyprexa each day, I got better.

But the event had significant residual beneficial effects I am still grappling to understand. The fact of the matter is that those confused, thoroughly disorienting days have everything to do with what I am doing right now. On the one hand, they left me with a residue of an angry voice in my head. On the other, they gave me a means of dealing with it in a most satisfying and creative fashion. I would not be writing without the psychotic episode. I thank my Higher Power every time I am fortunate to set down consecutive sentences.

No doubt other factors contributed to this persistent capacity to write. I was a student for an inordinately long period of time and earned two graduate degrees. I developed my creativity through a variety of art forms. But the fact remains that the writing did not begin in earnest until after my unsanitary but brief swim in the Hudson River. You figure it out.

Chapter Thirty-Nine

A Place in the Bronx – 1994-2014

In the winter of 2014, when most of this book is coming together, the Brooklyn craze may be on the wane. Still, it is safe to say Warren is not in fashion. It remains all about Brooklyn: the bands, the restaurants, the alternative concert venues. Everything is about Brooklyn. P.B.S. is running a series on the history of that borough. Artists from far and wide are choosing to relocate. I can't say I was never tempted to join them. I, too, had a choice to make, some twenty years ago, when it came time for me to leave Washington Heights, the Dominican neighborhood where I had lived for seven years. I gave the matter some thought and decided on Warren. To tell you the truth, it wasn't a tough decision.

I have lived here for some time now. I'd like to think that I have taken the intervening years one day at a time. But with the passage of time, Warren has become my home. None of this is entirely new; I was born and raised here, attended P.S. 42 through the second grade and went on to one of Warren's prestigious private schools, The Warren Country Day School, for the next eight years. I played in the Southern Warren Little League, both the minors and the majors, and was Bar Mitzvahed at the Warren Temple. Upon my return, I have walked the streets of Warren in every direction, exercising my heart and lungs. Finally, and by no means least important, I have become a client of the Warren Mental Health Association.

I really hadn't planned on saying a whole lot about the early years before I left for Andover in the tenth grade. Everyone seems more interested in the crazy part, and as a child I passed for normal. The early years are a backdrop, context. They make me more at home here. I stand at a bus stop awaiting the number 7 Bus, and know that it is the successor to the 100 and 24 Buses that used to follow a similar route and took me to and from school. I may not think about it at the time. It does not even cross my mind that the bus shelter used to be made of weathered, black wood and that it is now made of Plexiglas with a large space for advertising at one end. I like to think that I live in the present. And, in fact, the current perceptions comprise the content of my days.

It's almost a joke, or at least what passes for an astute observation. Warren is very unlike the stereotype most people think of when they think of the Bronx. This is most pronounced on the shoreline of the Hudson River. The Hudson River marks the western border of Warren. You know it's the eastern shoreline because in the evening the sun sets over the Palisades Cliffs on the opposite shore. These sunsets can be spectacular. The home I grew up in took in the view. Upon my return to Warren, I settled in an apartment complex to the north, just a ten-minute walk down a steep hill to the river. I've taken that walk many times as well, at least once when I was in real trouble.

The Hudson River is not Warren's only natural landmark. On the opposite side from the river, to the east, is Van

Cortlandt Park, a vast city park, complete with hiking trails that serve as a course for cross country runners, a golf course, a lake, and open fields for softball, soccer, cricket, curling, and rugby. The park serves a multicultural clientele who take the 1 Train to the end of the line, the 242nd Street station to enjoy it. This natural space has also consoled and healed me on more than one occasion, sitting on shady hillsides, waiting for equilibrium to return.

The sense of green stillness is found elsewhere in Warren in enclaves, parks, and tree-lined streets. Some people might argue that it is fading, that the natural charm of Warren isn't what it once was. Here, I beg to differ. There is a quality of peace here that you just don't find elsewhere in New York. The ballfields, of which there are three, the playgrounds, of which I count at least four, and the numerous churches and synagogues, landscaped to present a green and inviting face to the community, all contribute to Warren's distinctive charm. There are birds here, and I'm not just talking about pigeons, sparrows and starlings. There are blue jays and cardinals and doves, all of which might be seen on a walk through the neighborhood. Down by the river there are geese and ducks. Add to this the raccoons that come out after dark to feed on outdoor trashcans, and you might think you are off in the country somewhere, not in an outer borough of New York City.

The natural charms are part of what drew me back to Warren after the seven years of living in Washington Heights. I knew it would be Warren and seamlessly made the transition. Familiar landmarks, convenient bus transportation to the city, nearby family, all of that must have been considered. Rubin did not express an opinion, as best I can recall. And it has worked out. I write. Day by day, I write.

Epilogue

The Europan Café is still serving the tourists who continue to flock to the Times Square area. They come from all over the world to gawk at the electronic billboards and ride the double-decker buses. The café served its purpose for me as well. It was in no way approved behavior to compose a work of memoir in a Times Square tourist trap. There are coffee shops in Brooklyn where such activity goes on regularly with full peer support. At the Europan Café, I was very much on my own. I was the only one with a notebook and a pen. But when you consider the material I was working with, being alone was entirely appropriate.

I haven't been in for a while. Once I got the book mapped out, I didn't really feel the need. Still, I would like to think that there has been some element of the Europan Café in the book that has come together these past few years, some element of the small wooden tables and the coffee and the Linzer tarts, the employees wiping down table tops and serving coffee, the cute Greek manager. None of them knew me from Adam, but as the weeks drifted by, they came to expect me, even to accept me.

For better or for worse, the mentally ill remain on the edge, the often-shunned outskirts of American society. It was from this marginal position, sitting alone with a cup of coffee, that my book grew. The alone part may come with the territory, one of the rights and privileges of my condition along with the frequent visits to the counter at the back of a Duane Reade pharmacy. I cannot say with any certainty, however, that this is a liability. The case can be made that I have, of necessity, been forced to acknowledge a fundamental reality of the human condition: we are all fundamentally alone. If that sounds like a sad or negative statement, it wasn't meant to be. It is more of an observation that I believe lies at the heart of all the world's major religions.

Clearly, there are advantages to being around people as well, and if anything is to bring me to that eventuality, it will be the writing itself. Like a long, cool wave breaking off the shores of Maui, I will ride this one as long and as far as I can. Surfing has never been much in vogue in New York City but, with a couple of cups of coffee, I, too, can crouch over a surf-board, hide in that tunnel of water and make it to shore un-scathed, where, with any good luck, there will be people there to greet me. The act itself is undertaken alone. The camaraderie may, God willing, come later. The Good Lord makes all things possible.

Acknowledgments

The Dr. Rubin in this account is based on none other than Dr. Harry Reiss. He is the real hero of this story. This book would not exist without the capable, steady hand provided my agent, Liza Dawson. The author would also like to thank Kalindi Handler for her capable editorial assistance. So many others have played a role in the events upon which this story is based and have supported me in writing about them. I trust they know who they are and that they will accept these heartfelt thanks.

Credits

Parts of this novel have been published in the following literary magazines: *Better than Starbucks, Chaleur Magazine, The B'K Magazine, Prometheus Dreaming and Adelaide Literary Magazine.*

About the Author

Josh Greenfield spent his early childhood in privileged surroundings of Riverdale, New York. Along with his two older
sisters, he was raised in a beautiful home and attended the
exclusive Riverdale Country Day School through the ninth
grade. At this juncture, he made the independent decision to
uproot himself and to complete the final three years of his high
school education in the even more privileged environment of
Phillips Andover Academy.

Perhaps with at least some awareness that he needed a
greater exposure to the realities of the world, Josh, after his
sophomore year in Cornell's College Arts and Sciences, flew
alone to Alaska to try and support himself by working in a
salmon cold storage plant. Challenging himself in this manner
no doubt helped prepare him for the far greater challenge that
lay in his future. The following summer, he again sought to
broaden himself by taking on the responsibilities of an internship for a liberal congressman in Washington D.C. This
exciting opportunity opened the way to further involvement
in the Nuclear Weapons Freeze Campaign, a preoccupation
which in time became all consuming.

All of this was preamble to his greatest fight of all, the
fight to extricate himself from the grips of a devastating mental

illness, an illness with hereditary roots on the paternal line of his family. No doubt, his ultimate success in this endeavor was made possible by his strong educational foundation. While working with a skilled psychiatrist and doing the hard work of recovery, he not only completed his Cornell degree as a visiting student at Columbia University, but went on to earn two master's degrees from the City University of New York. This work provided essential structure and purpose when his illness made other forms of gainful employment impossible.

Josh knows that he has been among the fortunate few, given the resources and the support, which combined with his own hard work, has seen him to a brighter day.